# SHIFTERS OF BLACK FOREST RIDGE: MACK

## SEDONA VENEZ

# CHAPTER 1
## AURORA (RO)



I walked into the ranch with a huge grin on my face.

*I did it.*

Today I'd joined the Army, and in one week, I'd be sent to the Fort Dix, New Jersey, military base for basic training.

The plan to free me from the Rossi brothers—Nick and Guy—was almost complete. The Rossis were devious and cruel lion-shifters who treated their lionesses like breeding property. And I couldn't wait to be rid of them.

I hated the Rossi brothers.

According to Mom—a lioness—when she was younger, her father was so pissed with her for getting pregnant by her fated mate—a human—that he'd given her to the Rossi brothers in exchange for territory. Mom wasn't the only lioness the brothers had acquired over the years. All the lionesses in their pride were either given to them by the lioness's parents or stolen from another pride.

Mom and I had been plotting for years to extricate me from their clutches. Not that the Rossis wanted a hybrid shifter like me in their pride. They only kept me around to control Mom. Every taunt and threat against me kept Mom and the other lionesses who feared the same treatment as me in line. For years, I'd begged Mom to leave this toxic compound, but she was terrified to run. Nick and Guy were rich, powerful, and would never stand for their property escaping. Mom's fear was that the Rossi brothers would just hunt us down, dragging us back to their pride for punishment.

But I was done living in fear.

And after enduring eighteen years of Nick's and Guy's cruel taunts and lustful stares, I was finally going to be free of this pride.

I bounced into the kitchen, intending to grab a yogurt. After leaving the recruitment office today, I'd spent hours at the library, deliberately coming home after eight in hopes of missing the usual awkward, tense dinner with the pride.

I skidded to a stop at the sight of Nick caging Mom against the granite counter. They both turned to stare at me. My stomach plummeted at the grim expression on Mom's face.

Nick smirked at me. "There you are," he slurred. "Happy birthday, broken shifter."

"Thank you," I croaked, ensuring that I kept my eyes lowered in deference.

When I heard footsteps approaching, I glanced up.

My stomach soured from the stench of Home Brew wafting off his breath. "Turning eighteen means you're now a woman." He grabbed my chin tightly. My skin crawled from his touch, but I remained still and silent.

He released my chin. "I purchased a gift." His eyes moved to the small box wrapped in red paper on the table. "Go see what it is, broken shifter." He smiled indulgently.

Walking over to the table, I eyed Mom, who stared at me with a neutral expression. Snatching up the box, I ripped off the paper with trembling fingers, then opened the velvet-covered box.

My knees almost buckled when I saw what was nestled inside. It was a wide onyx metal ring. The same ring all the lionesses in the pride wore, marking them as property of the Rossis.

I didn't like the way his eyes roamed up and down my body or the way he was licking his lips like I was a tasty morsel. "My brother doesn't feel that a hybrid deserves the honor of becoming our mate, but I've convinced him otherwise."

I could barely breathe. *This can't be happening.*

"Tomorrow night, we'll claim you under the full moon," he stated matter-of-factly.

I tamped down the anger that surged through my veins. If Nick sensed my displeasure, he'd punish Mom.

"I understand," I replied.

"Good." He nodded. "Now get out of my face and go to bed."

Mom stepped forward and addressed him. "Alpha? May I walk her to her bedroom?"

He waved his hand as if Mom were a pesky fly. "Go on, but hurry back. Tonight we celebrate another successful Home Brew run." Home Brew was for Others, and the brothers were illegally selling it to humans.

Mom and I rushed through the house and into my bedroom.

Shutting the door, I whispered, "Mom. Tomorrow night? What are we going to do?"

She grabbed my arm. "Did you sign up today?"

I nodded. "I'm off to the Fort Dix, New Jersey, Army base for basic training in a week."

Mom's body sagged with relief. "Thank God."

"But…"

"You have to leave now."

My heart raced. "What? To go where?"

She marched over to my private bathroom, and I trailed behind. My eyes widened as I watched her pull a sealed plastic bag out of my toilet's tank.

"Put this in your backpack." Mom handed me the bag filled with rolled-up wads of cash and a cell phone. "There's a burner cell inside and enough money to get you someplace to stay until you can leave for New Jersey."

"Mom, what are you talking about?" I searched her face. "That's not our plan."

Mom cupped my face. "The plan has changed. I've programmed my sister's number into the cell. Call her when you get out of state."

I'd always wondered about Mom's younger sister, June. Mom had shown me an old photo of them together, young, happy, and laughing.

"Mom. Please. You have to get out of here."

Mom shook her head. "Ro, I can't leave the cubs behind." None of the cubs were hers, but Mom was the alpha female of the pride, so she was protective of the cubs.

"Why can't you run to Aunt June and come back with reinforcements to save the cubs?"

"I've told you a million times why." Mom's eyes glistened with tears. "I can't bring trouble to June's doorstep, and that's exactly what would happen if we sought refuge with her. Nick and Guy would find me, killing anyone who got in their way. That's why your going into the military is the safest option for you. After next week, you'll belong to the Army. They won't want to fuck with the human government to get you back."

Joining the Army was my lifeline, but it was dawning on me that I was just replacing one owner—the Rossi brothers—for another, the Army.

"But, Mom…"

"Go," Mom snapped. "And never look back."

"You have to fight them." I clenched and unclenched my fists.

Mom opened my bedroom window. "You and I know that the grasslands surrounding this ranch are littered with the unmarked graves of women who tried."

"April!" Guy bellowed. "Get your ass outside. We're waiting in the backyard."

"I love you, Ro." Mom kissed my cheek. "Now go."

Wrapping my arms around her, I hugged her tight before climbing out the window. My bedroom was on the first floor, so escaping was easy. I headed in the opposite direction of the back of the ranch, where the pride would be congregating. It would take me over an hour to make it on foot to human civilization, but I'd done it many times.

Fifteen minutes into my trek across the grasslands, my steps faltered from the sounds of unfamiliar roars.

*What the hell?*

Turning around to face the ranch, I peered into the inky night, waited, and heard the unfamiliar roars again.

*Something is wrong.*

Nibbling on my bottom lip, I contemplated my options.

Option one, continue running.

Or option two, go back to the ranch to check if Mom was okay.

Shifting from one foot to the other, I hesitated.

Mom would kill me, but I chose option two. I couldn't leave until I knew for sure that she was all right.

*Fuck it.*

I walked toward the ranch. It didn't take me long to get back, and once I did, I headed in the direction of the roars—the backyard. But I had to play this smart to avoid detection by the Rossis. Once I made it close enough to the back of the house, I crawled low through the grasslands on my belly. When I reached an ideal spot with a good view of the back, using the knee-high goldenrod grass as cover, I pressed my body to the ground.

What I saw chilled me to the bone.

The Rossis' bodies were bloody and lifeless on the ground.

Three unfamiliar lions were prowling around, roaring at the lionesses. Another smaller lion stood separate from the fray, watching the chaos like some sort of spectator.

Mom and Fiona were in their lioness form and blocked the back door to the ranch. I knew instantly that they were trying to prevent the intruders from getting to the cubs.

My body shook with fear for Mom, the other lionesses, and the cubs.

I wanted to help Mom, but I'd do nothing but make the dangerous situation worse. I had no fighting skills. I was a hybrid, so I couldn't shift.

My heart thudded faster when the scrawny-looking lion ran over to Mom and Fiona to… Wait… He was helping to block the entrance to the door.

*Why is he working against his own? Is this some trick?*

An older-looking lion roared at the young, thin lion.

The thin shifter roared right back.

And the two other lion intruders just stared at the thin lion.

The older-looking lion shifted into his human form. He was tall, with a potbelly and long, unkempt gray hair. "Buster. Glen. Guard the other lionesses." Two lions loped away to do what they were instructed, but the skinny lion remained steadfast by Mom and Fiona's side.

"Mack. Shift," the older man ordered the lion.

The lion transformed, and my breath hitched at the sight of the tall young man with shoulder-length dark brown hair. Lust slammed into me, and my uncharacteristic response to him made my heart race with fear.

*What the hell is wrong with me? This is a life-and-death situation, and I'm acting like I want to beg him to take me to the prom.*

"What the fuck are you doing?" the gray-haired man demanded.

"Enough!" the young brown-haired guy yelled at the old man. "I was brought here against my will because you, Glen, and Buster wanted to take over this fucking pride. This is wrong. I want no part of this."

The old man sneered. "You've always been weak."

The younger man flinched. "If being weak means defending

the innocent, then yes, I'm weak. I'm not going to let you kill their cubs."

The old man laughed. "Come on, son. You're no match for me or your brothers."

*Son? The intruders are kinfolk?*

"We'll see," the guy replied. This guy's body was thin in comparison to his father and his brothers. There was no way he'd win the fight against them, but I applauded his bravery.

The old man sighed tiredly. "Glen, get your ass over here." A large lion loped over. "Take these stupid bitches down."

My stomach plummeted at the old man's order. I dug my fingers into the ground as the lionesses leaped onto the shifter named Glen as a unit. Mom and Fiona were best friends and warriors, but they were no match for the gigantic lion.

The young brown-haired guy stood there, his eyes darting between the three fighting, the old man, and the door. I didn't envy him; there was no clear decision on which of the three situations was more dangerous.

My attention shifted to Mom when she fell to the ground in a heap before transforming into her human form. Tears flowed down my cheeks at the sight of her beaten and bloody body. "We'll do whatever you want," she pleaded. "Just don't kill our cubs."

The old man's lips twisted cruelly as his fingers transformed into claws. "Are you the alpha female of the pride?"

*Mom… please say no,* I chanted in my head.

My breath hitched when Mom got unsteadily to her feet and said, "Yes."

"Too bad." I watched in horror as the old man lashed out with his claws, striking Mom's neck.

*Oh God… no!*

"Mom!" I wailed from my hiding place on the ground.

Two heads—the old man and young guy—swung in my direction, instantly pinpointing me within the grasslands. But it was the young brown-haired guy's intense focus on me that held me in place. I wanted to run, but my body froze like a rat caught in a trap.

I snapped out of my haze when the old guy bellowed, "She's a hybrid."

I had to go. Now. Making sure that my backpack was still secure on my back, I quickly calculated the fastest route to safety.

"What's a hybrid doing here?" the old man directed to Mom, who was bleeding profusely.

"I. Don't. Know," Mom replied.

"Liar," the old man snapped. "She called you Mom." He called over his shoulder, "Buster, get over there and kill the hybrid."

Scrambling to my hands and knees, I prepared to flee even though I didn't want to leave Mom.

Suddenly, the young guy stepped forward. "No. I'll kill her."

The old man grinned. "Finally, you've grown a set of balls."

"No," Mom wailed before sprinting in my direction. "Run, Ro," she called out, prompting me to jump up and run.

"Get them, Mack," the old man ordered.

I knew this territory better than the intruders, so that advantage gave me a fighting chance. But I couldn't outrun shifters. With arms pumping at my sides and eyes focused on the terrain, I traversed it with expert precision.

The farther along I got across the grasslands, the more relieved I became, especially when I didn't hear anyone pursuing me.

*I did it. Just keep running, Ro.*

Then I heard the sounds of someone moving quickly behind me.

*Fuck. My. Life.*

Whoever it was, they were moving like a freight train over the grasslands. My lungs burned as my feet pounded against the ground. They were coming up fast.

*Shit. I'm going to die.*

Chancing a glance over my shoulder, I saw the young guy barreling after me. Fear raced through me, causing me to trip over my own damn feet. Stumbling forward, I felt a sharp tug on my backpack. I fell backward and found myself on the ground, clutched against the brown-haired guy's nude body.

Struggling to breathe, I felt my bare skin tingle where his skin pressed against mine. Nothing could have prepared me for how my body would react when I finally stared down at his face. His face was gaunt but handsome. His chestnut hair was wild. But it was his strange bright apple-green eyes that gave me all types of inappropriate, lusty feelings. Then common sense came back. This guy wasn't one of the jocks from my high school; he was here to kill me.

"No!" I yelled while struggling to free myself, but it was no use. Despite the fact that he was skinny as hell, he was stronger than he looked. "Let me go."

"Quiet," he hissed.

"Please," I begged.

"I'm trying to save your life."

"I saw what your pride did to mine. You're a monster."

"Well, this monster is the only man who can save you from my kin."

I squirmed. "Let go of me, asshole."

"Calm the fuck down. I can't save you until you stop fighting me."

*Is this a trick?*

"Why?" I demanded, momentarily ceasing my fighting.

"Why what?" he replied.

"Why are you saving me?"

He remained silent for what seemed like forever.

Just when I thought he'd never answer my question, he said, "I am not like my kin. I do not kill for sport." He paused. "I won't kill you. I'm going to release my hold, but do not run. We've wasted enough time as it is. And if I'm not back to my family soon, they'll come looking for me and you. And I don't want that."

Releasing his hold on me, he gently rolled me off him before getting to his feet. I was tempted to run, but this dude was fast. He extended his hand to me. I hesitated, then accepted it. When my hand touched his, a curious shock tingled across my palm, racing up my arm.

With wide eyes, I asked. "Did you feel that?"

Pulling me to my feet, he replied, "Feel what?"

I shook my head. "Nothing."

"Hold out your arm," he demanded while extending the claws on his right hand.

I backed up. "I thought you said you wouldn't kill me?"

"I won't. I need your blood as proof of the kill."

Nibbling on my bottom lip, I stared up at him, contemplating my new dilemma. Can I trust him?

He sighed heavily. "The clock is ticking…"

"Ro," I offered. "My mom calls me Ro."

"Give me your arm, Ro."

It wasn't lost on me that he didn't tell me his name, which made me even more suspicious of his true motives.

I hesitated. *Oh, fuck it.* I held out my left arm, and he swiped a dark claw against my bare skin. I screamed in pain. The slash was long but shallow. I muffled my cry as blood trickled down my arm and onto the ground.

I frowned when the guy rubbed his hand against my wound, coating his palm liberally before rubbing his hand against his chiseled bare chest. He collected more of my blood, putting it on his hands and face like war paint.

Stepping back, he said, "Run," then turned to walk away from me.

I didn't know what provoked me to do it, but I caught his arm, stopping him.

"Thank you," I whispered before hugging him. Heat licked my skin, and my nipples tightened. It wasn't as if I'd never hugged a guy before, but this felt… different. So I was disappointed when he stood in my embrace, stiff as a board.

*What did you expect, Aurora? This isn't some love connection.*

Pulling back and feeling awkward, I tugged my favorite bracelet off my wrist. "Here."

He arched a brow.

"I saved up for months to buy it. It's my gift to you for going against your kinfolk to save my life."

Turning on my heel, I took off running into the night.

# CHAPTER 2
# MACK



**TWENTY-THREE YEARS AGO...**

When Dad parked along the deserted dirt road, I silently mouthed to my middle brother, Buster, *What the hell is going on?*

I'd arrived home from my second job and hadn't even stepped into our small trailer home when Dad had ordered me to get in his SUV because "We have family business to take care of."

What family business was a mystery to me because I was the only member of the family who had a job, bringing in a paycheck. Everyone else in my family—Glen, Buster, and Dad—spent their days drinking Home Brew, watching television, or hanging out at the local shifters biker bar.

Buster shrugged, but I knew he was lying because his ears were now beet red—his tell that he wasn't being truthful.

I peered around in search of landmarks or anything that could tell me where we were. There was nothing in the landscape besides grassland that expanded to the left and right of the road like the sea.

Nothing about being on an unfamiliar, deserted stretch of

land in the middle of the night felt right. But I knew better than to pepper Dad with a bunch of questions—it would only piss him off and earn me a brutal ass kicking.

Dad got out of the vehicle. We dutifully followed.

"Let me hear it!" Dad shouted while glaring at Glen and Buster, ignoring me as usual.

"How many times do we have to go over your plan, Dad?" Buster whined.

*What plan?*

Dad's expression darkened. "As many times as I fucking want you to."

"We're not stupid," Glen grouched.

"I beg to differ," Dad snapped. "You three are so dumb that you can throw yourselves on the ground and miss."

Glen snorted but replied, "When we get into the Rossi pride territory, we kill the alphas first, then separate the lionesses from their cubs."

"Then we kill the cubs," Buster interjected robotically.

My shoulders stiffened. *Fuck my life.*

*We're taking over the Rossi pride?*

All the lion-shifters in Tennessee knew about the Rossi brothers—Nick and Guy. They were alpha lion-shifters who made their money by running Home Brew and illegally selling it to humans.

"Any of their lionesses that resist our pride takeover, we kill," Glen finished.

Dad's lips curled up into a menacing grin. "Exactly. We've staked out this pride for far too long to fuck this up." His body swayed, and I knew, as usual, he was tipsy. "I'm tired of those pussy-ass Rossi brothers controlling everything around here. Why should those greedy fuckers have it all? Money, territory, and control over all the illegal Home Brew distribution."

Glen and Buster nodded in agreement. I stared at the three, shocked to the core. The Rossi brothers were known to be ruthless fighters, and attacking their pride was a suicide mission.

And if Dad and my brothers didn't succeed tonight, we'd have a target on our backs for the rest of our lives. But most importantly, attacking a pride was morally wrong.

Dad continued. "I want everything they got."

Anger coursed through my veins. We'd never moved in on another pride.

"Dad," I croaked. "We shouldn't do this."

"You'll do this, or I'll kill you." He leaped forward, backhanding me so hard that I flew onto the dirt road with a thud. As I got to my feet, anger boiled in the pit of my stomach, but I lowered my eyes in mock deference.

*Fuck this. I'm not killing anyone.*

Dad yelled, "Eyes on me, boy!"

I raised my gaze to meet his, making sure my expression remained neutral.

Dad pointed a beefy finger in my face. "This is my fault. I've been too fucking soft on you."

I barely bit back a scoff. Forcing me to fight Buster and Glen for the right to eat first was far from being too fucking soft on me.

"But no more," Dad snarled. "It's time to be a man. Pull your damn weight in this family."

I was twenty-four—the scrawniest and youngest of three—and the only person in the family who worked two jobs, bringing in a steady paycheck. Dad, Glen, and Buster sat around in our trailer drinking while plotting get-rich-quick schemes. Tonight's plan to take over the Rossis' pride was just another one of Dad's harebrained plans. But this time, there was a one hundred percent chance of us all getting killed.

"Now get ready to claim that pride," Dad ordered.

I nodded even as disgust bubbled inside my gut. Dad could force me to come along, but I had no plans to take part in this attack.

We all undressed, shifted into our animal—a lion—then slowly moved across the grasslands under the moonlight. We passed a small grove of scrubby trees with still no sight of the Rossi pride, but I kept my guard up. If I made it out alive tonight, I was done with my family for good. And even though breaking ties with my kin would make me a nomad, I didn't give a fuck.

When we finally spotted the large ranch-style house and circled around the back, I couldn't believe what I was seeing… It was some sort of freaky orgy party. Fire torches were peppered around the area, illuminating the partiers. Loud music was blaring. All the women and the two men were nude. A few women were dancing lewdly while rubbing against one another. Some of the females were stumbling around while holding large glasses. And each man was sitting on a lawn chair with a woman kneeling between his knees while he got his cock sucked.

*This is the big bad Rossi pride?*

My thoughts were broken when I saw Dad, Buster, and Glen barreling toward the raucous party. I stood frozen, watching as the attack unfolded.

The Rossi brothers—Nick and Guy—shoved away the females who were sucking their dicks. But when Nick and Guy got to their feet, I noticed that they swayed unsteadily. *Fuck. They're drunk.* This meant Dad, Buster, and Glen had a greater chance of taking down the brothers.

Dad, Glen, and Buster tag teamed the Rossi brothers, who were putting up a good fight. But my kin were winning this brawl, and none of them noticed—yet—that I wasn't taking part in the fray.

*Fuck this. I'm not joining this fight…* despite the consequences.

The battle between my kin and the Rossi brothers was over in a matter of minutes. What was left of the brothers lay on the ground, bloody and lifeless. Dad, Buster, and Glen then set their eyes on the females, who were huddled together except for two who had shifted into their lioness form and blocked the back door to the ranch. For whatever reason, they did not want my kin to get inside. Then it occurred to me why—their cubs were probably inside.

The two lionesses roared and swiped their paws, warning off my kin. Dad, Buster, and Glen roared right back. The two lionesses were no match for my family, who was determined to get inside and kill the cubs.

*I have to do something.*

The cubs were innocent and weak.

*I have to help.*

I had to do what was right, no matter the cost.

Decision made, I ran over to the two lionesses guarding the door.

Dad roared, his eyes locked on mine.

He wanted me to get the fuck out of the way.

I roared back, telling him I wouldn't.

Buster and Glen just stared at me, stunned.

Dad shifted back into his human form. "Buster. Glen. Guard the other lionesses." They loped away to do as instructed. I remained steadfast by the two lionesses' sides.

"Mack. Shift," Dad ordered.

I hesitated but needed to communicate with him. I had to try to de-escalate this situation before he killed the cubs.

I shifted but remained vigilant.

"What the fuck are you doing?" Dad demanded.

"Enough!" I yelled. "I was brought here against my will because you, Glen, and Buster wanted to take over this fucking pride. This is wrong. I want no part of this."

Dad sneered. "You've always been weak."

I flinched as if he'd physically slapped me. "If being weak means defending the innocent, then yes, I'm weak. I'm not going to let you kill their cubs."

Dad laughed. "Come on, son. You're no match for me or your brothers."

I straightened my back. "We'll see." Yes, I was scrawny for a lion-shifter, but I was faster than my kin.

Dad sighed tiredly. "Glen, get your ass over here." Glen loped over. "Take these stupid bitches down."

The two lionesses leaped onto Glen as a unit, but they were no match for him. Dad had a huge grin on his face as he watched the three fight. Dad remained in human form, as did I.

I was torn between helping the lionesses fight Glen and keeping guard on the door to ensure Dad didn't get to the cubs.

One of the fighting lionesses fell to the ground in a heap before shifting into her human form. The female's body was battered, bloody, and bruised, but she glanced over to Dad and said, "We'll do whatever you want. Just don't kill our cubs."

Dad's lips twisted cruelly as his fingers transformed into claws. "Are you the alpha female of the pride?"

Unsteadily, she got to her feet. "Yes."

Dad lashed out with his claws, striking the woman. The woman screamed while clutching her now-bloody neck.

"Mom!" a female screamed in the distance.

Dad and I glanced over in the direction of the woman's voice and spotted a female lying on the ground within the grasslands.

My breath caught in my throat when the woman's alluring scent of sweet apple intermixed with creamy vanilla drifted over to me.

My inner beast roared before saying, *Hybrid. Mine. Mate.*

*Shut it,* I reprimanded. *She's not ours.*

Dad sniffed loudly. "She's a hybrid." He turned to glare at the alpha female, who was bleeding profusely. "What's a hybrid doing here?"

"I. Don't. Know," she gasped out, but I smelled her lie, and so did Dad.

"Liar," Dad snapped. "She called you Mom." He called over his shoulder, "Buster, get over there and kill the hybrid."

My heart raced with fear at the thought of the hybrid being killed. *I have to protect her. I have to stop my kin.*

"No." I stepped forward. "I'll kill her."

Dad grinned. "Finally, you've grown a set of balls."

"No!" the alpha female wailed before sprinting toward the hybrid. "Run, Ro," she called out, prompting the hybrid to get to her feet and run off.

"Get them, Mack," Dad ordered.

I didn't bother shifting and sped after the two. Halfway into my run, I found the alpha female bleeding out on the ground.

"You are a brave and honorable female," I said. "But you will not survive your injuries." Even if she shifted from animal to human and back again, her injuries were too severe to heal.

Resignation gleamed in her eyes. "Please save my daughter."

*Her daughter was hybrid?*

She continued. "Spare her life." Blood trickled from her mouth. "Please..."

"I'll try," I said before taking off in a run across the grasslands in pursuit of the hybrid, whom I could see slicing through the night. But she wasn't fast enough to evade me. Adrenaline surged through me as I sped faster.

As if sensing my pursuit, the hybrid kicked into high gear, her arms pumping at her sides. But she made a critical mistake when she turned, glancing over her shoulder at me. She tripped over her feet, and I pounced, grabbing the backpack she carried on her back.

I yanked her body against mine, and we tumbled to the ground. I landed on my back with her chest pressed against mine.

Growing up, I'd heard shifters talk trash about the existence of hybrids—children created from a mating between a shifter and human—as if they were the equivalent of the bogeyman. Most considered hybrids abominations. I'd reserved my opinion on the subject since, until tonight, I'd never met a hybrid before.

"No!" she yelled while trying in vain to tug out her arms that were pinned to her sides by my arms, which were wrapped around her body like a python. "Let me go."

"Quiet," I hissed.

"Please," she begged.

"I'm trying to save your life."

When she glared down at me defiantly, her beauty took my breath away. Thick black hair framed her heart-shaped mahogany face, and her clean, fresh, sweet scent captivated me.

"I saw what your pride did to mine. You're a monster."

*Monster?* My jaw tightened.

"Well, this monster is the only man who can save you from my kin."

The hybrid squirmed. "Let go of me, asshole."

"Calm the fuck down. I can't save you until you stop fighting me."

"Why?" she asked.

"Why what?" I replied.

"Why are you saving me?"

*Because my stupid animal thinks that you're mine.*

"I am not like my kin," I answered, which was true. "I do not kill for sport. I won't kill you." Which was also the truth. "I'm going to release my hold, but do not run. We've wasted enough time as it is. And if I'm not back soon, my family will come looking for me and you. And I don't want that."

Releasing her, I gently rolled her off me before getting to my feet. I extended my hand to her, but she hesitated before accepting it. And when her hand touched mine, an electric shock stung my palm.

"Did you feel that?" she asked with wide eyes.

I pulled her up to her feet. "Feel what?" I lied.

She shook her head. "Nothing."

"Hold out your arm," I demanded while extending the claws on my right hand.

She backed up. "I thought you said you wouldn't kill me."

"I won't. I need your blood as proof of the kill."

She bit her plump bottom lip, peering up at me.

I sighed heavily. "The clock is ticking, hybrid."

"Ro," she offered. "My mom calls me Ro."

I started to tell her my name but stopped. *Why waste my time? I'll never see her again after today.*

"Give me your arm, Ro."

She hesitated before holding out her left arm. I swiped a claw against her bare mahogany-hued skin, executing a long, shallow slash. The female's piercing scream was like a knife to the heart, but this had to be done. Her wail would give my kin the satisfaction of hearing her pain, and they would assume I was killing her as Dad ordered.

Blood dripped down her arm and onto the earth. Rubbing my hand against the wound, I coated my palm liberally before rubbing my hand against my bare chest. I collected more of her blood, making sure to get the fluid on both my hands and face.

Stepping back, I said, "Run."

"Thank you," she whispered before hugging me.

Every muscle in my body tightened with shock. I'd never been touched by anyone in such a gentle way. But before I could respond, she pulled back and unhooked a braided black leather bracelet with small silver beads from her wrist, handing it to me. "Here."

I just stared at her, dumbfounded.

"I saved up for months to buy it," she explained. "It's my gift to you for going against your kinfolk to save my life."

Without another word, the hybrid ran off through the night.

# CHAPTER 3
## AURORA (RO)

**PRESENT DAY…**

Standing several feet back from the baggage carousel, I swallowed a pill to calm my nerves, chasing it with water. I hadn't expected such a large crowd in such a small airport, one town over from Black Forest Ridge, Alaska. I watched people get elbowed or bumped in the knees by someone lifting luggage, and my mind buzzed with anxiety from being around so many people in such a compact area.

Shoving my water bottle into my backpack, I plucked out my ringing cell and smiled when I saw the name on the screen.

"Hi, Aunt June," I answered.

"Hi, Ro. How was your trip?"

"Long." I sighed tiredly. "My body is a throbbing mess of pain from being crammed in several planes for hours."

"I'm sorry, honey," June said. "But I appreciate you for coming all the way to Alaska for my birthday party."

"You're turning seventy-five. How could I miss that?"

"Because I know that you'd rather be anywhere but the Ridge," June said.

"You got that right," I murmured.

When I'd asked June what she wanted for her birthday, I had to swallow my irritation when she said she wanted me to come to the Ridge for her birthday party.

"I promise you'll love both my party and the Ridge."

I snorted. "Highly unlikely." Hanging out with a bunch of shifters was not my idea of a good time. "Anyhoo, let's not get into that subject again. I'm waiting for my luggage. I'll meet you outside in a few."

I was about to end our call when June said, "I'm not outside. I'm sorry, baby girl, but I can't pick you up. The damn pipes just burst in my bar, and I'm dealing with the aftermath."

"Damn. I'm so sorry about your bar. How bad is the damage?" June's bar was her world.

"Nothing that a few weeks of construction can't fix. You know me. I don't let shit get to me. Anyway, I've asked Mack to pick you up."

"He's the deputy," I replied, even though I'd never met Mack or any of the townsfolk from the Ridge. But frankly, I felt like I knew these people. I'd been hearing about them for years during my weekly phone conversations with June. She kept me well entertained about the who's who of the Ridge and all the shenanigans that frequently went on. June's gossip about the Ridge was better than a reality television show.

"Yes." June sighed heavily. "Poor Mack. He came by today on a routine visit, and I twisted his arm to do this favor for me."

"Why didn't you ask your cougar squad?" June's tales about her besties—Piper, Freya, and Bonnie—were a riot.

"Because I already had a hell of a time getting you to come to the Ridge. I don't need them rolling up on you like the mob, giving you the wrong impression about our townsfolk."

I arched a brow. "What wrong impression?" I paused dramatically. "Like that the Ridge is a cesspool of crazy people?"

"Well, yes, that. Anyway, be on your best behavior with Mack."

"Hey!" I frowned. "When am I not on my best behavior?"

"You've made it abundantly clear that you don't like shifters. Mack's a lion-shifter. So don't you dare give him any of your sassiness." Someone in the background yelled June's name. "Hold your horses," June snapped at the person before directing her conversation back to me. "I've got to go, Ro. Mack will be outside, holding up a piece of paper with your name. And when you get to my house, my keys are under my front mat."

I spied my bag on the carousel. "Putting your key under the mat is not safe."

"Crime in the Ridge is nil. Besides, not many residents want to deal with the big bad lioness." June laughed. "Anyhoo, see you later."

When our call ended, I shoved my cell into my front pocket and hoisted my heavy duffel bag off the carousel. I was instantly rewarded with a sharp pain that zinged up both arms.

"Fuck!" I muttered under my breath.

It had only been a week since I was released from the hospital. The doctors had warned me against lifting anything heavy. Striding through the small airport, I felt my arm tremble from the exertion it took not to drop my bag. It frustrated me that the things I once took for granted, like the ability to carry a damn bag, were now a challenge.

Finally exiting the airport, I moved over to the side, heaving a sigh of relief when I dropped my bag. Gently massaging my aching arm, I scanned the area for Mack, who was supposed to be holding a piece of paper with my name.

My eyes stopped on the tall, muscular man—who looked like an older version of Chris Hemsworth but with dark brown hair—holding up a paper with my name, "Aurora Darabont," scrawled across it. And even though he wore mirrored sunglasses, I could tell that the deputy was checking me out... thoroughly.

"Well, ain't you a pretty kitty," I murmured. His dark jeans molded to his muscular thighs and narrow waist. A gold shield was hooked on his leather belt, confirming that he was, indeed, law enforcement. And his long-sleeved black V-neck shirt barely contained his massive biceps and wide chest.

Sexy Kitty pressed all my Yes Please buttons.

Tall, check.

Muscular, check.

Exceptionally handsome, double check.

*He's damn near a perfect ten.*

Except for the one important thing…

Sexy Kitty was a shifter, which meant that he was a hard pass for me.

# CHAPTER 4
## MACK

My primal instincts rose to the surface when I recognized her captivating scent—fresh, clean, and sweet.

*It's Ro.* The hybrid whose life I had saved twenty-three years ago.

*How is this even possible?*

But the impossible was confirmed when I spotted the eight-inch scar—made by my claw—on her left forearm.

Discreetly, I tugged down the left cuff of my long-sleeved shirt to hide her bracelet that I still wore every day.

She picked up her bag, striding over to me before dropping it again. "Hi, I'm Aurora." She smiled like I was a perfect stranger.

Yes, I was older. More muscular. And my hair was shorter. But why didn't she recognize me?

*Is she playing some sort of game?*

"I'm June's niece." She stuck out her hand. "Nice to meet you, Mack."

I played right along and said, "Hello, Aurora."

When our hands connected, a frisson of static skated across my palm. Aurora jerked her hand away, staring down at it like it was some sort of foreign object before eyeing me. "Sorry for the static electricity."

She laughed nervously. "Haven't had that kind of static jolt since…"

*Since me?*

She shook her head as if trying to clear away a memory of me—of us.

I arched a brow. "You okay?"

"Uh…" She bit her bottom lip. "Yes. Of course. Don't mind me. I just had an uncanny feeling I've experienced that static electricity before."

*Uncanny feeling?*

*Is that code for she doesn't remember me?*

*That I'm not memorable?*

*What the fuck?*

# CHAPTER 5
## AURORA

Suddenly, I did remember when and with whom I'd experienced that same static electricity. It had happened twenty-three years ago. The night of the pride attack. With the guy who saved my life.

"You ready to go?" Mack asked.

I nodded, reaching for my duffel.

"I got it," he said while edging me back and grabbing it.

"I can do it myself," I snapped with way more heat than was warranted.

"I know you can. However, it's the gentlemanly thing to do," he replied simply before walking over to the back of his SUV, stowing it away.

I stared at him for a beat. It had been so long since I'd allowed a man to do anything for me that his kind gesture had both surprised and annoyed me.

Mack strode to the passenger's door, opening it for me. "Get in, Aurora."

"I see chivalry isn't dead," I joked before walking over to him.

"Not when it comes to you, darling," he replied.

*Was that a compliment?*

*Or a sarcastic jab?*

I couldn't tell which from his neutral expression.

Taking off my backpack, I slid inside the SUV before he shut the door. As he strode around the vehicle, I boldly checked out his spectacular ass. When he hopped behind the wheel, he turned on the radio before pulling away from the airport.

Minutes drifted by, and there was no conversation between us. I also noticed how tightly he was gripping the steering wheel. *Do I make him uncomfortable?*

I shifted in my seat, unsure what to do to break the tense silence.

Normally, I didn't give a shit about making polite conversation. I was too socially awkward for that shit. Yet here I was, probably giving off unfriendly vibes when I should be grateful he took the time to pick me up from the airport. So I attempted something that I tended to be very bad at, small talk.

"Is Alaska supposed to be so hot at night?" I asked as sweat dripped between my large breasts.

"The weather is unpredictable in this area," he replied.

"Why is that?"

"Most shifters think that having a high concentration of us living in the Ridge affects the weather and temperature, not only inside the town but in the surrounding areas."

I arched a brow. "That's an interesting theory."

"You asked a question, and I answered," he snapped.

Not liking his snippy response, I turned to glare at him. He ignored me.

*Oh boy, this is going to be a long ride.*

"Can you put on the air conditioner please?" I asked.

"Nope," he replied.

It was his vehicle, but... "Are you always such an asshole, Mack? Or is this a special occasion?"

Instead of a snarky comeback, he chuckled. "I'm always an asshole."

I couldn't help the laugh that slipped out. "At least you're honest about it."

"Most townsfolk think I'm too blunt," he remarked.

"Yeah, well, I can deal with blunt."

"And for the record, I wasn't trying to be an asshole. I hate the AC. I prefer my two-seventy AC." He rolled down two windows—the driver's and passenger's.

I glanced over at his speedometer, and he was going seventy miles per hour. So to say he had a two-seventy AC—two windows down and going seventy miles per hour—was a true statement.

"Smartass," I murmured as the air rushed into the SUV, whipping my hair around my face.

He just grinned. "So June told us that you're military."

I arched a brow. "By us, do you mean the whole town?"

"Yup. She's proud of your accomplishments. Special Ops is a big deal."

It was, and I'd had to work harder than most for my place on the team. But nothing in life ever came easy for me. I trained hard to be a better, stronger soldier, which was how I moved up the ranks fast. But there was also a negative side to my focused ambition. Life at the top was lonely.

"Yes, that's June. My biggest supporter." I couldn't be mad at her for bragging about me. "I'm former military," I explained while shifting to ease the ache on my right hip. "I was medically discharged with honors this week." I sighed heavily before turning to stare at the passing scenery. "I've been in the military since I was eighteen. Now, I'm a forty-one-year-old woman who doesn't know jack shit about being in the civilian world."

He took his eyes off the road momentarily to peer at me. "It's scary, but it takes time to adjust to being a civilian. I'm former military too. Special Ops. It's been over five years since I retired and relocated to Black Forest with my friends who are also former military."

"How did you adjust to civilian life?" I asked.

After moving every three to four years to different countries, the thought of settling down in one place scared the shit out of me. In the military, I followed orders. Now I had to start making decisions about my life for myself.

"I had a support system. My band of brothers. We helped one another when we retired. If you decide to make the Ridge your home, we can be your support system."

"Thank you, but I'm just passing through. Two weeks max, then I'm gone." I felt more comfortable and safe in the human world. I could never make a town filled with Others—a society of witches, vampires, shifters, and other supernatural beings— my home.

I noticed his hands were back to gripping the steering wheel like he was about to rip it off. *What did I say to upset him?*

Trying to ease the sudden tension between us, I said, "So tell me about your band of brothers."

"We're a pack. Quinn is the appointed leader. He's also the town's alpha and a wolf-shifter. Rhett is the town's sheriff, aka the Protector, and a jaguar-shifter. Emmett owns the only garage in town, and he's a rhino. Jasper is into real estate and a tiger-shifter. And Brody owns a renowned brewery and distillery and is a wolf-shifter. There's also Imani, Quinn's mate and wolf-shifter. Nova, Rhett's mate and jaguar-shifter. And Piper, Quinn's mother, she's the pack matriarch."

"I've heard all the names you've mentioned from June. But she never explained your pack dynamics. I didn't know that different breeds could peacefully coexist in a pack." Growing up, I'd seen quite the opposite. Breeds killing and fighting one another over territory and females.

"We can and do. We're family. Yes, it's uncommon for more than one breed to form a pack, but it works for us. But I ain't going to lie, most of the townsfolk hate our different breeds' dynamics. In fact, they call us misfits."

"Misfits?" I was offended for them. As a hybrid, I knew

exactly what it was like to be ridiculed by your own kind and treated as less than.

I touched his leg lightly. "Mack, fuck those bigoted people." The muscles under my palm tightened. I quickly pulled away. "Apologies. I didn't mean to overstep by touching you." I didn't even know what had gotten into me. I wasn't even a touchy-feely kind of chick.

"You didn't overstep," he said.

I eyed him, trying to figure him out while continuing our conversation.

"June told me about the hybrids—Imani and Nova—who moved into the Ridge and all the chaos that ensued."

"Yes, it was rough in the Ridge for a while. Others tend not to like change or differences. But it's been pretty quiet for months. I'm hoping it stays that way, but I'm not holding my breath. Freya's mating spell is bound to bring more fated mates into the Ridge, and if they turn out to be hybrids, the haters are just waiting in the shadows for an excuse to act a fool again."

I shook my head. "It's a shame the Others can't get over their prejudice against hybrids even for their own betterment. From what June told me about Freya's spell, it's the solution to finding unmated males in the Ridge their mates."

"The spell is working," he said. "Two of my pack members found their mates. Imani, she's a hybrid wolf-shifter and Quinn's mate. She also co-owns the only B and B in town. Nova, she's a hybrid jaguar-shifter, the town's midwife, and Rhett's mate."

"You know, when June told me about Imani and Nova now being able to shift after finding their mates, I couldn't believe it."

"Why?"

"Because as a hybrid, I was never told by anyone in my pride about the possibility of me being able to shift into my animal when I meet my fated mate. In fact, growing up, the message had been quite the opposite. That I'm a broken shifter." An outcast no one would ever want or love.

"Broken?" he shouted. "What kind of bullshit is that? You're not broken. There's nothing wrong with you."

I laughed dryly. "It took years and lots of therapy sessions to figure that out, Mack. I've also learned to live with the fact that I can't shift. I don't fit in the shifter world, but I do among humans. So that's the life I've chosen. To live as a human."

An uncomfortable silence filled the SUV.

"But you can shift when you find your fated mate," he informed me.

"I don't want to find my mate," I snapped. "Why do Others assume that all female shifters will die broken and alone if they don't find their fated mate? That's such a narrow view of life. It's like saying that all women want children. I'm here to tell you that they don't."

"I'm not one of those shifters who thinks that all females need to be barefoot and pregnant. When I find my fated mate, if she doesn't want cubs, I'd be perfectly cool with that because I'm not looking for some fucking breeding machine."

"I didn't—"

"Excuse me, I'm not done, Aurora."

"Fine." I crossed my arms.

"Second, there's a big damn difference between needing a mate and wanting one."

"And that is?" I demanded.

"Needing a mate is a first-class ticket to the land of codependence. Wanting a mate is the first step in learning how to love and trust someone."

His words hit something deep inside me. A longing to have a man in my life whom I could love and trust.

"No snappy comeback, lioness?"

"No," I grumped.

"So you agree with my distinction between need and want?" he asked.

"Yes. Agreed."

He nodded. "Good. Now we're making progress."

I frowned. *Progress with what?*

# CHAPTER 6
## AURORA

The vibe in the SUV became more companionable halfway through our ride.

After his alpha smackdown on the difference between need and want, I had a whole different perspective on the sexy kitty.

Yes, he was an alpha asshole with a dominant air that made me want to put his ass in a choke hold. But I also sensed that—way deep down inside—Mack was a bad boy with a heart of gold who was going to make a loving mate for some lucky shifter.

"This is the thruway that leads right into the Ridge," he informed me after turning onto the road, his headlights brightening the way ahead. He sped along the serpentine road that had twists and turns and dipped and arched over the imposing waves of the crashing sea that flanked both sides of the freeway.

"It feels like being on a roller coaster," I commented. "And I love it."

He chuckled. "Driving on this road is like teetering on the edge of the sea. The brutal waves often crash over the road during storms. Most people hate driving on this thruway, and that's under the best conditions. But it's the only way to get into the Ridge."

"So the only destination at the end of the road is the Ridge?"

"No," he answered. "There are numerous villages along the way. And if you keep driving past the Ridge, the road will bring you out to the very farthest point, where the land ends and the ocean begins. Black Forest Ridge is one of the towns along the way, but only Others can see the entrance. For humans, the entrance to the Ridge is undetectable because of the magic in the veil."

"Fascinating," I remarked. "At first, I couldn't wrap my mind around the concept of the veil when June explained it to me. I mean, a veil created by a witch coven that cloaks the town from human entry and detection? That's some unbelievable shit."

"Yup, that's the same thing I said to Quinn when he told me about it. But it's true. That's why Others love living in the Ridge. They're safe and protected from humans there."

Mack continued driving for a bit before turning left, driving through the huge hole that was carved into a mountain. Only his headlights illuminated the darkness within the tunnel.

When we got to the end of the tunnel, I saw a wall of shimmering crisscross lines. "Is that the veil?" I asked.

"It's the second part of the veil," he informed me before driving right through the light show. "The first part was at the mountain entrance, but it's not as showy as this one."

Popping sounds echoed within the SUV, and a pulse of energy licked my skin before disappearing. I shuddered. "God, it's been so long since I've been around Others that I've forgotten how weird and mystical shit can get sometimes."

He chuckled, still driving along the road. "Yeah, weird and mystical pretty much sums up the Ridge and the townsfolk."

Suddenly, the scenery changed to a dirt road flanked by a lush forest instead of mountains. The forest had an Amazonian vibe. A landscape I recognized that was similar to my travels around the world.

"Is this really a freaking rain forest?" I asked.

"Yes, it is," he replied, never taking his eyes off the road.

"If I hadn't seen this for myself, I would have balked at the possibility of a rain forest in Alaska," I admitted.

"Black Forest is a place you have to see to believe," he said as he continued driving. "I've traveled a lot in my time in the military, but the terrain inside the rain forest is unlike anything I've seen. The land is so old and steeped in magic that it's created its own ecosystem that defies logic. We have mountain ranges to fast-flowing streams, waterfalls, and gorges. It's home to many animals and plants you won't find anywhere else on this planet."

"On the planet? That sounds more like an Amazon-rain-forest thing. Isn't that strange for Alaska?"

"It is. The topography and weather in Black Forest are unique. That's why Quinn doesn't allow rural residential development inside the rain forest. He doesn't want any displacement of wildlife."

"He sounds like a great alpha. Protecting the rain forest and animals is important," I agreed. "How many residents live in Black Forest?"

"Registered, 773, but there are more who refuse to take part in the yearly census and prefer living off the grid."

I laughed. "Yeah, that's Others—paranoid as fuck." I marveled at the beautiful terrain until a barely perceptible deviation in the landscape caught my eye. It was a turnoff that looked ominous as hell. "What's down there?" I asked.

"Wolf-shifter territory," he clipped out. "If you ain't a wolf-shifter, you don't trespass on their territory. Quinn, Rhett, and I go there occasionally to visit their alphas—Wilder and Hugo—to verify things are peaceful. But for the most part, they keep their pack in line."

Mack kept on driving before turning off onto a road that opened into a lush valley bordered by a stream. He drove along the road for a bit before pulling up in front of a stone thatched cottage that looked like something straight out of a fairy tale.

"Well, this is June's home," Mack announced.

"Whoa," I whispered while gawking at the strikingly picturesque property. "This is impressive."

"You ain't seen nothing yet. Wait until you see the inside." He shut off the engine and got out, coming around to open my door.

Getting out, I quickly stretched my torso left then right, hoping to ease the tension along the scar tissue over my right hip.

Mack wrinkled his eyebrows. "Are you all right?"

I nodded. "Yes. My body ain't what it used to be."

He stared at me for a bit before walking off to get my duffel from the back of his SUV. Mack lugged my bag as if it weighed nothing. "Let's go," he ordered, heading to the front door with me following behind him.

Once we made it to the porch, I lifted the mat and found the key Aunt June had left.

I shook my head with the key in hand. "I'm not comfortable with her leaving the key in the most obvious hiding place."

He laughed. "Hell, most people in the Ridge don't even lock their doors at night."

"Well, all righty," I chirped before opening the door. I was greeted by a light casting a warm glow into the foyer, and instantly, I felt at home.

"Thank you for the ride, Deputy," I said when Mack set my duffel on the floor.

"My pleasure," he said but made no attempt to leave.

We stared at each other silently, and again the feeling that I'd met Mack before came over me.

"Why do I feel like we've met before?" I asked him.

"Because we have, Ro." He ripped off his sunglasses, revealing his eyes, and I nearly staggered back from shock.

I recognized his bright apple-green eyes, but he looked nothing like that man from my past.

Mack was older, taller, and way more muscular, with sun-kissed skin. His hair was the same color—chestnut—but he had a buzz cut on each side of his head, with a longer mop of hair on top. I had to physically stop myself from reaching up to run my fingers through his hair.

"Do you know who I am now?" he demanded.

"Yes." My heart raced with surprise and happiness. "You're the lion-shifter who saved my life twenty-three years ago."

"Yes," he rasped.

Without thinking, I leaped forward, wrapping my arms around him, hugging him tightly. And just like on that night years ago, he didn't reciprocate my gesture.

*Is it me? Or does the deputy just have a thing about hugging?*

Embarrassed, I released him, stepping back. "Apologies. I invaded your personal space again."

"No." His green eyes locked on to mine. "You didn't. It's just that when you didn't recognize me…"

"You look nothing like you did twenty-three years ago." He didn't. He'd grown into a masculine sexy kitty whom, under different circumstances—like, if he wasn't a lion-shifter—I'd be all over. "But your eyes. I'd never forget them." They were beautiful. "I'm a hybrid, Mack. I don't have your keen sense of smell. Honestly, with those sunglasses, I had no clue." I pushed his arm playfully. "Why didn't you say something earlier?"

"I didn't know how you'd react when you realized who I am."

"React?" I frowned. "Like how?"

His jaw tightened. "My kinfolk killed your pride, Ro. Yes, they paid the price with life in shifter jail, but that will never bring back your mother, the cubs, or the rest of your pride."

I touched his arm. "I'll never forget what they did, Mack, but their punishment brought me closure."

The expression on his face looked doubtful.

The night of the attack, after I'd reached safety, I'd called Aunt June, telling her what had happened. June had contacted the shifter authorities, who hightailed it over to the ranch. Everyone from the Rossi pride was dead except for a few cubs and lionesses. They'd arrested Mack and his kin, but June had told me they'd later let Mack go after the judge read my statement about his role in the attack and him saving my life.

"Look, Mack, I spent years in therapy just to get my head right after that night. But eventually, I did. You weren't to blame for your kin's actions. I heard everything you said and saw what you did that night. You didn't even want to be involved in the attack."

His eyes hardened. "I could have walked away before the attack, never going with them in the first place."

"And if you had, I'd be dead." I pointed out. "You were there that night for a reason. I know that, and so do you. Let go of all that guilt I hear in your voice and see on your face." I meant every word I said to him. Mack's family would have killed me if he hadn't been there. His being there that night was divine intervention.

He sighed heavily. "Thank you." When he grabbed my hand, weaving his fingers through mine, my stomach fluttered with all the feels.

"What are you thanking me for?" I asked. "I should be thanking you… again."

"Thank you for not hating me for the sins of my kin." He lifted my other hand, pressing his lips against it. And that was when I saw the bracelet on his wrist. The gift I'd given him that night.

"You kept it," I whispered, feeling a deep sense of contentment that he wore something of mine. "My bracelet. Why?"

"At first, it was a punishment. A daily reminder of the lives we'd destroyed. But as I grew older and had more life experience, your bracelet became a symbol for my moral compass. When shit got rough, and I was tempted to make fucked-up decisions like choosing between doing what's right and what's wrong, I'd look at your bracelet on my wrist and remember what it felt like to do the right thing. This bracelet reminds me of you."

The beauty of his words caused my heart to thump hard in my chest. "Mack…"

"Aurora…"

We both stepped closer, nearly chest to chest, not taking our eyes off each other.

From outside, Aunt June called out, "Aurora? Mack?"

We stepped away from each other quickly.

"Hey," June said, stepping into the foyer. "I'm sorry I'm late."

"I should be going," Mack announced, still eyeing me. "Can I call you?"

I nodded. "Absolutely." I rattled off my number, and he memorized it before striding past with a "See you later, June."

"Bye, Deputy," June said. "And thanks for picking up Aurora."

He stopped, turning to stare at me. "It was my pleasure." Then he left without another word.

June shut the front door, then eyed me. "What was that?"

"What was what?" I hedged.

"Oh no you don't," she replied, swaying over to me with her ass-length braids swinging behind her. "There was something going on between you two." June jabbed a finger at me. "I smelled it." She tapped her nose. "Chemistry. Attraction. The prelude to hot, dirty sex. It was wafting through the air right when I walked inside. So spill."

I put my hands on my hips. "So I'm not even going to get a hug before you start interrogating me?" I sassed back with my lips curled into a smile.

"This is a temporary reprieve, young lady," June said before pulling me in for a tight hug. I embraced her right back. "It's so nice to finally have you here, Aurora."

"There's no way I'd miss your birthday," I replied, giving her another squeeze before releasing her. "Seventy-five, huh?"

June didn't look anywhere near seventy-five. She only had a few strands of silver in her neatly braided waist-length hair, and her ebony-hued skin had no wrinkles.

June shooed me. "Age ain't nothing but a number. I still make both the older and younger men in this town wish for a taste of my honey," she finished with a saucy wink.

I laughed. "I bet you do. So did your pipe issue get resolved?"

"Yes. Thank goodness. But there's water damage. I hired someone to take care of the cleanup, but I need to oversee the progress." She pinched my cheek. "Why are we still standing here in the foyer? Let's get you settled." We reached for my duffel at the same time.

"No, Aunt June. I got it."

"You're a guest in this house, Aurora Darabont," June rebutted.

"It's too heavy for you," I countered.

"And it's easy for you?" she asked, pinning me down with her gaze. "You're still recovering, honey."

I felt my cheeks warm up, and I sighed heavily. "How about we compromise? Let's leave my duffel here for now and go have some tea."

"Sounds good to me." She looped her arm through mine, tugging me away from the foyer. "I can't wait to hear what's going on between you and Deputy Mack."

# CHAPTER 7
## MACK

Dripping with sweat, I pummeled the punching bag. With every swing of my arm, my mind was still trying to process that Ro was in Black Forest.

*She's yours,* my inner beast announced. *Her scent has already told me so.* And this time—unlike twenty-three years ago—I didn't disagree with my beast.

*Aurora is mine.*

*And the only person who doesn't know it yet is her.*

My punches against the bag got harder.

I was a fucking impatient man. The need to dominate, claim, and mate her pulsed through me. But there was no getting around the fact that I'd have to wait for her inner animal to wake up and claim me.

*What if her beast doesn't pick me as hers?*

My inner beast snorted. *Unlikely.*

But there was a possibility.

Closing my eyes, I went at the bag harder.

Common sense told me that Aurora needed time to settle down inside the Ridge before I charged her like a bull.

Then there was the other issue that I'd sensed. Pain

emanating from her body. Aurora had hinted that she'd been injured in the military, but to what extent was unclear.

Opening my eyes, I stood, breathing hard, when Quinn walked into the gym with his cell pressed against his ear.

"Mack," he called over to me. "Imani wants to know if you're coming over to the ranch for dinner tonight."

"No." I walked to the bench. "I don't have much of an appetite tonight." Unwrapping the tape from my hands, I sat down.

"Yes, he did say that he's not hungry," I heard Quinn say into his cell while striding over to me. "Imani, calm down. Okay, I'm putting you on speaker."

"Mack? You all right?" Imani probed.

"What makes you think I'm not?" I asked.

"One, you've never missed a family dinner," she answered. "And two, that's what you lion-shifters like to do… eat."

*She's right. We lions do love to eat. Well, we love to eat, fight, relax, and fuck, but not necessarily in that order.*

"I'm okay." I tossed my tape onto the bench. "It's just been a long day."

Quinn stared at me silently.

"What?" I grouched at him.

"Imani," Quinn said. "I need to find out what's going on with Mack."

"Oh, for fuck's sake!" Imani exclaimed. "Before you do that, Mack, just tell me what happened."

I eyed the cell that Quinn held in his hand. "What happened with what?"

"Did Aurora arrive safely?" Imani asked.

I arched a brow. "Why wouldn't she?"

Everyone in the town knew Aurora was arriving tonight. All week, townsfolk had been gossiping about the new hybrid coming to the Ridge. June was the one who had spread the news that her niece—a hybrid—was coming to her birthday party next Saturday.

I couldn't blame June for feeding the gossip mill. After the surprise arrival of Imani and Nova and the ruckus that had caused, June's strategy had been to give everyone in town enough time to mentally and emotionally prepare for another hybrid in the Ridge.

"June told Piper that Aurora was waffling about coming," Imani said.

"Well, she's here," I informed her. "I dropped her off at June's."

"What is she like?" Imani asked.

*Beautiful. Intelligent. Sassy. Everything I want in a woman.*

"Imani, will you stop interrogating Mack?" Quinn demanded while taking a seat beside me on the bench. "If you want more information about Aurora, call June."

"Would you stop being such an ass, Quinn?" Imani sassed. "We're just excited to meet Aurora."

Quinn and I rolled our eyes. We knew who *we* was. Nova, Rhett's mate. Freya, the head of the witch coven. Piper, Quinn's mom. Bonnie, Nova's grandmother and a member of the council. And Imani's crew—Nyx, Rose, and Izzy.

"Well, go over to June's and introduce yourself," I argued.

"We can't," Imani admitted. "June's put us on the no-visiting list until tomorrow." She snorted. "Something about not wanting us to scare Aurora away with our pushiness."

I laughed because June was on point with her concern.

"Hey. We're headed to the ranch for dinner," Emmett announced from downstairs in the forge.

"Hold on a minute. I need you up in the gym," Quinn barked. "We have a problem."

"What problem?" I turned to glare at him. "There's no problem."

I heard a stampede of footsteps on the stairs before Emmett, Brody, Jasper, and Rhett arrived inside the gym.

"Imani, I'm going to be late for dinner," Quinn said.

"No problem," she replied. "Love you, babe."

"Love you more, mate," he said before ending the call.

"What's going on?" Rhett asked, barreling over to us with the other guys trailing behind.

Quinn jabbed a thumb at me. "I sense one pack member is down."

"I ain't down." I stretched out my legs. "I'm just not in the mood for company."

Emmett crossed his arms. "Mack being grumpy because he hasn't been fucked in years is not a damn emergency."

"His cranky 'I haven't fucked anything but my hand' attitude, that was this morning's conversation," Quinn said. "This is different."

My eyes narrowed. "You fuckers been talking about my sex life behind my back?"

Brody started punching the bag. "You don't have a sex life."

"Neither do you," I snapped. "The only two that are having sex on the regular are Quinn and Rhett."

"I'm missing dinner for this shit," Jasper said before plopping onto the mat and stretching out like the lazy tiger he was.

"Hey. Guys, stop bickering," Quinn ordered. "This is important."

"Yo, Brody," Rhett called. "Quit fucking around with that bag."

Brody stopped midpunch. "If this is going to be another 'let's learn how to get in touch with our feelings' conversation, then I'm out, motherfuckers."

"Brody!" Quinn shouted. "Come over here and get supportive."

My lips quirked. Ever since Quinn and Rhett had met their fated mates, they'd been pushing their "let's learn to communicate on a deeper level because mates love that shit" agenda.

Brody stomped over to the bench where everyone was gathered around. "Okay, I'm here. Get to talking."

They all glared at me. Waiting for me to say something. Ain't nothing more annoying than an alpha being stared down by a pack of alphas.

"Aurora, June's niece, is Ro," I rushed out.

Rhett's, Emmett's, Quinn's, Brody's, and Jasper's jaws slackened.

"What?" Jasper demanded, sitting upright. "Ro, the girl you told us about when we were in the military?"

I nodded. "Yes."

"The girl whose life you saved twenty-three years ago?" Quinn asked.

"Yes. Her," I confirmed.

"Wait." Brody grinned, his face finally coming alive. "Did she go all batshit 'I will avenge the lives of my pride' crazy on your ass?"

"What?" I exploded. "No. She didn't."

Jasper cut in. "Dude, if I were her, there would be major avenging happening right now."

Emmett nodded. "Like plotting to take you down while you sleep."

"She's not going to do any of that!" I shouted. At least, I didn't think she was.

"Why not?" Rhett asked with a perplexed expression.

Before I could respond, Brody asked, "Why aren't you bleeding, crying in a corner, and licking your wounds like you big-ass cats tend to do?" He shook his head. "I expected more from that lioness."

I crossed my arms. "So you wanted her to kick my ass?"

Brody nodded. "Someone needs to."

Brody and Emmett gave each other a high five.

"Frankly, I expected more from that lioness," Rhett chimed in. Then he gave me a wide grin.

"Hell, I wouldn't blame her," Quinn started, "if she went high drama with all the jazz hands on your lion-shifter ass."

"Whose side are you guys on?" I growled.

"Aurora's," they said in unison.

I huffed. "I just love all the pack support I'm getting right now."

"Lighten up, man." Quinn clapped my back. "We're just joking with you."

"I wasn't," Brody muttered.

"All kidding aside," Rhett said. "How did she react when she first saw you?"

I shrugged. "When she stepped out of the airport, she had no reaction. She didn't know who I was." Truth be told, it was a blow to my ego that I hadn't rated highly enough to elicit some type of emotion from her.

"She didn't recognize you?" Emmett asked.

"Nope." I paused. "But I was wearing my sunglasses, and it's been years since we've seen each other."

"She's an unmated hybrid," Quinn replied. "That's why she didn't pick up your familiar scent."

We'd learned from our experiences with Imani and Nova that when it came to hybrids, their senses—sight, hearing, smell, taste, and touch—were like those of humans until they met their fated mate and their inner animal awoke.

"What happened after that?" Rhett asked.

"I dropped her off at June's, took off my glasses, and when she saw my eyes, she recognized me." I paused. "She was excited to see me. There was no drama. In fact, she thanked me for saving her life. I thought she'd still be reeling from the loss, but she said she got therapy to deal with it."

Brody shook his head. "She's a better person than I am. I wouldn't have taken what your kin did so calmly."

"It was more acceptance of the loss than calm," I said. "Honestly, I thought she'd go ballistic on my ass when she found out who I was, but obviously, she didn't." I twirled her bracelet with my fingers. "I'm grateful for that, because for so long, I'd felt guilty that I didn't do more to save her pride."

"Do more?" Jasper demanded. "You did all you could have done in that fucked-up situation."

"In a nutshell, that's what Aurora said," I admitted. "She actually said that she was grateful I was there that night because if I hadn't been, she'd be dead."

"She has a point," Quinn said.

They all nodded in agreement.

I continued. "She seems to want to put that night all behind her."

"Well, that's good," Brody declared. "It's a clean start between you two."

"Is she hot?" Emmett asked.

"Very, and she's former military. Special Ops."

"So did you tell her she's your fated mate?" Quinn asked, looking at me knowingly.

"How did you know?" I said.

"Because when I walked in, you were hitting the bag like it owed you money," he countered. "And I could smell frustration and confusion in the air."

I sighed heavily. "No, I didn't tell her she's mine."

"Why not?" Emmett asked.

Rhett shoved him. "Because it's too soon, man. Trust me. Hybrids need space to figure shit out on their own."

"Her scent calls to me," I said. "And my inner beast is adamant—just like he was twenty-three years ago—that she's my fated mate. My primal instincts are telling me to pursue her hard and fast, but logic dictates that I slow down, give her space and time to get to know and trust me."

"Believe me," Rhett said, "that's the best thing to do. My relationship with Nova started out on the wrong foot. We wasted way too much time on bullshit misconceptions about each other. But once we finally got our shit together, we never looked back. That woman is the love of my life. She completes me. But if I had to do it all over again, I'd do it completely differently. I would spend more time communicating in a meaningful way. You know, building trust. Not bickering on irrelevant shit that at the end of the day doesn't mean anything."

Quinn nodded. "Ditto. I love my female. She's my rock. My everything. But when we first met, it was chaos, miscommunication, fear, and denial." He turned to stare at me. "If Aurora's yours, then don't let that shit happen between you two. I'm not saying relationships are easy, especially in the beginning. But start off on the right foot. Tell her what you want from her, then let her set the pace. That's part of the hybrid courting process. And in time, Aurora's animal will wake up and choose you."

"It's more complicated than that," I answered. "Aurora is former military, medically discharged with honors. I don't know the details of her injury, but I suspect she might need time to adjust to civilian life."

"Well then, let her make the first move," Rhett stated.

"What if she doesn't?" I asked in earnest. "I'm alpha to the bone. I'm used to charging in to take what I want. I'm not a patient man."

Quinn and Rhett chuckled.

"Welcome to our world," Rhett said. "We had a hell of a learning curve when we met our mates."

Quinn nodded. "Yup. And it didn't help that Imani has an alpha personality like me. Lines get blurred outside our bedroom, but behind closed doors, she's all submissive."

"Same with Nova," Rhett said. "But I've learned that the path to a happy mating is becoming friends first, then lovers. You have to build trust in a healthy relationship."

"That sounds to me like the way to go," Jasper chimed in.

Emmett and Brody nodded.

"Just send her a text telling her to call you anytime," Quinn said. "Leave the door wide open for her until she's ready to come right on through."

Patience wasn't my virtue, but if I wanted a relationship with Aurora, I had to leave the ball in her court or risk losing her forever.

"Okay." Brody clapped his hands. "Now that we're done sitting around talking like a bunch of girls, can we go eat dinner? Or do you want to start braiding one another's hair while we listen to sappy love songs?"

Emmett raised his hand. "I vote for hair braiding."

# CHAPTER 8
## AURORA

"So tell me, Aunt June. What's your beauty secret?" I asked as we made our way to the kitchen. Unlike vampires, shifters did age.

"I wash my face with black soap, then smooth on shea butter. I drink eight glasses of water every single day, starting with a big glass first thing in the morning. I exercise regularly." She paused. "And I have a very active sex life."

Aunt June and I had talked openly about sex since I was eighteen years old. So nothing about this conversation made me uncomfortable.

I broke out in laughter. "Aunt June, you're a hot mess."

"I'm just keeping it real, baby girl."

June turned on the light when we entered the kitchen, illuminating the modern but comfy space.

"Wow, it's beautiful," I marveled, scanning the stone walls, decorative plasterwork, timber beams, and medieval-style doors. "When you said you lived in a cottage, I wasn't expecting all this."

"When the previous owner—a fairy—put this cottage on sale, I had to have it." She gestured to the space. "I felt an instant connection to this property the moment I stepped inside. It's a little quirky, but it's my sanctuary. I hope it will be yours too."

"Thank you, June. You don't know how much it means to me to be here. But this is not a permanent arrangement. I'm here two weeks max."

June arched a brow. "You're family. I love you, but you're stubborn as hell. Why can't you get over this shit about being around shifters?"

"I won't live where I'm not wanted. I spent too much of my childhood feeling trapped in a toxic situation that I couldn't get out of. Do you think I'm going to voluntarily decide to live in a town that hates who I am?"

"Nova and Imani are hybrids like you, and they're happy here. I don't understand why you can't give it a try. You need a place to heal while figuring out what your life will look like after the military. Why not the Ridge?"

"Because I don't want to live in a town where I have to justify my existence."

June sighed. "Now you're just being dramatic about it. Majority of residents in this town are over the hybrids-versus-shifters debate. Hybrids are welcomed and are official residents of the Ridge. Imani and Quinn made sure of that. Who gives a shit about the rest who have issues with hybrids? They don't matter." She grabbed my hand. "I know the pride put you through some shit growing up, but that was then and this is now. All shifters are not prejudiced assholes. Look at me. I'm a Black woman with a successful business in a small Others town. My friends are as diverse as can be, and I'm welcomed here."

I knew she was right. It was time to let go of the fear, anger, and angst I had about living among Others. I'd faced lots of adversity in the military because I was female and Black, but I didn't let anyone stop me from achieving my goals in the mili-tary. I trained harder—did more pull-ups, ran more miles, became faster on the obstacle course—to be a better and stronger soldier than any of my peers, which was why I moved up the ranks fast.

I squeezed her hand. "I'll be here for two weeks, so I'll work on my bias against shifters."

"Good." June released my hand. "I want you mingling with residents, which means being socially engaged."

I rolled my eyes. "Fine. I'm all in for two weeks." I wasn't a social butterfly, but I wasn't a hermit either. "And I'm making your birthday cake."

"I wouldn't have it any other way. You're a fabulous baker. The grocery store at Main Square is top-notch. You'll find what you need there."

She bustled over to the stove. "It's teatime. I'll put on the kettle."

"Let me help," I insisted.

She turned on the water, filling the kettle. "The cabinet to your left has the teacups and plates. And the pink-and-green canister on the granite countertop has a variety of tea. I'll take mint." She placed the kettle on the stove, then set a beehive-shaped crystal honey jar with a dipper on the counter.

I did as directed and opted for ginger tea, putting a tea bag into each cup. "You have any sliced fruit for a snack?"

"Check the refrigerator. I should have a bowl of diced pineapple mixed with grapes."

Finding the fruit, I scooped a serving into each bowl before taking a seat. When the kettle whistled, June poured water into each cup.

"So you're attracted to Mack, huh?" She popped a grape into her mouth and chewed.

"Yes," I answered, putting a dollop of honey into my cup. "But it's complicated."

She arched a brow. "Explain."

"One, he's the guy who saved me that night of the pride attack."

June's eyes widened. "He's the same Mack?"

I nodded. "Yes."

"That's interesting," June replied before pursing her lips.

"Very." After stirring my tea, I took a sip.

"I don't get it. What's so complicated about you and Mack having history?"

"It's dark history."

"Aurora, don't make a mountain out of a molehill. You met. You survived. You're together."

"We are not together," I corrected.

"Yet." She waggled her eyebrows.

"Anyhoo. Moving on." I popped a grape into my mouth, chewed, and swallowed. "You know I have PTSD. I still have nightmares at night, and loud noises trigger my PTSD." I swallowed hard. "I don't need a savior, June. He saved me twenty-three years ago, and if I start a romantic relationship with him, he'll think he has to save me from my PTSD." I speared a piece of pineapple and chewed.

She stared at me like I'd lost my mind. "Save you? How about if he cares enough to help you?"

"Save. Help. Same thing. I don't need it."

"Asking for help is not a sign of weakness, Aurora."

"Forget it." I picked up my cup. "You don't understand."

"Make me understand." June reached out, grabbing my other hand.

"Growing up in the pride, I had to depend on myself." I bit my bottom lip, fighting the tears that pricked my eyelids just thinking about the way they'd ostracized and belittled me. "Yes, I had Mom, who was there for me, but she had her own shit she was dealing with inside the pride. I learned quickly that I had to protect myself. Depending on anyone else was a weakness I couldn't afford to indulge in. Not then and not now."

June clucked her tongue. "Oh, honey, I know what you went through growing up in that toxic pride was hell. But you have to let go of that pain. You're allowing those fuckers to steal your happiness. The pride is gone. You're here."

I shook my head. "I hear you, Aunt June, but I'm not dragging Mack into my emotional shitfest. I want to deal with my PTSD alone."

"Aurora, pretending that you've got everything together when you don't is not actually being mentally strong, it just means that you're acting tough. Ignoring your pain, hiding your weaknesses, and concealing your emotions won't make you any better. And last but not least, there's nothing weak about letting Mack in and leaning on him when you need to."

"Mack and I are not happening," I said, yanking my hand away. "Drop it, Aunt June."

There was no amount of convincing June could do to change my stance on this topic.

"Okay, but let me say this," June insisted. "Then I'll drop it."

With narrowed eyes, I drummed my fingers against the granite island.

"Getting help is not a sign of weakness," June continued. "It's a sign of strength. It means that you're strong enough to admit that you don't have all the damn answers." She grabbed my hand. "And that is the real sign of strength. It means you're trying to deal with uneasy emotions like humiliation, fear, and embarrassment head-on. It also means you're willing to be vulnerable. I love you, Aurora Darabont. You deserve joy, happiness, and love... and that's my final say on this topic."

"And I love you, June Darabont," I said.

She released my hand. "So I'm starving. What shall we order for dinner?"

"Surprise me," I said, my lips curling up into a smile.

She rubbed her palms together. "I like that you're adventurous. Well, we can—" She stopped short when her cell chirped. "Let me get this, Aurora. Hi, Freya. What's up?"

There was a long pause.

"Yes, Aurora's here. Don't act like Mack hasn't told you so already."

She rolled her eyes.

"I'm not being snippy. I'm just stating facts."

She paused several beats.

"Now look who's being snippy. There's a reason I didn't ask you to pick Aurora up from the airport."

She pursed her lips and waited another beat.

"Because I knew that you'd roll up to the airport three deep —you, Piper, and Bonnie—peppering my niece with questions and scaring the shit out of her."

June took another sip of her tea.

"No, you can't come over. Aurora needs rest before you all descend on her like a swarm of locusts."

There was silence.

"No, we haven't eaten dinner yet. What's it to you?" She pursed her lips. "What?" She sat up so fast that she spilled tea over the front of her blouse. "Aurora hasn't even been in town for a day, and y'all are seriously rolling up on her like the mob?"

I burst out laughing when the doorbell rang.

"I have a good mind not to answer the door," June snapped. "And no, it has nothing to do with not loving y'all."

The doorbell rang again.

"Do you want me to get it?" I asked.

"No." June ended the call and got her feet. "I'll get it." She headed out of the kitchen.

It wasn't long before I heard several unfamiliar female voices announcing in unison, "Dinner is here."

I laughed and shook my head. I hadn't met them yet, but I could tell June's friends were spitfires, just like her.

Sounds of women laughing and talking got closer. Minutes later, four women, including June, burst into the kitchen carrying large food containers before placing them on the granite island.

"She's way too pretty to be your kin, June," said the female with thick white hair that contrasted sharply against her beautiful ebony-hued skin.

June chuckled. "Shut your face, witch." She walked over and wrapped her arm around my waist. "Aurora, that's Freya." She pointed to the woman with white hair. "She's the head of the coven."

Then she gestured to a woman with dark hair. "That's Piper. She's Quinn's—the alpha of the town—mother."

She pointed to a woman with ass-length jet-black braids that were pulled back into a ponytail that clearly showcased the youthful appearance of her glowing sienna-hued skin. "And that's Bonnie, but we call her Bo. She's a member of the town council." She sighed heavily. "They're my pain-in-my-ass friends, but I love them."

"Hello," I said, getting to my feet.

Freya walked up to June, then playfully shoved her aside to hug me. "Welcome to Black Forest Ridge, Aurora." I hugged her back quickly. "We would have been here sooner..." She gave June the side-eye. "But your aunt is a selfish lioness who doesn't like sharing with others."

"She just got here," June complained.

Freya's eyes narrowed on June. "We're family. You can't keep us away." Then she turned to eye me. "What's this I hear that Mack was the guy who saved you twenty-three years ago?"

"What?" I sputtered. "How did you know that?"

"Mack told the pack," Piper replied.

June stepped forward. "And years ago, I told Piper, Freya, and Bonnie about the attack. It's their connections that helped me get the shifter authorities to the pride that night."

"Thank you," I said to all of them.

"No thanks necessary," Piper said, walking over to me. "It's so nice to meet you, Aurora. June's been telling us about you for years." She wrapped her arms around me. I hugged her before we both stepped back.

"Stop hogging her." Bonnie nudged Piper aside to hug me.

"Welcome to the Ridge, Aurora." She grinned at me. "We need all the help we can get for June's birthday party next Saturday."

"I'm here to help," I volunteered.

"Good," Freya said. "Now, will everyone get their ass in gear? We don't want dinner to get cold." She walked over to the cabinet and started pulling out dinner plates.

"Who made it?" June's eyes narrowed on the containers as if they were snakes. "I hope not you. The last time you cooked, we all got food poisoning."

Freya swung her head around to glare at June. "One damn time. Ten years ago. And you won't let me live it down."

Bonnie shuddered. "Good, it was awful. The four of us vomiting like we were actors in the movie *Exorcist*."

Freya pointed a finger at her. "Shut it."

"Don't worry, June. Imani made the food," Piper said before we all started buzzing about the kitchen, taking off the lids from the containers of food, grabbing utensils, glasses, bottles of sparkling water, wine, and napkins. Once everything was laid out, we milled around the island with plates in hand, serving ourselves buffet-style.

With my plate filled, my mouth watered from the delicious aroma of baked chicken with rosemary, mac and cheese, flaky biscuits, string beans, and mashed potatoes. I sat down, wasting no time digging into my food.

"Isn't it exciting, Aurora?"

I jerked my head up when I heard my name.

My eyes widened when I saw the four of them sitting across from me, on the opposite side of the island like it was a boardroom table and they were a panel about to interview me for a position.

"What's exciting?" I asked, totally confused.

"Freya's mating spell calling you to the Ridge to find your fated mate," Piper clarified.

I snorted. "First, the spell didn't call me. I'm here for June's birthday party. Second, I'm not interested in a mate. I have way too much shit that I'm dealing with."

Simultaneously, Freya, Piper, and Bonnie swiveled to stare at June.

"What are you old biddies staring at me for?" June sassed. "I can't make her do anything she's not interested in doing."

"But what about Mack?" Piper asked. "Do you think it's happenstance that you've met again after all these years?"

I put another forkful of mac and cheese into my mouth, chewing thoughtfully. I'd seen, done, and experienced a lot of things—good, bad, and ugly—during my time in the military. So I was a big believer in things happening for a reason. But I refused to jump to conclusions about Mack and me.

I answered truthfully. "I don't know why Mack and I reunited after all these years."

"See." Freya nudged June with her elbow.

"Ouch," June protested.

"Hold on," I said. "That doesn't mean that he and I are mates."

With an anxious gleam in her eyes, Piper leaned forward. "But you're willing to explore the possibilities, right?"

I sighed heavily, not willing to cave in to their matchmaking shenanigans. "Nope."

Freya's eyes widened. "But…"

"Nope." I leaned forward with my palms pressed against the cool granite. "I'm not interested in your mating club."

I was unapologetically firm on my stance, even though I knew about the feral-sickness problem consuming unmated males in the Ridge.

June told me Freya cast the mating spell in a last-ditch effort to bring the fated mates of the unmated males to the Ridge in the hope of saving them from going feral.

June took a sip of wine. "See. I told you so. She's not having it."

"This is not a mating club," Bonnie complained. "It's just what we shifters do. Mate."

"Yup," June chimed in.

"Shifters also like to eat, hunt, fight, dominate, and fuck," I said. "So what's your point?"

"The point is that finding your fated mate is more important. It's about experiencing a deep level of love, passion, trust, and connection with your fated mate. That's what both the human side and animal side of every shifter craves."

"I'm going to keep it real with you four. I'm a forty-one-year-old woman who's met a hell of a lot of Mr. Wrongs. So the possibility of finding Mr. Right—a man I could have everything that you described with—sounds like some fantasyland bullshit."

It had taken years to climb to the top in the military, but I did. But my focused ambition also had a negative.

Life at the top was lonely.

I couldn't risk dating or having sex with anyone in my unit or in the military. There was too much at stake—my credibility and my career—to allow sex and the job to mix. I'd seen way too many of my fellow female soldiers go down that path of sleeping with a soldier who let his ego get in the way when their relationship went sour. That was when the ugly rumors and gossip started spreading about the woman. *No. Not me.* The few men I'd fucked had been civilians whom I'd kicked out of my bed right after sex. My motto was no romantic relationships ever.

"That's what Nova thought before she fell in love with Rhett," Bonnie said.

"Ditto for Imani, before she and Quinn fell in love," Piper remarked.

June had told me about how the two couples met, their tribulations, and ultimate mating.

"I'm happy for them," I said with full honesty. "And maybe one day I'll find what they found. But that day is not now or tomorrow or the day after that." I arched a brow at them. "You get what I'm saying?"

"Oh, we get it," Bonnie answered. "But hear me, young lady. This is not up to you. It's up to your inner animal."

I shrugged. "And if she wakes and makes that decision, I'll deal with it. But for now, let's eat, drink, and be merry."

I could tell from the frowns on their faces, they were not pleased with my response. But they'd have to deal with it.

After what I'd been through in Afghanistan, I wasn't interested in happily-ever-after with anyone but myself.

# CHAPTER 9
## AURORA

*The high-mobility multipurpose wheeled vehicle—HMMWV—pulls up in front of the mess tent, and Brown, the driver, sticks his head out of the window and yells, "Saddle up! Time's a-wasting."*

*Glancing over at my team, I order, "Gear up. Mission first. Let's go."*

*Brown pulls away when we get inside the vehicle.*

*My team is in the back. I'm up front with Brown.*

*Suddenly, all hell breaks loose.*

*Machine-gun fire.*

*Mortar fire is coming from every direction.*

*"Get ready. Safety off!" I yell to my team.*

*I can hear sounds of loading weapons, them taking off the safety, getting ready to engage.*

*My nerves are steady as I call in over the radio for backup.*

*Then I yell to my team, "Get ready for a hell of a firefight!"*

*Brown starts to pull over to a group of buildings when I hear an enormous boom.*

*We've hit a roadside bomb.*

*My racing heartbeat causes pains in my chest as the HMMWV flips over on its top, and it's on fire.*

*My weapon's gone.*

*"Report!" I yell, dizziness nearly consuming me.*

*I hear screaming and gunfire. I turn my head and flinch when I see Brown dead and on fire.*

*My leg muscles tighten as my body readies itself to get me out of my vulnerable predicament. But I can't move my legs. The roadside bomb has twisted the metal from under the HMMWV, and I'm pinned between the dashboard and door with metal wrapped around my limbs.*

*The pain is throbbing in my legs, but I am more concerned about my team.*

*I can smell the burning of human flesh.*

*I can feel the heat from the burning of the vehicle.*

*I hear someone scream my name, "Sergeant Darabont!" But I can't move.*

*Men are trying to pry the crushed metal from around my body to pull me out of the vehicle.*

*The pain and heat are unbearable, and I pass out.*


My eyes snapped open, and I felt the weight of something pinning me down. Panic set in. I thrashed and kicked.

*Ro, you're in bed.*

*Not in Afghanistan.*

*You're at Aunt June's home.*

Closing my eyes, I forced myself to take deep, calming breaths.

*You're safe.*

I breathed in through my nose and out through my mouth.

*One. Two. Three. Four. Five.*

*I am in a safe place.*

*It was a nightmare.*

After a few minutes, my heart started to slow down, and some of the adrenaline evaporated from my system. And I realized that my body was wrapped like a mummy by the blanket.

"It's going to be okay," I whispered over and over while wiggling side to side, easing out of my blanket. With my limbs free of the material, I scooted back against the upholstered headboard.

Sweeping a shaky hand across my forehead to get rid of the sweat, I felt tears well up behind my eyelids. I took in the sunlight and the comforting sounds of nature streaming through the small windows lining the opposite side of the bedroom.

Placing my feet on the wood floor, I sat on the edge of the bed, feeling like a weak, defeated mess.

*How much longer are my nightmares going to last?*

It'd been months since Afghanistan, but just like clockwork, almost every night, I'd relived the roadside attack with brutal clarity.

I rubbed my eyebrows.

*How many more nights of nightmares can I take before literally falling apart?*

*Ro, get your shit together,* I chastised myself. *You're lucky to have survived when most of your team did not.*

I owed it to myself and my team to never give up.

With chin high, I stood up and strode over to the dressing table, reaching for my cell phone where I'd left it charging last night. I was relieved to have a signal, courtesy of Aunt June giving me the password to the town's private network. I checked the time. It was six in the morning, which was early for some but not for me.

Leaving my cell behind, I padded inside my private bathroom. I turned on the shower, allowing the water to heat up while peeling off my T-shirt and sleep shorts. Putting on my shower cap, I jumped in the shower, lathering up with lavender-scented body wash that worked to soften and replenish my skin as it gently cleansed. I let the water beat against my skin for a few more minutes before stepping out and wrapping myself with a fluffy white towel.

The steam in the bathroom started dissipating, so I took a quick look at my reflection. My dark skin glowed from the humidity, but I looked sleep-deprived, with hanging eyelids, darker circles under my eyes, and droopy corners on my mouth.

I needed to get my nightmare problem under control. I'd hoped that the frequency of my nightmares would taper off, and they had but not to a bearable level.

Carefully running the comb through my big, thick cloud of hair, I braided the strands into one large plait that dangled down to my shoulder before leaving my bathroom.

Marching into my bedroom, I dropped my towel, eyeing myself in the full-length mirror anchored to the wall. My five-four frame was no longer the toned, muscled fighting machine it once was in the military. Now, my stomach was softer. My breasts, thighs, and hips were fuller. And my ass, which was always rounder than the average female, now had a sexier jiggle.

In all honesty, I loved my new, more feminine curves, but I did need to get back to some form of exercise to stretch my achy body. I traced the large swath of puckered, discolored skin across my right hip with my fingers. The scar would be there forever... a reminder of my survival of the roadside bomb.

This was me now, and any man who wanted into my life could either take it or leave it.

I wrapped my arms around my body, giving myself a big hug. "I love you." I whispered my self-love affirmation. "And no one is going to love you as much as you love yourself. No more woe-is-me episodes. Today is my acceptance of what was, is, and will be." And with my affirmation, I got dressed, tugging on lingerie, black leggings, a T-shirt, and bright-pink sneakers.

Grabbing my cell, I headed out of the bedroom and through the small sitting area of the guest cottage I was staying in. I was grateful for the cozy space to unwind when I wanted time for myself. But I loved hanging around June too. After stepping outside the guest cottage, I traipsed across the manicured green lawn, heading to June's house that was only a few feet away.

My stomach rumbled as I opened the back door leading into the kitchen. Once I walked into the kitchen, I instantly felt my anxiety lessen. Sun from the multiple windows illuminated the space. The house was quiet, so I assumed Aunt June was still asleep. I'd planned on surprising her with breakfast while satisfying my need to bake, which was the one thing that soothed my stress and relaxed me.

Rubbing my hands together, I wondered aloud, "Now what shall I bake?"

Padding over to the refrigerator, I checked out the contents and was delighted when I saw that it was well stocked. The cabinets also had gourmet ingredients any foodie would die for.

After pulling out the items I needed, I placed everything on the counter, then turned on the oven. In a bowl, I added sour cream, butter, sugar, and eggs and stirred, loving the vigorous arm workout. I added cinnamon, flour, and baking powder into the bowl, popping a few morsels of chocolate chips into my mouth before adding them inside. Next, bananas and walnuts went into the large bowl.

Satisfied with how the banana bread dough had come together, I poured everything into the pan, inserting it into the oven. "Okay, that stays in for an hour." Leaning my hip against the counter, I searched my mental repository for another quick recipe.

Three hours later, I had several baked goods cooling on a wire rack.

Aunt June walked into the kitchen, her lips curled up into a smile. "Look at you, my little baker." She ogled the baked items. "What's all this?"

I pointed to each item. "Banana bread. Norwegian custard buns. Homemade buttermilk donuts with a rich whisky chocolate glaze." I eyed her. "What would you like to try first?"

"All of them," June replied. "I'm greedy as hell."

I laughed. "Me too."

June walked over to the already-brewed coffee and asked me, "How do you like your coffee?"

"With almond milk and one teaspoon of raw sugar."

June nodded. We worked in companionable silence as she prepared our coffee. I cut a piece of bread, placing a slice on each plate, then added a donut and a bun.

"Table or counter?" I asked.

"Table. I love sitting near the bank of windows with the sun beaming on me."

With all the food and the coffee on the table, we dug in.

When June bit into the donut, she groaned as if she was having an orgasm. "These are delicious," she said around a mouthful of doughy goodness. "Like professional-baker delicious."

"Thank you. I love to bake. It's what keeps me centered and calm." I popped a morsel of bread into my mouth and chewed.

While in the military, I'd moved around a lot. I'd been to Germany, Japan, Italy, England, Belgium, to name a few spots. It was my culinary adventure. While some of my peers were drinking and partying, I was baking in my spare time. Everything that I knew about baking I'd learned through trial and error.

I took a swallow of coffee. "When I bake, I become very focused. I don't have time to think about anything but the present. Worries and stress just melt away."

June leaned forward, examining me. "And how are you, stresswise?"

I shrugged. "I'm still having the nightmares I told you about. I'm also worried about what I'm going to do for a living." I took a bite of my bun. "Working in an office is not my thing."

"But baking is…"

"That's for sure." I devoured my bun.

She tapped her chin. "Imani and Piper are having a Ridge baking championship that starts next week. I think you should participate."

"Isn't it too late for me to join?"

"No. According to Piper, there's only one contestant so far."

"I've never thought about putting my baking skills to the

test." I bit my bottom lip, contemplating the possibility. "What's the grand prize?"

"An exclusive one-year contract to provide all the baked goods their B and B serves. A storefront on Main Square in a prime spot, and $2500 in prize money."

I sat back. "I don't know anything about owning a business." Even though I'd always dreamed about opening my own bakery, I'd never thought I could do it—not with being in the military.

"I can teach you everything you need to know."

"Well, it's that and the fact that if I win, I'll have to commit to staying in Black Forest to run my business."

"Would that be so bad?" June asked.

My eyes narrowed. "Is this your sneaky way of getting me to stay in the Ridge?"

"The competition is real, Aurora. It's been planned for months. Your baking is that good. It deserves to be on display. Besides, I know how competitive you are."

I loved to push myself and go against the best in anything I did.

"I'll think about it," I replied, taking a gulp of coffee. "Now let's talk cake. What is your vision for your birthday cake?"

June shrugged. "I'm not fussy. Surprise me. You know what I like."

"Sounds good." I'd mix my wants with hers and come up with something fabulous. "I'll need to get ingredients. Are you going into Main Square today?"

"You can get everything you need at Sanders. It's a grocery store in Main Square. I'll give you directions on how to get there." June bit into a donut and moaned. "This is better than sex."

I arched a brow. "Really?"

"Almost." She winked at me.

"When should I get ready to head out with you?"

"I have to see how far they got with my bar repairs; then I have to take care of a few other things. I won't be home until late. You take my SUV. I'll use my other car. I don't want you stuck inside the house. Get out and mingle with the townsfolk."

I wasn't interested in mingling, and she knew that. "What about the actual party? Is there anything you need help with? Decorations? Organizing?"

"Piper, Freya, and Bonnie are handling everything." She pursed her lips. "Which is making me crazy because they won't tell me anything about what they have planned."

I laughed because June was a control freak like me and didn't like surprises.

"I'll call them," I offered, "and see if they need help with anything." Piper, Freya, and Bonnie had given me their numbers as I'd given mine.

June perked up. "Good. Then you can tell me what they're planning for Saturday."

"I will do no such thing," I said. "I'm not snitching. Snitches get stitches."

June frowned. "Whose side are you on?"

"Theirs." I winked at her.

My phone vibrated and lit up. I picked it up to see a new text message.

MACK (TEXT):

Good morning. This is your asshole deputy, officially welcoming you to the Ridge.

The text from Mack caused fluttery sensations in my chest and stomach.

ME (TEXT):

Lol. Asshole? Whose ass do I have to kick for calling you an asshole?

MACK (TEXT): Yours... I ain't mad at you. Being an asshole is what I do.

I laughed out loud and texted back.

ME (TEXT): *Lol... Acceptance is the first step to change.*

MACK (TEXT): *I'm not changing, darling. I'm an asshole for life.*

My lips curled up into a smile.

ME (TEXT): *A man with a purpose. I love it. But you deserve better… How about a nickname for the rare occasions when you're not being a total asshole?*

MACK (TEXT): *I can't wait to hear this…*

My thoughts drifted to his hot body. I grew wet just thinking about how his lips would feel against my skin.

MACK (TEXT): *????*

ME (TEXT): *Hold on… I'm thinking…*

Mack was all my hot-man fantasies come true. He was a big, hot, sexy kitty. And right then, the nickname came to me.

*Don't do it…* I chastised myself even as I tapped out my response.

ME (TEXT): *Sexy kitty.*

I didn't have to wait long for his response.

MACK (TEXT): *I ain't mad at it… You can call me sexy kitty. In my bedroom. With me between your legs.*

I sighed softly as my cunt pulsed and nipples pebbled, just imagining him licking my pussy like the sexy kitty he was.

MACK (TEXT): *Did I scare you, lioness?*

His words didn't scare me. In fact, they made me wetter, hotter.

ME (TEXT): *No. Not scared. Just intrigued. But not ready for any sexy kitty action.*

I unapologetically loved sex. I also only did hookups. I didn't need the hassle of a romantic relationship. But I knew instinctively that if Mack got me into his bed, he'd want more, and I wasn't ready for forever.

MACK (TEXT): *Just say when. Your sexy kitty is ready, willing, and able.*

My pussy pulsed. *Damn. I'm going to need to change my panties.*

ME (TEXT): *I bet you are.*

MACK (TEXT): *Seriously, Ro, no pressure. Call me if you just want to talk. I'm here.*

Tipping my head to the side, I stared at my cell.

*No pressure?*

Sexual banter with a man wasn't new, but deep conversations about other topics besides sex? This was new for me.

ME (TEXT): *Thank you. Talk to you later.*

With a grin on my face, I set my cell on the granite island. I glanced over at June when she cleared her throat loudly.

"Text from Mack," I told her.

June's eyes were filled with laughter. "So…" She took a long sip of her coffee. "Are you sure there's nothing between you and Mack?"

"Nothing." I shoved a large piece of banana bread into my mouth, causing my cheeks to puff out like a chipmunk.

June cackled. "You'll be in his bed within a week."

My eyes narrowed as I chewed.

June got up from her chair and kissed me on the cheek.

Turning on her heel, she started walking out of the kitchen. "When you're at Main Square," she said without looking back, "make sure you stop by the station to say hello to your deputy."

*My deputy?*

*Fuck… I'm screwed.*

# CHAPTER 10
## MACK

My mind was still firmly stuck on my text conversation with Ro from this morning.

*Sexy kitty?* I chuckled aloud, just thinking about the nickname.

*Shit. This kitty can't wait for the chance to get between her legs and lick all her sweet cream.*

My thoughts snapped back to the present when I heard, "Hey, Deputy." It was Ambrose, the owner of the only hardware store in the Ridge.

I strode up to him as he locked the front door of his hardware shop.

"Hey, Ambrose. How's business?"

"Today is one of our slow days."

I nodded in agreement. Main Square was quiet and deserted today, which was why I'd decided to take advantage of the lull to head over to Bessie's Coffee Shop for pie and coffee.

Ambrose jingled his keys. "I'm heading home early. Tonight's pot roast night, and Hazel gets mad if I'm not home to help her cook dinner."

I smiled but felt a twinge of envy. It must be nice to have someone to go home to every night.

"Well, you better hurry," I coaxed. "Don't want to make your mate angry."

Ambrose nodded. "For sure. Ain't nothing scarier than a pissed-off hippopotamus-shifter." He waved goodbye and got into his rusty, beat-up jalopy, pulling out of his parking spot and starting down the road.

I was about to continue on my trek to Bessie's when a familiar SUV—June's—pulled into a parking spot in front of Sanders grocery store. The car door opened, and Aurora hopped out.

I started to call out to her when Ambrose's vehicle backfired with a loud kaboom sound. Aurora released everything in her hands—keys and handbag—and she dropped low to the ground, cowering next to her SUV.

My stomach plummeted when I saw her trembling body as she held her head in her hands. My primal instincts—to protect her and to provide for her—rose to the surface. Her eyes were blank, as if she had no clue where she was. I knew exactly what was happening. I'd seen plenty of soldiers with shell-shock or PTSD—post-traumatic stress disorder—act identically to her. She thought that the loud sound was gunfire and that she was back in the war.

I ran over to her side but didn't touch her—if I did, it would make this precarious situation worse.

"Ro, it's okay," I coaxed in a soothing voice. "You're not at war. It was a car that backfired."

She squeezed her eyes shut. "No. No. No. This can't be happening again."

I tried again to verbally pull her out of her panic attack. "Listen to the sound of my voice, darling, and breathe deeply."

I stood, waiting patiently.

A few minutes passed before her eyes snapped open. When she dropped her hand from her head, her eyes were wide, white showing around the whole iris. "Give. Me. My. Handbag," she demanded in a high-pitched voice.

Reaching down, I picked up her bag, handing it to her.

She reached into her bag and pulled out a prescription bottle. She fumbled with trembling fingers to get the top off with no success.

Stepping closer, I said, "Aurora, hold on a second. Don't take the medication." I knew the most common drugs prescribed for PTSD were antidepressants.

She tightened her fingers around the bottle. "Why?"

"Let's try something new," I coaxed.

"No!" she yelled. "I need my fucking medication."

I crouched down next to her. "Ro, breathe deeply," I said, my eyes locked with hers. "Then try to breathe normally. Then I want you to talk to me about what you're feeling."

She took a breath, her eyes still locked on mine. "Did you see what happened? I lost my shit. That's what the medication is for, to calm me down."

"I've seen this multiple times in combat and when people come home from war."

"This is not war," she hissed.

"But at that moment, when you heard a car backfire, you thought it was war," I explained. "You were not on the battle-field." I reached out my hand to her. "So put the medication away, and let's go talk about it."

A couple of minutes ticked by before she put the pill bottle back into her handbag and took my hand.

Rising to my feet, I pulled her up. At that moment, I saw her face transform from panicked to relatively calm.

"Let's go to Bessie's and get pie and coffee," I suggested. "We need to talk about what just happened."

"Okay," she said softly.

Pressing a hand to the small of her back, I ushered her toward Bessie's.

# CHAPTER 11
## AURORA

Our entire walk over to Bessie's, my mind was a typhoon of angst as I dissected my PTSD episode.

When I'd stepped out of June's SUV, I was mentally prioritizing my grocery shopping list. Then out of nowhere, the kaboom sent me into a panic. Fear raced through my body along with the roadside bomb flashbacks and sudden, vivid memories of gunfire ricocheting outside the HMMWV and the smell of my burning flesh.

My brain went into a state of alarm—my heart raced, sweat dripped down my face, and my breath sped up. I couldn't move or think. Then I heard Mack's voice breaking through the mental storm raging inside my head. He was my mental lifeline that saved me from drowning beneath the dark waves of fear.

"In here," Mack said while ushering me inside the coffee shop. The few patrons sitting in the front of the shop turned to stare at us as Mack directed me past the tables and toward a booth at the far end of the shop.

I slid into the large booth bathed in sun from the bank of windows, and Mack sat in the seat across from me.

An older female walked up to the table. "Hey, Mack."

"Hi, Bessie," Mack said.

Bessie smiled at me before saying, "Hey, Aurora. It's sure nice to finally meet you."

"Hi, Bessie," I said.

"June told me you were coming to Main Square today, so I hoped to see you," Bessie volunteered.

All the customers in the front were still staring at me.

Bessie turned to glare at them. "Go back to eating, y'all, and leave her in peace," she said. They grumbled but did as told.

"Pay them no mind, Aurora," Bessie said. "Everyone has been all abuzz about you, the new hybrid in town. Anyhoo…" She looked over at us and said, "Mack, you having the usual? Coffee and a slice of cheddar apple-pear pie?"

He nodded.

I wasn't hungry, but I knew that a jolt of caffeine and sugar would even out my still-shaky equilibrium. "That pie sounds delicious," I said. "I'll have the same."

"Be right back," she replied and hustled away.

"You all right?" he asked.

I blew out a breath. "No. Just need time to settle down a bit. Thank you for being here for me."

"If you need me, I'm here." He reached across the table, grabbing my hand.

My stomach fluttered from the warmth and the touch of his fingers.

"Mack, I—" I started, only to be cut off when Bessie came back to our table with two cups of coffee and enormous slices of pie.

"Here you go." Bessie placed our order in front of us, then walked away to tend to other customers.

Wasting no time, Mack and I dug into our pie.

"Dang good pie," Mack mumbled.

"Yup." The pie was gooey, tart, and sugary while the cheddar was sharp and savory—a naturally perfect salty-sweet combo.

Comfortable silence stretched between us while we ate and drank coffee. I liked that Mack didn't pepper me with questions about my PTSD episode. He patiently waited until I was ready to discuss it.

I took a sip of coffee. "I was in Afghanistan with my team." My fingers started trembling, so I placed my cup down.

Mack grabbed my hand. "If you're not ready, I won't push."

"I'm ready, Mack. This is the first time I've talked to anyone about the details of what happened." With everyone else, I'd glossed over the specifics. "I want to tell you because I know that you'll understand." He was a former soldier and Special Ops, so I knew he'd seen the horrors that came with war. War was ugly, and as soldiers, we knew this.

I continued. "I was in an HMMWV with my team, and about thirty minutes into our scouting mission, all hell broke loose. There was machine-gun fire and mortar fire coming from every direction. I told my team to get ready. They loaded their weapons and prepared to engage. I called in over the radio for backup before telling my team to get ready." I swallowed hard when I felt the panic creeping up on me again.

"Breathe," Mack instructed. "Stay with me."

I nodded, then took a deep breath.

I continued. "We were getting ready to pull over to some buildings when I heard an enormous boom. I realized we had hit a roadside bomb when our HMMWV flipped over and was on fire. I heard screaming and gunfire, and when I turned around, I saw a member of my team dead and on fire." I yanked my hand away from his. "I could not move my legs. The roadside bomb had twisted the metal, and I was pinned between the dashboard and door. I felt the pain, but I was more focused on my team."

It was comforting that Mack just listened, which was what I needed.

I didn't want to be soothed.

I needed to be heard.

I bit my bottom lip. "I could smell burning flesh, and I knew it was one of my team members. I could also feel the heat from the burning of the vehicle. Finally, backup arrived. I could hear them screaming my name, but I couldn't move. When they pried the metal from around my body, I passed out. The next thing I remember was waking up in the hospital in Landstuhl, Germany."

"What were your injuries?" he asked.

"Shattered bones in my knees and a cracked hip. I still have a burn scar on my right hip. After multiple surgeries to put me back together, I was sent to Texas for recovery and was assigned a therapist to help me work through my emotional trauma." A therapist I'd refused to talk to. "I knew my military career was over. They were done with me, and I was done with them. So I retired."

"Would you have gone back if you could have?" he asked.

"Yes. The military was my life. They were the pride that accepted me with no questions asked. Their only requirements were that I believed in the mission and followed orders. I did, and I took shitty jobs that no one wanted, which allowed me to move up the ranks quickly. But that was then and this is now. I don't look back, only forward. But my PTSD won't allow me to move on. I know it will take time for me to unravel my emotional issues. At least the frequency of my nightmares has decreased. But just when I think I've moved two steps forward, something happens, like losing my shit when I hear loud noises, and moves me four steps back."

He leaned forward, his green eyes latched on to me. "Ro, you have to be patient with the healing process."

"Patience is not my virtue." I stirred my cup of coffee. "This is the first time in years I've allowed myself to think about want I want. For years, it was what the military wanted. It's difficult facing the hard truths about my life."

He frowned. "What hard truths?"

"About who and what I am. I'm a forty-one-year-old woman who's scared to death about starting over in a civilian world that I know nothing about."

"Years ago, I felt the same thing. I never thought I'd retire from the military when I did. Like you, the military was my life." He took a big gulp of coffee. "The military gave me the discipline and structure my father never instilled in me. My team—Rhett, Quinn, Brody, Emmett, and Jasper—was my family, my band of brothers. But I knew it was time for me to retire when I started to want more."

Intrigued by his statement, I asked, "What do you mean by more?"

"A life that was my own," he replied. "I was physically and emotionally tired of moving every four years. I had no roots, no foundation to ground me in a life outside the Army. I longed for my fated mate, but there no way in hell that when I found her, I'd drag her into a military-wife life."

From what I knew and heard, being a military spouse was hard. The spouse had to hold it together when the service member left to work in a really dangerous place for months on end or more. They had to be okay with moving halfway around the world from their family. They had to be okay with their service member missing all the special stuff, like birthdays, holidays, anniversaries, or, gasp… the birth of their child.

Boldly, I asked, "So you were one of those fuck-them-and-leave-them men?"

"Never." He shook his head. "I was always straight up with my lovers. I never played games. I gave them what they wanted, my total focus during our sexual encounter, but I made no promises of a future together. I was waiting for my fated mate." He grabbed my hand. "My mate will get my love, devotion, caring, and protection for the rest of our life together."

Butterflies fluttered in my stomach with every stroke of his finger across my palm.

My heart thudded faster. "What are you saying, Mack?"

His eyes were unwavering. "You're mine. My fated mate."

"But we just met," I croaked. "How can you know that?"

"I'm a shifter, Ro. You know that we recognize our fated mate by scent and attraction. For us, it's clear-cut—you're either our mate or not. There's no in-between. And if that's not enough to convince you, my inner animal has been clawing my insides in protest because I haven't claimed you yet. Hell, he insisted that you were ours twenty-three years ago. You're mine, and I'm yours."

I knew full well from growing up in the shifter world that there was no waffling about the distinction between just a fuck buddy and a fated mate. So I knew that what Mack said and believed was his truth. But my inner beast hadn't awakened. And when she did, would she pick Mack?

"Mack, I'm attracted to you, and what I feel for you is not just about sex. It's more complicated, which scares the shit out of me. But I'm a hot mess. You deserve more. You deserve perfection."

"I'm not looking for perfection, Ro. I'm looking for real, and that's what you are to me. I have no blinders on when it comes to you. I know that you need time to heal. But healing is not a solo act. So I'm here for you… anytime and anyplace."

I stared at him. This man's words and actions were everything I needed, but the fear of him rejecting me when shit got rough gave me pause.

I couldn't risk opening the gate around my heart only to be hurt when he decided that being with me was too complicated. That I was broken just like my pride called me.

"I need time, Mack."

"You need time to heal," he replied. "We'll do it together."

My eyes widened. "What? Why?"

"You're my female. I'm here for you." He squeezed my hand before releasing it. He pulled money out of his wallet, placing it on the table. "See you tomorrow night." He got up, walking away.

"Tomorrow night?" I murmured to myself. "What just happened?"

It didn't take long for Mack to appear outside. My seat by the window gave me a perfect view of him standing on the sidewalk, texting.

Seconds later, my cell buzzed. It was a text from him.

MACK (TEXT): *7 p.m. Tomorrow. MMA grappling session. Here's the address.*

When I looked up from my cell, his green eyes were locked on mine. A challenge was in his gaze, as if daring me to back down and text him back with some lame-ass excuse why I couldn't accept his invitation.

I never walked away from a challenge... ever. It didn't hurt that I loved mixed martial arts. All Special Operations members honed their fighting skills, including mixed martial arts, aka MMA—as former Special Ops, Mack knew that.

ME (TEXT): *Prepare to get your ass handed to you, sexy kitty.*

He pointed one finger at me, then pointed to the ground, gesturing that he was going to take me down.

I laughed while giving him the one-finger salute before he walked away.

# CHAPTER 12
## AURORA

After leaving the diner, I decided to do a little sightseeing, passing multiple shops along the tree-lined street. But one of the shops caught my eye, a brightly painted storefront with a hanging Nyx's Yoga sign.

Opening the door, I stepped inside the spa-like atmosphere. The space was accented with a soothing neutral color palette, blue yoga mats, and lit candles subtly wafting a sophisticated scent through the space.

"There's nothing small town about this," I said aloud.

"I hope not," a woman with dark skin and short, natural hair replied as she walked up to me with a huge smile. "Hello, Aurora. I'm Nyx. Nice to finally meet you."

"You're Freya's daughter."

"Yes, I am. I've been dying to meet you, but your aunt insists that you need more time to acclimate yourself to the Ridge before meeting your new girl crew." She winked at me.

I laughed. "June would surround me in Bubble Wrap if she could." I panned my eyes across the huge, open space with lots of natural lighting. "I love your studio. It has a safe, relaxed vibe."

"That's my goal. Inner peace." She arched a brow. "Have you ever taken a yoga class?"

"Yes, but it's been a while. But I'm looking to take a class where the focus is not on stretching or strengthening, but on releasing tension."

"I have the class for you. Restorative yoga can help reconnect with your parasympathetic nervous system and strengthen your ability to move between states of stress and rest with more ease. By helping you learn to relax, restorative yoga can also reduce the production of stress hormones—cortisol and adrenaline—improve the function of your immune system, reduce muscle tension, help with insomnia, and so many other vital benefits."

"Sign me up. When is your next class?" I asked.

"Monday night at seven in the evening, and your first class is on me."

I frowned. "I'll be here, but I'm paying. You can't stay in business by giving away classes, Nyx."

"It's my welcome-to-the-Ridge gift, Aurora. Besides, like a good drug dealer, your first one is always free." She winked at me. "That's how I lure in unsuspecting residents. Give them a free class, and they're hooked."

I smiled. "Sounds kind of scammy if you ask me. But I'm a sucker for a good marketing gimmick."

"Well, see you Monday, and be prepared to get your yoga on."

"I'll be ready. Bye." I walked out of her studio feeling a lot lighter.

I headed to the grocery store, picking up some items before heading back to June's cottage, unpacking the groceries, and making a quick dinner by myself since June was still at her bar, taking care of business.

All through dinner, I couldn't get my mind off my encounter with Mack today. The lion-shifter was a gentle giant who truly saved my ass—again—when I'd lost my shit during my PTSD episode.

I was grateful for his help talking me down from the proverbial ledge. But in retrospect, the fact that he'd seen me at my absolute lowest didn't sit well with me. I'd always been the strong, show-no-weakness chick. Frankly, I didn't understand why such a powerful alpha lion-shifter wanted me—a hybrid—who felt lost for the first time in my life.

Typically, I wasn't a woe-is-me kind of woman, but I'd changed—a lot—after Afghanistan. I'd lost my life's direction and had no clue how to find my way back to any semblance of normalcy.

I was jarred out of my thoughts by my cell ringing. When I picked it up, I didn't recognize the number.

"Hello?" I answered.

"Hi, Aurora. This is Imani, your friendly hybrid stalker. I finally got your number from June, so don't freak out."

I laughed, loving her quirky humor. "Hi, friendly stalker. Nice to finally talk to the woman I've heard so many good things about from June."

Imani chuckled. "Well, damn, that's a hell of a lot to live up to, but I'll try. Hey, I'm calling to welcome you to Black Forest and invite you to girls' night at my place on Wednesday night. It's potluck. Everyone brings something."

My eyes widened. I wasn't a social bee; in fact, I bordered on the loner side. "Well... I... uh..."

"I'm not accepting no, Aurora. You're coming. We're a real chill crew. No mean girls here. There'll be drinks, food, music, and no drama. It'll be fun, I promise you."

I shrugged. "Okay."

"Good. I'll text you directions. See you Wednesday night at eight." Our call ended.

"What the hell is happening?" I grumbled, even though the idea of hanging out with Imani filled me with more dread than excitement.

# CHAPTER 13
## AURORA

Sunday night, I pulled up in front of an enormous building with an EMMETT'S AUTO SHOP sign on the left and a BANE'S FORGE sign on the right.

"Aurora," I muttered aloud. "What are you doing?"

Here I was, getting ready to spar with a man built like a fucking tree compared to my five-four frame. Prior to my injuries, I wouldn't hesitate taking on Mack, but now I'd lost all my muscle mass.

"No fear, Aurora," I coached myself. "Just get your ass in there." I hopped out and took the next door into the forge and what looked like converted stables. When I walked inside, the enormous stone forge took up the entire back wall. Several racks of forged-iron artwork lined the other walls along with bins of raw materials and shelves of tools.

I spun around, trying to take in all the artwork, which was mostly nature-themed and primarily of animals or mythological creatures. I couldn't take my eyes off the mesmerizing masterpieces. "This is fucking amazing."

"Ro," Mack called out. "Up here."

I stared up at the second story before walking up the stairs. My eyes widened at the massive gym with glass doors that had been opened, revealing a balcony. One side of the space had black floors covered in mats with bags lined up and hanging from the ceiling. The other side had a boxing ring with all the walls covered with mirrors.

My heart raced like that of a schoolgirl with a crush when I saw Mack sitting on the matted floor. Today, he was wearing all black—knee-length basketball shorts, fitted T-shirt—with bare feet. His eyes traced me from head to toe, making me happy I'd spared the time to pull my outfit together—tight yoga pants, T-shirt, paired with pink-and-green sneakers.

"Hey." I greeted him.

"Sneakers off," he said with no smile.

"Oh, I see," I said, taking off my sneakers as instructed. "No hello. Just let's get down to business, huh?"

"Something like that," he replied, getting to his feet.

I strode over to him and tried not to drool. Mack was powerfully built, with muscles bulging everywhere.

With his muscular forearms crossed in front of him, he stared pointedly at me. "Next session, get here on time, Ro. I don't like waiting around."

"I got lost," I replied. That was the truth. It had taken me a while to get myself back on track after I'd made a couple of wrong turns.

"It didn't help that you sat outside, waffling about coming in here to meet the big bad lion-shifter."

"How…"

"I heard when your car pulled up," he answered.

*Damn. Busted.* My cheeks heated that he knew about my trepidation regarding coming inside.

"I've got cold bottles of water." He pointed to the ice chest pushed against the mirror. "I want you hydrating frequently tonight. I can't have you losing steam right in the middle of your ass kicking."

I rolled my eyes. "Ass kicking? Don't underestimate me, Deputy."

"I'm not the one doing the underestimating. You are. You've lost sight of who you are and what you're capable of. Tonight begins your rebirth."

I blinked, no clue how he'd read me so well, so fast. He was right. My confidence was at an all-time low since Afghanistan. Between my nightmares and yesterday's panic attack, I questioned if I could function in my everyday life. Now Mack was here, pushing me to face my fears, to start my healing process.

"You don't even know me, Mack. Why do you have so much confidence in me?" I wasn't used to any man having my back or giving a shit about me beyond what I could give them in bed.

He cupped my face, and my gut flipped faster. "Because you're a fighter. Are you ready?"

I nodded. "I'm ready. So what's my mission tonight?"

"We're going to grapple." He sized me up with his green eyes. "You were Special Ops, so this will be easy for you."

He was right. I had plenty of experience with grappling from my time in Special Ops. The goal of grappling was to gain a physical advantage, improve your relative position, escape your opponent, or force your opponent to submit.

"Yes, but it's been a while since I've grappled."

He nodded. "My body is already warmed up from cardio. You'll need to warm up, then stretch."

It had been quite some time since I'd moved my body in any rigorous movements besides physical therapy. My doctors had advised me to get back into the gym to keep my muscles loose and body limber, but I hadn't been motivated until now.

Mack and I jogged in place for ten minutes. I felt good after our light warm-up.

"All right, let's get you stretched," he announced before striding over to the wall.

We were both standing in front of the section of the wall covered with a wide floor-to-ceiling mirror. Our reflection in the mirror was a graphic representation of the huge difference in our bodies. His massive frame was Mount Everest, and my short, curvy frame was the valley eclipsed by his body.

"Have you ever stretched using the wall?" he asked while staring at me in the mirror.

I gazed at the floor-to-ceiling mirror with a sliver of wall on each side. "Yes," I answered. "But not in front of a mirror."

He grinned. "Hmm, so you're a mirror virgin. I'll have to rectify that."

"Mirror virgin? Why does that sound sexual as hell?"

"Have you ever had sex in front of a mirror?" he asked.

His bold question did not embarrass me. In fact, just the thought of doing something so kinky made my pulse race. "No. But I'm not afraid to give it a whirl." I winked at him in the mirror.

"Well then, I can't wait to introduce you to how incredibly sexy it can be to watch yourself getting taken by me."

Lust slammed into me, just imagining what it would be like to catch glimpses of myself in the mirror while Mack fucked me hard.

"Unfortunately, that won't be tonight."

I turned to glare at him. "Did you just cliffhanger my ass?"

"Yup." His eyes roamed over me from head to toe, making my skin tingle as though he'd stroked me. "The first time I take you will be long, slow, and memorable."

*Well… damn.* My nipples throbbed and pebbled, and I had to fight not to cover them.

He pointed to the mirror. "Now get to stretching, lioness."

Shaking myself out of my lust-filled stupor, I walked up to the mirror. Glancing up and into the mirror, I saw Mack's eyes firmly on my ass.

"You like what you see, Deputy?" I asked.

"Absolutely."

"I'm loving that you're into a woman with lots of junk in the trunk." I wiggled my ass suggestively before bending my knees slightly.

"I'll love it even better when I take you from behind." He moved to stand directly behind me, placing his hands along the sides of my hips.

I nudged him back. "Stop distracting me, Mack. I have stretching to do." Keeping my neck relaxed and lower back in its natural arch, I slowly pressed my chest toward the floor, folding at the hip joints as much as possible.

"Breathe deeply," he said while deepening the stretch by rotating my hips forward to lengthen my hamstrings. "And hold this position for sixty seconds."

I groaned while pressing my heels to the mat. My legs were tight and hips were stiff, so it took me a little bit longer to work out the kinks.

I glanced up, and Mack's eyes locked with mine in the mirror. Talk about getting an up-close-and-personal view. "Damn, this isn't as easy as it used to be," I complained. "Before I got injured, I was extremely flexible."

In the mirror, I watched his eyes narrow with interest. "How flexible?"

"Full-on splits and backbends were my thing."

His hands that were still on my hips squeezed. "We're going to have to get your flexibility back so you can show me those moves behind closed doors."

"I'm not making any promises, Deputy," I sassed back.

He grinned. "What happened to sexy kitty?"

"Reserved for times when you're being nice to me."

He ran a hand over one ass cheek. "Like this?"

"Keep going," I said, now standing with my back pressing against his chest.

He wrapped his arms around my stomach, and we gazed into the mirror together, sharing superintense eye contact. His muscles jumped when I raked my nails across the front of his thighs.

"There's my sexy kitty," I purred.

He growled before swooping down, nipping and flicking his tongue against the side of my neck. My breath hitched. Transfixed, I watched him flick his tongue against the skin of my throat.

"Mack," I whispered, raising one hand and pressing my fingers against the back of his head. "More."

My hands fell away when he snapped his head up, his eyes locked with mine in the mirror. "You'll get more when you're ready to give yourself to me fully." He released me.

And just like that, he walked away.

My eyes narrowed on his wide, retreating back.

I'd never been so turned on by a simple touch. But he was right; I wasn't ready to give myself to him fully. I was more than willing to have sex with him, but he wanted more than a quick fuck. He wanted commitment. He wanted forever. Two things I wasn't ready to give.

I strode over to the center of the mat to meet him.

"Take me down," he instructed as we both faced off.

Mack was a huge guy, but I'd taken down bigger when I was at the top of my fitness game. I wasn't as fit right now, so I had to be strategic with my takedown.

I attacked, getting a solid grip on his collar, then sidestepped, pulling strongly before attempting to swing around his body like Tarzan on a vine. It did not work as expected. Instead of Mack dropping facedown and me getting on top of him, he stood steady on his feet while I slid to the mat in an embarrassing splatter.

"Try again, lioness."

Breathing hard, I rolled to my feet.

We faced each other again.

"Did I tell you how sexy you are?" he growled.

My heart rate increased. "Are you trying to distract me, sexy kitty?"

"Of course not. I'm only stating a fact." He winked.

"Well, just for the record, I find you extremely sexy. But none of that is going to stop me from taking you down." I blew a kiss at him.

"I wouldn't have it any other way."

Mack stepped forward, grabbing me and easily hefting me across his side, tossing me down to the mat. I rolled away before he could get to the mat and cover me with his body.

Getting to my feet, I said, "Again."

We went at it hard for a few minutes, and I loved and respected the fact that he didn't go easy on me. For every move I made on him, I had to work for it. There was also a sensuality to our movements and the way we touched each other. Every touch of his hands on my back, butt, arms, or hair ratcheted up the sexual tension between us. I gave him everything right back— trailing my fingers across his chest, back, arms, and ass.

We took breaks in between, taking sips of water.

For my next move, I grabbed him from behind, pressing my chest against his back while wrapping my arms around his narrow waist. He twisted left, then right to shake me off him. Feeling bold and cheeky, I loosened my grip to graze his cock with one hand. He hissed as if he'd been burned. I used his distraction to take him down.

Lying on his back, he stared up at me. "If you wanted to touch my cock, all you had to do was ask."

I grinned while gazing down at him. "This lioness doesn't ask for what she wants, she takes it."

I knew it was a long road back to my physical body feeling strong again. The roadside bomb didn't kill me. It only made me stronger. I had to move on. That didn't mean I needed to bury or ignore what happened. It just meant that there was a way to move forward.

He chuckled before getting to his feet. "It's getting late." He glanced over at the clock. "And I don't want you overworking your body tonight."

I nodded because I was already feeling the soreness of working my body in ways that I hadn't done in months.

"Come here," he demanded.

Without hesitation—surprising the hell out of me—I walked straight into his arms. Pressing my cheeks against his broad chest, I sank into his warm embrace. It felt like home.

Stroking along my spine, he said, "You did good tonight. You're beautiful, courageous, fierce, brave, and strong. Thank you for giving me the gift of trusting me enough to come here tonight."

His words were like a balm to my battered body and mind. I wanted to let him in… closer to my heart, but I didn't know how to look past the pain of being emotionally hurt and abandoned by my pride because they viewed me as lesser than—broken.

*How can I trust Mack without getting hurt again?*

*I need time to figure out how far I want things to go between Mack and me.*

*I need distance.*

Gently pulling away from him and avoiding his gaze, I said, "Time for me to go, Mack." Without another word, I walked away from him.

"Ro, what's going on?"

I didn't answer him, but Mack didn't approach me. I knew that he was allowing me to bide my time, gather my thoughts before he approached me. Quickly putting on my sneakers, I ran down the stairs and out of the forge. I was under no illusion that he wasn't coming for me.

I'd made it to the driver's side of my SUV before Mack demanded, "Look at me."

Turning around, I faced him, my eyes locked on his.

With his hands on his hips, he asked, "What's going on?"

"Nothing."

His nose flared. "I'm a shifter, Ro. I can smell a lie."

"I'm fucking scared, okay," I admitted. "This"—I gestured between us—"I don't understand what it is, and it scares me."

It would be better to keep whatever we had strictly sexual. Sex I understood. Relationships and emotions were not in my vocabulary. All my previous sexual encounters had been fast and hard, with no foreplay required. Pretty much wham, bam, thank you, ma'am. But Mack already made it clear that he expected a lot more from me.

He moved in closer. My back was pressed against the SUV. "I've already made it clear, Aurora. There're no ifs, ands, or buts about it. You belong to me, and I belong to you. I'm giving you space to figure this out on your own, but I'm damn sure not allowing you to walk away from me and us."

My body stiffened. I felt raw, exposed, and confused.

He stroked my hair. "Don't overthink this. Just feel," he coaxed.

Too late. My mind had run through all the scenarios of me getting hurt by Mack. Feeling was what had allowed me to get rejected and hurt by the pride over and over again. Feeling was what I'd sworn not to do because it would break me when a man eventually broke my heart by rejecting me. And that was exactly what would happen with an alpha lion-shifter like Mack.

My heart raced, nearly exploding. "This is bullshit. I don't want to fucking feel." My voice broke. I cleared my throat. "I want to fuck you and be done with all this." I wanted him to get angry, rejecting me now before this shit between us got too deep.

I needed Mack to save me from myself.

He grabbed my chin. His eyes were clear and determined. "It will never be done between us, Ro. You're mine. All of you. I'll never leave you." He released my chin.

Before I could stop myself, I blurted out, "Don't make promises you can't keep."

His eyes turned to slits. "Do you trust me?"

I looked away from him.

Everything inside me rebelled at the notion of trusting him. But rationally, he'd done so much good for me that couldn't be denied. Logic and emotion warred inside me. I couldn't ignore the emotional scars I still had from growing up in the pride. Their rejection was the model for how I now saw myself—

broken. And the message I'd internalized was that it's not okay to just be me. I grew up believing, to varying degrees, that something about me was flawed or shameful. As a result, I expected that I wouldn't be accepted and that others would fail me. I was trying to protect myself by keeping my guard up.

"Ro, look at me," he growled.

*Don't show him who you really are.*

*He'll want nothing to do with you.*

I met his eyes. "No. I don't trust you."

He studied me until I felt uncomfortable.

"Why are you staring at me?" I yelled.

"I want to know why," he growled.

"Why what?"

He sniffed hard through his nose, then slowly released it. "Don't play games with me, Ro."

I threw my hands up in the air. "Because I'm broken. I was a broken shifter growing up in the pride, and now I'm a broken woman with PTSD." Something inside me split wide open, allowing all the fear, anger, and confusion to pour out. "It has never been okay to be just me."

"And what's wrong with being you?"

"Didn't you hear me? I'm flawed." The air became thick in my lungs. "You'll fail me when you realize that I'm not the woman you think I am."

"Look at me," he growled.

I met his eyes.

"There is nothing wrong with you. So what, you're a fucking hybrid who has PTSD. That doesn't mean you're not worthy of love, because you are. You're beautiful, strong, intelligent. You are my lioness. And this lion will always be on your side. My need for you isn't going to fade. It will grow more powerful with time."

My stomach fluttered nervously.

He continued. "And when you give in to what you feel for

me, I will love, care, and protect you in ways you never anticipated."

My heart pounded faster. His words ignited a strange feeling —hope—inside me.

"No." My voice trembled. "Friends with benefits."

The muscles jumped near his jawline. "I'll have all of you or none of you," he clipped out. "That's the only way it will be." He pinned me with his hardened eyes.

I held back a scream of frustration.

His mouth compressed into a thin line. "Ro, you can waste a whole lot of time pretending this isn't happening, but it is. The sooner you come to terms with your new reality, with me in it, the sooner I can claim you as mine." His nostrils flared, and every muscle in his body seemed to tense. "But that's not going to happen until you let go of your fear. Trust yourself. Trust me. And trust us."

He brushed a hand against my breast and teased the tight bud of my nipple between his fingers. Liquid heat poured through me, and my stomach quivered.

*Jesus.*

The mere thought of surrendering to Mack on an emotional level made me dizzy with fear. My hands started shaking. I swallowed hard and bit my bottom lip to hide the emotion that had set it trembling. Clasping my fingers together, I tried to remember how to breathe.

Emotionally, I was falling down the rabbit hole. It was dark, cold, and disorienting.

He stepped closer before settling his lips across my mouth. My breath caught. He slid his tongue between my teeth. His kiss was long, slow, and deep—the stamp of his possession. No one had ever kissed me like that.

*Jesus, I'm so fucked.*

He sucked my tongue into his mouth. My stomach contracted as a rush of heat flooded my entire body. I wrapped my hands tightly around his lean waist. Lust curled deep in my damp, hot, needy place. Mack was slowly crumbling my resolve to remain emotionally detached.

He pulled his lips away from mine, and in one sinuous motion, he yanked me forward and cupped my ass cheeks.

I leaned up, my teeth grazing his throat, before I inched back ever so slightly. Releasing one hand from his waist, I grazed his face with the backs of my fingers, moving from his cheek to his full lips. As I caressed his chiseled mouth with my fingers, he opened his lips and licked my knuckle with a quick flick of his warm tongue. A feeling of excitement fluttered like butterflies in the pit of my stomach. The sensation ratcheted up my emotions like a kid on a roller coaster.

He fastened his mouth on mine. My womanhood was drenched, everything inside me shattering from his kiss. I desperately clutched his shoulders with my hands to anchor myself. My soft lips were on his hard ones. A stinging nip of his teeth made me open my mouth, and he plunged in, his tongue stroking mine.

I dug my nails into his muscular shoulders as the searing need burned between my legs. Nudging my legs apart, he moved between them. With his hands on my ass, he slid me closer until my sex rubbed across the aching bulge in his shorts. Our kiss deepened. I rubbed against his hard-on with a slow and steady motion.

Abruptly, he released me. "Open your door." His voice was deep and caressing, sliding across my skin like silk.

I blinked, confused from my lustful stupor. "Huh?"

"It's time for you to go before I forget my promise to give you space and take you home with me tonight."

With shaky fingers, I unlocked the SUV. He opened the driver's door, nudging me inside. While I was buckling my seat belt, he said, "Text me when you get to June's. I want to make sure you arrived safely." He pressed a quick kiss to my lips, then shut the door.

It took me a while to calm my nerves, but when I did, I

turned on the SUV, pulling away with Mack standing outside the forge staring at me.

* * *

I walked inside the kitchen to find June sitting at the island with a plate laden with cheese and sipping a glass of wine.

June waggled her eyebrows. "How was your workout session with the deputy?"

I gave her a quick kiss on the cheek. "Hot and hard." Leaning a hip against the island, I snagged a piece of cheese from her plate.

"Are you talking about the session or the deputy?"

"Both," I admitted.

"Yes!" June clapped loudly. "Just so you know, townsfolk know that you and Mack were making out outside the forge."

I felt my cheeks heat. "What? How?"

"It's a small town. It takes just one person to see something, and gossip spreads faster than wildfire."

"So I'm the skanky chick of the town now?"

"What? No. Shifters don't give a crap about that. Hell, they fuck out in the open, Aurora. You should know this." June rolled her eyes.

I did. I'd witnessed many orgies within the pride. Shifters loved to fuck, whenever, wherever, and with whomever struck their fancy.

June continued. "The rumor is that you and Mack are a couple, and boy, is that making the single females hotter than fish grease. First Quinn, then Rhett, now Mack. You hybrids are not messing around. You all are snagging the hottest males in town."

"Well, nothing is confirmed between Mack and me."

"Are you sure about that?" June arched a brow. "Because Mack doesn't get around. In fact, he's been here for years, and he hasn't dated or slept with anyone since he arrived."

"That can't be true," I whispered.

"Again, this is a small town, Aurora." She sipped her wine. "If he did, everyone would know. Now..." She waggled her eyebrows. "About your make-out session with Mack. I need details. Was it hot? Is he a good kisser?"

"Nope." I pinched her cheek. "Not happening," I declared, walking toward the kitchen door.

"But..."

"Good night, Aunt June," I chirped before closing the door behind me. It didn't take me long to get inside the guesthouse. Pulling out my cell, I called Mack while walking to my bedroom.

"Hi, Mack. I'm home."

"Good. I was worried about you. We don't have streetlights in the Ridge, so navigating the terrain can be difficult."

"Thank you for caring," I said, sitting on the edge of my bed. "No. Thank you for everything."

"You're welcome, Ro. But you don't have to thank me. I do it because I care about you, and I hope that one day you'll care about me too."

My heart raced when I admitted, "I already do."

There was a beat of silence as we both took in what I'd just confessed.

"Thank you," he said. "I know it took a leap of faith for you to admit that to me."

I flopped back onto the bed. "Mack, I have a hell of a lot of issues. It's not just my hang-ups about being treated like shit when I was younger. And it's not just about my PTSD." I paused, gathering my strength for what I was about to say. "I don't have any examples of what a healthy romantic relationship looks and feels like. And what I'm starting to feel for you is foreign to me. Frankly, it terrifies me."

"I suspected that," he confessed. "But what terrifies me is that you'll run without giving us a fighting chance."

I sighed. "I've thought about it several times, but I'm not a runner, Mack. Well, not when it comes to you. Just..." I bit my bottom lip. "Don't give up on me. It would break me if you did."

"Oh, baby... I'll never give up on you and us. I meant what I said. I'm in this for the long haul."

My breath lightened.

"I want to spend more time with you. How about a picnic on Tuesday?"

"I've never been on a picnic." There were so many normal, everyday things that I'd never done.

"Is that a yes?" he asked.

"Yes. What should I bring?"

"Yourself. I'll take care of everything. I'll pick you up at three."

"Okay."

"Get some rest, Ro. Talk to you later."

"Night, Mack."

"Night, Ro."

When our call ended, I stared up at the ceiling. My stomach fluttered with excitement, just thinking about seeing him again. Getting off the bed, I put my cell on the nightstand and undressed. After walking into the bathroom, I put on my shower cap and stood under the hot water for a long time, letting the heat sink into my sore muscles. When I stepped out of the bathroom wrapped in a towel, I felt more relaxed than I'd been in months.

Putting on black boy-cut panties and a racerback T-shirt, I opened the windows, letting the cool night air inside. I slipped under the soft sheets and, for the first time in a long while, fell into a peaceful sleep.

# CHAPTER 14
## AURORA

Stepping into Nyx's yoga studio, I nearly turned around when I saw the number of women sitting on the lined-up yoga mats.

With the doorknob still in hand, I contemplated backing out, but Nyx was fast, pulling me inside. "Hey Aurora, come on in."

"What's going on?" I asked.

"My restorative yoga class is always a hit with the ladies." She grinned while looping an arm through mine. "Hey." She looked at the container in my hand. "Is that for me?"

I nodded, handing it to her. "I made granola clusters as a thank-you."

"Yummy. I didn't know you could bake." She ushered me past the eclectic mix of females of every race, age, and size. "We always have snacks for our guests at the end of class, so this will make a nice addition." She pointed to the corner. "Drop off your shoes and water bottle there." I did as instructed. "Take two blankets." She pointed to the blankets stacked along the sleek wall unit. After I got what she suggested, Nyx led me over to an empty mat. "I've been saving this mat for you." She turned around to everyone. "Attention, everyone. This is Aurora, June's niece."

Most of the women waved at me, but some did not.

"Enjoy your class," she chirped.

I frowned when Nyx walked right past the mat at the front of the class.

The lady next to me said, "Hi, my name is Darcy. I own Things on a Stick."

"Hi," I said. "What kinds of things?"

She shrugged. "An assortment of exotic meats. Stop by, and I'll hook you up with my best sellers."

*Yeah, like that didn't sound ominous as hell.*

Darcy pointed to two women on her left. "That's Missy." She indicated the redhead. "And Pandora." She gestured to a woman with purple hair. "And Hazel, her mate Ambrose owns the only hardware store in town." She nodded to a woman on her right.

They waved at me. "Pandora and I work at the library," Missy replied. "Welcome to the Ridge."

"Thank you," I replied.

Hazel smiled at me. "Is this your first yoga class?"

"No. But it's been a while." I scanned the area. "I had no idea that yoga was so hot in the Ridge."

The instrumental music stopped, and the lights dimmed. Several ladies started clapping like they were at a concert. My eyes narrowed when I really focused on the attire most of the ladies wore. I saw a lot of boobs and ass on display for a yoga class. And most of the women had on full makeup with their hair shining and done up as if they'd just left the hairstylist.

Darcy laughed. "Nyx always has a crowd, but this class is by far the most popular. You have to get here early, or you won't get a mat."

Hazel nodded. "That's for sure. I've seen fights break out when the class sells out."

I frowned. "Why is it so popular?"

My question was answered when Mack came strolling into the room.

"Hello, Deputy," the ladies said in singsong voices.

"Good evening, ladies," Mack replied in his gruff voice before he strode to the front mat, looking like Adonis.

*Damn, he looks good enough to lick like an ice cream cone. He's a deputy and a yoga instructor?*

"The unmated females love the deputy," Missy pointed out.

My eyes narrowed on her, not liking her statement at all. An unfamiliar feeling slithered through me, and I struggled to name it until… *Fuck, I'm jealous.*

*What the hell is wrong with me? Mack is not my man.*

But even while I tried to convince myself that Mack didn't belong to me, my heart raced as I looked him up and down. Even wearing a tight black T-shirt, long joggers, and bare feet, the man was sexy as hell.

"I come to this class because I love lying here listening to his voice. It's relaxing," Hazel informed me. "Plus it's a nice break from my husband, but don't tell him I said that." She winked at me.

Mack sat down with a neutral expression as his gaze scanned the class before stopping on me. "I see we have a new student," Mack said. "Welcome, Aurora."

I nodded even as women swung their heads around to glare, giving me the stink eye like I'd stolen their man. I glared right back, not at all intimidated.

"This is a thirty-minute class," Mack said, his eyes sweeping the group. "We're going to start and finish with Savasana to rejuvenate the body and relax the mind. Do your best to be still as the deeper you relax, the more benefits you receive from the pose." He frowned at the scantily clad women. "Please add layers or a blanket for warmth."

I snorted when the blonde in the front stuck out her breasts that were barely contained in her spaghetti-strap T-shirt. The blonde raised her hand like she was in school.

"Yes, Josie," Mack said.

"I'm going to need lots of hands-on assistance," she cooed.

I heard sounds of snickering. Josie whipped her head around to shoot daggers at the class before turning back to stare at Mack.

He didn't respond to Josie's request.

I bit back a laugh when Josie huffed like a spoiled child.

"Let's begin Savasana," Mack ordered. "I will offer everyone an assist to help you find more ease in Savasana. If you don't want my touch, fold over a corner of your mat."

I wanted all his hands-on assistance, so I did not fold over the corner of my mat, and I noticed no one else in the class did either.

"Lie down on your back," Mack instructed. "Bring your feet as wide as your mat and let them flop open. Relax your arms a few inches away from your body, palms facing the sky."

I didn't think I'd enjoy being told exactly what to do by Mack, but I did. There was something freeing about letting go and not having to think.

"Tuck your chin toward your chest to lengthen the back of your neck. Close your eyes." He paused. "Make any final adjustments so that you are completely comfortable. Breathe naturally."

Lying on my back, I closed my eyes. It took me some time for my mind and body to settle down. I knew from my internet search that restorative yoga wasn't like other classes where practitioners moved at a fast pace. On the contrary, this class expected students to slow down—which I wanted—opening and stretching the body.

"Relax your whole body," he instructed in a gentle voice. "Allow your whole body to sink into the floor." I could hear his voice nearing me. "Your whole body is relaxed."

There were seconds of silence.

"Relax your whole right leg, then your left."

My body sank into my mat.

"Relax your whole right hand then your left."

Silence reigned for a few seconds.

"Relax your whole physical body." He paused. "Relax your mental body."

My eyes popped open when I heard soft footfalls.

"Relax your emotional body." He paused. "Your whole body is relaxed." He knelt behind my head, his eyes locked on mine. I didn't know how I knew, but there was something in his eyes asking for permission to touch me… to invite him in for more than just this moment. Subtly, I nodded, letting him know that I trusted him to take this moment in time wherever it should go.

Closing my eyes, I could smell his scent of warm cinnamon and mint citrus notes entwined with patchouli, lulling me further into relaxing.

His warm hands fell gently to the juncture between the muscle covering my shoulder joint and my collarbone and upper chest. His blue eyes locked with mine, and I inhaled, breathing in. With each touch, it felt as if the door to my mind was cracking open inch by inch. I didn't understand what or why it was happening, but I could feel our connection deepening on an emotional level that, quite frankly, was scaring the shit out of me. It was as if he was listening to my body through his hands, and I could emotionally feel our connection growing and strengthening.

When I exhaled, he applied a gentle pressure down. When my breath deepened, it was as if that was his cue to deepen his pressure.

His touch was simply magical.

Mack placed his fingers just under the ridge of my cranium. I could hear his exhale before applying a tiny amount of pressure, which drew my head away from my spine. He inhaled, releasing my head back to center. My breathing remained even as he repeated it twice more.

His fingers moved to the top of my forehead, and then his fingertips were above my hairline. He took a deep breath. I wasn't aware of how much emotional and physical tension I was holding in my head, neck, and forehead until now. Mack was releasing my tension through his physical touch, opening the door to my deep relaxation in Savasana.

I could feel him drawing his fingers away from each other along my forehead, then making circular motions at my temples with his thumbs. His touch was incredibly subtle but meaningful. He finished by giving three mild tugs at my earlobe before I felt him moving away.

"We'll now release the practice of Savasana," Mack announced. "Very slowly and gently, begin to make small movements with your fingers and toes."

Opening my eyes, I wiggled my fingers and toes.

"Take a deep breath into your belly," he instructed. "Reach your arms over your head and take a nice long stretch, from your toes to your fingertips."

He paused before continuing. "Roll onto your right side in a fetal position, resting your head in the crook of your right arm. Then rise to sitting."

He gave everyone time to rise; then he paused again. "Thank you for your trust and openness," he said with a sweeping gaze before his eyes locked on mine. I nodded to him in gratitude. I felt awake and refreshed.

He rose to his feet, walking over to a panel on the wall, turning up the lights. Nyx reappeared and said something to Mack before the throng of women rushed him.

I stood, putting away my mat where I saw the others had done.

"So? How did you enjoy the class?" Nyx asked me.

"It was great. I'd do it again." Especially if Mack was the instructor.

"Great, I was hoping you'd say that," Nyx said. "Let's head to my lounge. The class loves to mingle there after the session."

She looped her arm through mine before turning to look at me. "I tried your granola, and it was delicious. Have you thought about selling it?"

My eyebrows rose. "No. I bake for a hobby. I've never

thought about going into any type of business. The military was my life before I retired."

"Well, all I'm saying is that I'd buy it from you in a heartbeat." She paused. "Hey, did June tell you about Imani and Piper's upcoming baking championship?"

"She did, but I don't know… I've never…"

"Why not?" Nyx asked, escorting me into a well-lit area with plenty of seating amid the bright, airy space. "This can be your restart. Just think about it, okay?"

"Nyx!" a woman called out to her.

"I'll be right back," Nyx said. "Order a drink."

I nodded and smiled when I saw that Nyx had my granola poured into beautiful bowls. I used the spoon to put some into my palm.

I felt him even before I heard his voice. "So how did you like it?" Mack asked.

I turned to face him mere inches from me. "Loved it, but you know that already." I grinned at him.

"My ego needs stroking." He wrapped an arm around my waist, tugging me closer. "Do you want to stroke it?"

"Hmm." I felt his hard cock against my stomach. "Is this a trick question?"

He grinned, waggling his eyebrows.

I heard a loud clearing of a throat. "Don't mind me," Nyx said, strolling into the room.

I took a step back, breaking contact.

"I'm busy, Nyx," Mack growled.

"I can see that," Nyx replied, taking a spoonful of granola. "But I don't think that my assistant can keep your fans out of this room for long. So I'm giving you a heads-up."

I got more granola and stared at him. "What's the deal with your groupies?" I asked, chomping on a mouthful of granola.

"Can I have some of what you're eating?" he asked me.

I held a piece to his mouth, and he gobbled it, taking my

finger into his mouth and licking it. My pussy pulsed while his tongue flicked my finger.

"Wow, that's hot," Nyx exclaimed.

"That was delicious," Mack replied, his eyes on me. "Where did you get it?"

"Aurora made it for me," Nyx answered. "I told her she needs to make more and sell it to me."

He reached over and took a heaping portion from the bowl, popping a handful into his mouth, chewing thoughtfully. When he was done, he said, "I'd buy it. It's better than any of that stuff I've bought in the grocery store. You should sign up for Imani and Piper's baking championship."

"I already told her that," Nyx said.

He cupped my cheek. "So you're beautiful, smart, and can bake. I've hit the mother lode in a woman." His touch made me yearn for something I'd never thought I'd want. Him. And companionship.

"Don't let your groupies hear that," I admonished him with a smile.

He tugged me to him. "You're mine, and I don't give a shit who knows."

I heard a woman's whiny voice say, "You all can't go in there!"

"Why?" a woman shouted.

"They're here," Nyx announced.

Ignoring her, he pulled me over into a corner, ushering me to sit down before he did.

Josie marched over to us, bringing along her troupe of women. She gestured from me to Mack. "What's going on between you two?" she demanded.

I arched a brow. "That's none of your business."

"What do you want, Josie?" Mack asked.

Ignoring his question, Josie said, "Are you two together?" She placed her hands on her hips, pushing out her breasts. "Is that why she hogged up today's session?"

"Yes," another woman said. "I saw that. She did get all his attention."

I rolled my eyes. "You women have lost your shit."

Mack stood, his hulking form making the women back up. "First, I don't answer to any of you. Second, Aurora's mine, and I'm hers. So go run tell everyone that."

*Well… damn. A formal declaration for all to hear.*

"Ladies," Nyx called out. "Granola and water over here."

The women gave me the evil eye before walking away.

Mack sat down with an arm thrown behind me, cradling me closer to his body.

"Do you think that was wise?" I asked. "We don't know where our relationship is going."

"*I* know," he barked. "I'm waiting for you to admit it."

"Hey, Aurora," Hazel called out from across the room with her cheeks puffed out like a chipmunk. "Your granola is delicious."

Missy and Pandora nodded, also chomping on it.

"Thank you," I replied before glancing back at Mack.

Josie rolled her eyes before making a big show of spitting her mouthful into a napkin. "I've had better."

"We have a date tomorrow," he said against the shell of my ear.

"The picnic. I haven't forgotten. You change your mind and need me to bring anything?"

"Yourself. I'll pick you up at three."

"Well, it's time for me to head home," I announced. "But I'm going to need you to walk me to my car," I said jokingly. "I feel a girl fight coming on." I nodded in the direction of the women staring at us.

We walked up to Nyx on our way out. "Thank you for coming," Nyx said before giving me a hug.

"I had a great time," I replied while hugging her back.

We walked past the women, and I called over my shoulder, "See you, ladies. Don't be a stranger."

# CHAPTER 15
## AURORA

Standing outside on June's porch, I was dressed in jeans, a T-shirt, and sneakers, taking in the fresh air while waiting for Mack. Despite the fact that he'd told me I didn't need to bring anything to the picnic, I couldn't fight my need to stress-bake, so I'd whipped up some lemon bars that I'd packed into a container.

I watched as a black SUV pulled into the driveway, and Mack got out and strode over to me. "You ready for me?" he asked, grabbing my hand and kissing my fingers.

My stomach flip-flopped with every touch of his lips. "It depends on what you've got planned for me," I responded. "I still don't know why you told me to make sure I wore a bathing suit. Is this going to be a freaky, naughty picnic?"

He gave me a bad-boy smile. "I'm down for that, if you are." He released my hand and ushered me toward the passenger's side.

"I'm adventurous, so let's play it by ear," I replied as he opened the door for me. I slid inside, and he shut the door before striding around the vehicle and getting behind the wheel.

He looked at the container on my lap. "Couldn't help yourself, huh?"

I shrugged. "I bake when I'm stressed."

He took the container, reaching behind him and placing it on the back seat before eyeing me. "Anything you want to talk about?"

"Huh?" I asked, distracted by the fact that his scent seemed a lot more potent and delicious today. My nose twitched, distinctly picking out the notes of his scent. It was strange.

"You said that you were stressed," he recalled. "Are you still having nightmares?"

"Yes, but not as frequent." I pressed a hand against his thigh. "Let's not talk about my issues today, okay?"

He frowned but didn't press me further. He drove off, and I stared at the scenery, relaxing. A few minutes later, he turned on his radio, and R&B music streamed through the vehicle. When he started to hum along, I grinned.

I turned to glance at him. "You leading last night's practice was surprising."

"Why?"

I shrugged. "I didn't peg you as a yogi."

"I turned to yoga when I came to the Ridge. I wasn't coping well with the changes that I felt happening between my inner animal and me. So Nyx convinced me to take a yoga class. It was the best decision ever. After just one class, I was hooked. It was as if I'd had a spring clean of my mind."

"What's going on with your animal?"

"I'm going through what the majority of men in the Ridge are suffering from, feral sickness."

My heart raced. "You're going feral?" My voice croaked.

"Yes. It's not full-blown yet. I'm in the early stage. I still have control of my animal, but I can feel the disconnect happening. My animal has been discontent for a while now without our fated mate, but it's gotten a lot worse. When I shift, there's this battle between us when it's time to transform back to my human side. I've been spending more time in my animal form, which is never good. A shifter can lose touch with their humanity that way."

"How much time have you spent in your animal form?" For healthy shifters, anything more than a day in their animal form posed a high risk for disconnecting from their human side. Shifters who lost touch with their human side often returned to the wild and were never seen by their pride or pack again.

His brows furrowed. "Two days."

I gasped, my heart fluttering like a bird. "That's not good, Mack." The thought of Mack going feral and roaming to the outer edge of the Ridge like June had told me so many of the town's unmated males had made me very sad and uneasy.

"I know, but yoga and meditation help. My mind is quieter and clutter-free, so it's easier to direct my energy when I feel my inner animal trying to take over control of my mind and body." He paused. "I thought he'd be content since you've come back into my life, but he's become sullen because I haven't claimed you."

"Why are you and your lion so convinced that I'm your fated mate, Mack?"

"I already told you, Ro. Shifters just know. The feelings I have for you transcend physical attraction. It's a connection that I feel forming inside my heart. When I'm not with you, I feel a part of me is missing. And if that's not enough to convince you, my inner animal has said that you're ours since the night I met you twenty-three years ago." He paused. "Why is it so hard for you to believe that we're meant to be together?"

My shoulders sagged. "Because I'm so emotionally damaged that I can't believe a man like you would want to spend your life with me."

He took his eyes off the road briefly. "You're beautiful inside and out, Ro. I'm the one who can't believe that fate has matched me with you. Don't you trust me to treasure your heart?"

My stomach tightened when the truth of this situation finally dawned on me. "This has nothing to do with you and everything to do with me." I turned to face the passenger's window as I blinked back the tears threatening to spill. This man was strong, beautiful, caring, and protective—and part of me wanted to surrender to him. But the other part rebelled. I sighed deeply and decided to take the first step by revealing a peek into my vulnerabilities. "Mack, I'm afraid of opening up to you only to be abandoned if my PTSD doesn't go away."

"PTSD is not a life sentence, Ro. Some people have a complete resolution of symptoms with proper treatment. Even those who do not generally see significant improvements and a much better quality of life. Have you thought about speaking to a therapist?"

"I've been assigned one, but I haven't reached out to her."

"Why?"

"I'm not ready, Mack." And might not ever be, I left unsaid. All my life—in the pack and the military—I'd been taught to project an image of success, perfection, and strength. To ask for help from anyone, especially a therapist, would be perceived as a weakness.

*I'm not weak.*

*I'm strong.*

*I'm not some damsel in distress who needs to be saved.*

He shook his head. "I'm not going to push you, Ro. But know this: I'm embracing you as you are."

His words touched me to the core, but I'd learned a long time ago that words were meaningless when push came to shove and the going got rough.

# CHAPTER 16
## AURORA

Thirty minutes later, we reached a thick section of the forest and Mack pulled into a spot on the side of the road. He hopped out and came to my side of the car, opening the door.

Stepping outside, I inhaled the fresh and clean air deeply as I peered around at the tall trees rising out of the earth, brushing the sky. "This is beautiful," I marveled.

"It's my secret spot," Mack said while reaching into the back of his vehicle. "I love it because it's not far from Main Square. If I want to go for a quick swim during lunch, I head here." He handed me my container of bars before draping a large towel around each of our necks and then taking out a big woven picnic basket.

"Ready?" he asked, grabbing my hand.

"Yes."

He led me from his vehicle and into the forest until we ventured along a path that cut through the middle of the forestry.

I gasped at the soaring stalks of bamboo that surrounded both sides of the path. It felt as if I were walking into another universe.

"Bamboo in a rain forest?" I asked.

"Black Forest Ridge is an ecosystem all to itself," Mack explained. "Nothing makes sense, but it is beautiful."

I marveled at the thick bamboo stalks that continued endlessly in every direction and the soft light that filled the gaps between the trees beautifully.

"Piper told me there's a beach in the Ridge," I said. "It's hard for me to wrap my mind around a beach in Alaska. What's the origin of this land?"

"Quinn said that this oasis—all the land in the Ridge—was created centuries ago by the Faerie. The Ridge was one of their vacation spots in the human realm."

"Holy hell! Now this unbelievable landscape makes sense." The Faerie were a race of magical beings with a close connection to nature. They were rumored to be the guardians of the trees, mountain streams, and forest pools. "But how did this land fall into the Bane family's ownership?"

"Quinn's great-grandfather, Boris Bane, purchased the land. So the land belongs to the Bane bloodline. They are the owners and guardians of this territory." The grove opened up to a large swath of land covered with vines dotted with pink flowers and a breathtaking waterfall.

"It's spectacular," I whispered, staring at the beautiful crystalline-blue pools. "Can we go in?" I asked. The weather was warm, and I was excited to feel the water on my skin.

"Sure, let's do it."

Mack took my container and was looking for a spot to rest it along with the basket. I kicked off my sneakers and started peeling off my jeans, when I stopped self-consciously, remembering this would be the first time he'd see my large, ugly scar.

*It's now or never, Aurora.*

If he wanted me, he'd have to accept and love all my scars—emotional and physical.

I sloughed off my jeans and top, revealing my sexy two-piece swimsuit. If there was one thing I'd indulged in while in the military, it was my clothes. When I wasn't in uniform, I loved to look and feel sexy, so fashion was my thing. I'd gained weight since I'd bought this swimsuit, so more ass and breasts were hanging out, but this was me, and I wasn't ashamed about it. I waded into the water and headed for the waterfall. Sticking one hand underneath it, I was pleasantly surprised that the water was warmer than I anticipated, so I stepped directly under the spray.

I nearly jumped out of my skin when I felt Mack's fingers brush along my spine. Turning me around, he wrapped his arms around me, and I sank into his touch. We stood there for I didn't know how long as the water beat against our bodies before he released me and guided me over to the base at the right of the waterfall that was covered with plush moss.

Before I could take a seat next to him, he said, "Come here," and guided me onto his lap, facing him. Chest to chest, I wrapped my arms and legs tightly around him. With eyes locked on mine, he traced his fingers along the bumpy scar tissue that started at the top of my right hip. I flinched.

"Easy," he said softly. "There's nothing about you I can't and won't love."

My lips trembled at the emotion I heard and felt in his words.

He flattened his palm, skating it farther along the scarred skin. My body stiffened with tension.

"Mine," he hissed while watching me closely, the look in his eyes making me feel precious and beautiful.

I blinked back the tears. His touch and words were my undoing.

He leaned forward, biting my bottom lip. I kept my mouth determinedly shut.

"Let me in, Ro," he demanded against my ear.

I knew he wasn't just asking for entry into my mouth, but into my heart.

His palms traversed farther down my right thigh while he looked at me.

He nipped my lip again, caressing and skimming his hands along the scar that stopped midway down my right thigh.

I wanted to moan from the pleasure of his touch and cry from the shame of the ugliness of the scar that marred my once-beautiful skin. It was as if he were peeling me emotionally, revealing my soft underbelly.

"You are mine," Mack said in his quiet, rough voice. "And I'm yours."

I swallowed hard. The thought of having a man who was so strong and good to love and care for me was overwhelming.

He tugged on my bottom lip before trailing scorching kisses along my jaw. My heart and breathing slowed. My muscles relaxed. He pulled back slightly, letting me know he wanted me to take the lead. To show him that I wanted him as much as he wanted me.

My heart thumped hard in my chest. Getting emotionally close to Mack terrified me, but I had to know what it felt like to surrender to him, if only for this one time.

Leaning closer, I flicked my tongue against his lips. He groaned and opened his mouth. I inched my tongue into his mouth.

"More," he growled.

Inside his mouth, I explored and teased. His tongue slid over mine, claiming me. He reached one hand up, fisting my hair, angling my head back, giving him deeper access. His growl of hunger vibrated through me, making me clench my thighs. I felt both out of control and safe, which were opposing emotions.

Mack's sensual assault was soft and controlled, a contradiction to his alpha personality. He teased and coaxed. My body burned with the need to be taken by him. I pressed my ass against his hard, hot length. I shivered, just imagining being fucked by him. *Would he take me hard and fast? Or slow and deep?*

Abruptly, Mack broke away from our kiss. I could feel his

muscles tighten with tension. "Move slowly to my side, but stay close," he said. "And whatever you see, don't run."

Confused, I did as instructed, unwrapping my legs from around him and sliding down to his left side, sitting on the moss.

I quirked a brow in his direction. "What's going on?" I whispered, scanning my eyes over the area.

"I smell a wolf approaching," he replied, slowly getting to his feet. "And there's something off about his scent." I grabbed the hand he extended to me.

I didn't see or sense anyone in the vicinity, but I also didn't have acute hearing or smell like Mack, so I trusted his instincts. We waded through the waters and onto land.

"You get dressed," Mack said, his gaze assessing the clearing.

I started putting on my clothes. "But what about you?" The only thing he was wearing was shorts.

He didn't answer. His attention was focused on something I couldn't see or hear.

"Get behind me," he said while kicking off his shorts. I was instantly alert when I heard the distinct cracking of branches. Someone or something was approaching. "It's a male. I don't know its intention. I have to shift."

I didn't have time to respond. Mack's shift was fast. One second, he was a human. The next, his body had shifted into a lion with a strong, compact body and powerful forelegs. His coat was yellow-gold with a long, shaggy chestnut mane. He nudged me with his massive head, and I got the hint, getting behind him.

My nose wrinkled when I smelled a sour scent wafting in the air. Three things immediately concerned me. One, the scent wasn't coming from Mack. Two, my sense of smell had never been this acute. And three, from the growl I could now hear, my stranger-danger internal alarm was ringing off the hook. The wolf coming definitely did not want to make friends with us.

Mack's lion's tail went rigid. That was a bad sign for the wolf that was approaching—it meant his lion was hunting it.

I heard approaching footsteps. I froze when a black wolf

appeared—it was perhaps forty yards away from us—looking confused and disoriented. Mack's lion roared so loud it was deafening. The wolf froze. This animal was clearly sick; it was foaming at the mouth and making strange clicking sounds with its mouth. It also had several large patches of fur missing from its body, showing raw pink skin.

The wolf swayed on its feet as if it were drunk.

Mack's lion stood on its tiptoes, lifting its tail and hunching its back—he was showing dominance. He charged the wolf while roaring, then stopped not too far away from it.

The wolf started to back away slowly.

Mack's lion began to move again. The wolf froze immediately.

Mack roared. The wolf turned and ran back into the woods.

His lion stood alert for a few minutes before he strode up to me.

I'd seen plenty of lions in my lifetime, but Mack's animal was massive, beautiful yet deadly. When he reached me, I dug my fingers into his mane, and his tail swished back and forth. His fur was so soft. I smiled when he started huffing and puffing—those were happy lion sounds.

"Oh my," I cooed. "My sexy kitty is enjoying my touch."

He purred softly when I ran my fingers over his nose, then his ears.

"Thank you for protecting me, kitty." It was comforting yet strange to have someone protecting me. Leaning forward, I kissed the top of his head.

He puffed again before transforming back to his human form. I tried not to let my eyes drift down, but I was curious, and yep, the man was well-endowed even when his cock wasn't erect.

With his hands on his hips, he asked, "You like what you see?"

I licked my bottom lip. "It's sufficient." That was putting it mildly; his cock looked like an anaconda.

He arched a brow. "I would challenge that mediocre assessment, but we have to get going." He cupped my cheek. "Can I get a rain check on our picnic?"

I found myself nuzzling his hand before I caught myself and stepped back. "Sure. I don't think this place is secure, not with the appearance of that wolf."

He nodded. "Exactly. It's not common for a feral wolf to come so close to town. They normally never leave the outer edge." He frowned. "I need to get back to my pack and tell them what happened. We need to figure out what's going on with the feral shifters and if there's a possibility of more heading into Main Square."

"So that was a feral shifter?" I asked.

"Yes. When he was approaching, I picked up his scent. It smelled wrong. The scent was sick... sour. That's the trademark of feral sickness."

My brows furrowed. "I didn't smell him approaching." That wasn't new for me; my sense of smell was not acute like a shifter's. "But his scent was real potent when he broke in to the clearing."

Mack's eyes narrowed. "You smelled him?"

I nodded. "Of course. He smelled like sour milk." I scrunched up my nose, just thinking about how strong the wolf's scent had been.

"That's interesting," Mack replied, staring at me like I had two heads.

"It's not that fascinating, Mack. That wolf reeked."

"I hunted feral shifters during a Special Ops mission for the Shifter Council. There was one incident where the feral shifter was right on a human campground, and none of the humans smelled him."

"What are you saying?"

"Humans can't smell feral shifters."

My mouth dropped open. "But... how..."

He touched my face. "I suspect your inner animal is coming awake. Which is a longer and deeper topic to discuss, but not now. I need to get you out of here immediately. I'm not sure if the feral wolf might come back with company."

I nodded but was still stunned by his revelation. "Makes sense. I'll help you gather."

"We need to travel back to my car light because I'm shifting into my lion. I need to be prepared in case the wolf tries to ambush us." He gestured to his clothes. "Just take them and my boots. Leave everything else. Stay close. Keep your head on a swivel. And if something pops off, get behind me. I'll take care of you."

He gave me a quick kiss before shifting back into his lion. I gathered his stuff and walked by his side as we ambled out of the clearing and back to his vehicle.

Along the way, I picked up a large stick to use if shit got real and we were ambushed. But thank goodness we made it back to his SUV without incident.

I got into the SUV while Mack shifted back, got dressed, and started texting on his cell. When he slid into the vehicle, he patted my leg. "You okay?"

"Yes. It's just wild that I was so freaked out by that feral shifter. I've been in several life-and-death situations during my time in the military and never batted an eye."

He turned on the car. "There's something about encountering an animal with feral sickness that makes even a badass warrior quake in their boots. No one wants to get bitten or scratched by a feral shifter for fear of getting a bacterial infection." He pulled out, heading back to June's.

"What are you talking about? Shifters don't get sick."

"Typically, we don't, but Piper told us about an incident that happened when Quinn's father was alpha. A female got scratched by her brother, who had the feral sickness. She didn't think anything about it. A week later, she fell sick, the sickness having made its way to her brain. But by then, it was too late for Freya to help her. She died."

"That's sad and bizarre. I assumed shifters couldn't get sick."

My mind whirled as I processed what he'd said, then something occurred to me. "Mack, you could have gotten scratched or bitten by that wolf. Why the hell did you put yourself in danger like that?" My heart raced, just thinking about all the horrible outcomes of that clusterfuck.

He grabbed my hand, his eyes still on the road. "There's nothing I wouldn't do for you, Ro. You're mine to protect, care for, and love."

"Oh, Mack." I squeezed his hand. "What did I do to deserve you?"

He brought my hand to his lips. "That's how I feel about you every day." He continued to drive. The ringing of his cell echoed throughout his SUV. "I have to take this," he announced before tapping the button on his steering wheel. "Hey, Quinn."

"I just got your text," Quinn replied. "I'm assuming you and Aurora didn't get injured by the feral wolf."

"We're okay. I didn't give him the chance to attack."

"This is nuts," Quinn barked. "What the hell is a feral wolf doing so close to town?"

"That's what we need to find out. I'm dropping Ro home. I'll come over to the ranch after."

"Okay. See you there."

Their call ended when Mack pulled up to June's cottage and hopped out of the vehicle, coming around to my side and opening my door, clasping my hand in his.

"I'm staying in June's guest cottage," I said to Mack, guiding him to the back of the cottage and through the backyard. The sweet smell of flowers filled my nose while we walked toward the house.

When we arrived at the guest cottage, I said, "This is me."

"Yes, it is." He released my hand, backing me against the door.

I cleared my throat. "Yeah, well, I had a great time today, minus the feral wolf incident."

"I did too." He trailed his fingers against my cheek. "Can we do it again? This time dinner at my place. I'll cook."

I bit my bottom lip. I knew that if I ever went over to his place, I'd end up with him between my legs, and I wasn't sure I was ready for the ramifications of having sex with him. Mack was looking for commitment, and I wasn't sure I could give him what he needed. "Me coming to your house is a bad idea, Mack."

He circled my nape with his hand. "I don't bite… much."

My pussy pulsed, just imagining what his sexy lips could do to my body.

I leaned into his fingers. "I'm not naive, sexy kitty. I know where this"—I gestured between us—"is going."

"And that is?"

"Sex," I whispered. "Lots of it."

He grinned. "Sounds good to me." He dipped his head, planting his gorgeous lips on mine. I wrapped my arms around his neck, clinging to him as he deepened our kiss, dipping his tongue into my mouth. He groaned, and I moved my tongue deep into him. My breath became ragged, nipples strained against my bra, and warmth pooled between my thighs.

I broke off our kiss. My breathing was heavy. "Call me later."

He tugged me to him, brushing a hand down my back.

"Okay," he said in his quiet, rough voice. As he caught my chin, his gaze bored into mine. "And just for the record, I would never push you into having sex with me."

"I know that. You wouldn't have to. I already want to feel you against me in all the ways that scare the shit out of me."

"Then we'll wait." He released me, watching me closely. "Until you're ready to surrender to me."

I nodded. "Good night, Mack."

"Good night, Ro."

Turning my back to him, I opened my door with trembling fingers. I walked inside, shutting the door and pressing my back against it.

My heart thumped as my mind tried to sort through all the conflicting emotions I was experiencing. Fear that I wasn't the woman he deserved. Joy that he was the first man I'd ever wanted to spend more time with and explore the possibilities of our relationship. Which was a surprise, because finding a man like Mack after all these years was astonishing but nice.

Pushing away from the door, I strode through the cottage, needing to take a long hot bath. After peeling off my clothes, I ran bathwater, dropping in lavender bath salts.

My cell chirped.

JUNE (TEXT): *How was your picnic with Mack?*

ME (TEXT): *Nice but eventful.*

JUNE (TEXT): *More info please.*

I turned off the water.

ME (TEXT): *We never got to the picnic. We were interrupted by a feral wolf-shifter.*

My cell rang; it was June.

"What?" June screeched.

"We went swimming in his secret spot, and right after, this feral wolf-shifter showed up out of nowhere."

"Were either of you hurt?" June asked.

"No. Thank goodness. Mack shifted into his lion and scared him off." I sat down at the edge of the tub. "How come you never told me about the danger of getting scratched or bitten by a feral shifter in the Ridge?" I was still amazed that even though I grew up in the shifter world, there was so much that I didn't know.

"Because the chance of an encounter with feral shifter outside the outer Ridge is nonexistent." She paused. "He didn't bring you near the outer Ridge, did he?"

"Nope. It was a swimming hole not more than thirty minutes from your house. Mack seemed real concerned about the incident."

"He should be. Hell, we all should be. Feral shifters don't venture outside the outer Ridge, and if they do, it's certainly never in their animal form. What happened is different and not in a good way."

"It was scary. That's all I can say," I replied. "And the animal's scent…" I swallowed hard. "June, I could actually smell his sickness." I rubbed my nose as if I could still smell it now. "It was sour and… wrong." I shivered.

"Wait. You could smell the animal?"

I nodded. "Mack acted like that was some bizarre feat."

"Because it was. Only shifters can smell a feral shifter." She paused. "Is there something you want to tell me?"

I frowned. "Like what?"

"Like that your animal is awakening. That's the only way you could have smelled the feral sickness."

I sighed. "I don't hear her talking in my head, but I do admit that my sense of smell seems to be becoming more acute." I nibbled on my bottom lip.

"Oh my goodness. It's happening. You and Mack are fated mates."

"Hold on a second." I cautioned her. "Let's not start planning my mating ceremony. There's nothing else going on but a change in smell. We need more time to discover what's happening."

"I don't care what you say," June retorted. "Mack is yours."

"He seems to think that," I said.

"And what do you think?"

I shrugged. "I admit that I like him a lot. But damn, I just don't know. Everything seems to be moving so fast between us. He wants me… The man is all in despite the fact that I have a hell of a lot of unresolved emotional issues."

June sighed heavily. "There's no such thing as perfection, Aurora. Mack knows this. You're wasting a lot of time pushing him away, which is terrible because you're living for someday."

"The rational part of me knows that I'm chasing something that doesn't exist—perfection—and expecting it to make me happy. But it would break me if I let Mack into my heart only find out that he can't hack the dark, lonely places my PTSD sometimes takes me."

"Does Mack seem like a man who doesn't know what he fucking wants?" June asked.

"No."

"Ro, he's walking into a relationship with you with eyes wide open."

"I need time," I snapped.

"Time for what? To run? To pick apart his motives? To watch him like a hawk, waiting for him to make a mistake so you can use it against him?"

"I don't want to talk about this anymore, June."

My fingers were trembling with rage because she'd hit a soft spot. I was waiting for him to fuck up so that I could say "See, I told you so."

"My bathwater is getting cold."

"Aurora, don't shut me out. I just want you to be happy."

"That's the problem, June. I'm not happy, and I need to resolve that before I let Mack into my heart. He's a wonderful man whom I would love to have a relationship with, but it's not his job to provide happiness I can't find in myself."

I didn't believe in the philosophy of "Someday I'll be happy. I just need to find the right person."

"All I'm saying is that I don't want my relationship with Mack to be the emotional Band-Aid on my pain. I need to fix myself before—"

"You need to heal, and the only way that can happen is if you shed the layers of yourself that no longer serve you. There's no magic bullet to happiness, Aurora. It's working on being a better version of who you used to be. You have to be strong and vulnerable to grow. But I can talk until I'm blue in the face, and it still won't change things until you stop talking about wanting to heal and actually do it. Call your therapist, open the communication channels, and start healing."

"I know," I said.

"Good," June replied. "I love you, Aurora. Talk to you tomorrow."

"Love you too."

I slipped into the now-lukewarm water and shut my eyes. She was right. I knew there was no miracle cure for happiness and emotional healing. I had to do the work, and that was the hard and scary part.

# CHAPTER 17
## AURORA

I was a bundle of nerves when I walked into June's kitchen to pick up the baked goods I planned to bring with me for Imani's girls' night.

June whistled. "Well, don't you look pretty."

"I clean up nice, don't I?" I twirled left, then right like a runway model, showing off my sleeveless, backless cream top with an open crisscross design at the cleavage that I'd paired with a short skirt and ballet flats. I had a thing for nice clothes since I'd worn a military uniform most of the time.

"Yes, you do." She winked at me.

I eyed her outfit. She was also dressed up. "You're going out?"

"Yup, my cougar squad is taking me to the Dark Room for drinks."

"The Dark Room sounds, well… dark for a restaurant."

"It's a high-end sex club that's on the other side of the Ridge. It's owned by Wilder and Hugo, the wolf-shifter alphas."

My internal danger radar rang. I remembered passing by the road that Mack told me was the entrance to the wolf-shifter territory. "Mack made it seem like that area was off-limits."

"The Dark Room is on neutral territory. It's safe. The wolf-shifter alphas own the club, so there're no shenanigans."

It seemed the Ridge wasn't just some sleepy small town; there was also a darker side. "And remind me again, who are Wilder and Hugo?"

"Two alpha brothers who run and own the wolf-shifter territory. They're also members of the town council, though they don't see fit to attend any meetings. They're rich but reclusive. Rumor is that they're into some dirty criminal shit in the human world, but I know them personally, and I've never had any issues with them."

I frowned. "Well, be careful. Stay alert. Don't put your back to the door ever. That will leave you vulnerable if some shit breaks out."

June patted my cheek. "Stop worrying. I've been to the Dark Room several times. It's a members-only club, and I'm a member. Besides, if trouble happens, I'm a lioness. I can take down most shifters without breaking a sweat."

I blew out a calming breath. She was right. June was a tough badass and could take care of herself.

June gestured to the containers lined up on the counter. "That's a lot of baked goods. Are you planning on feeding an army?"

I laughed. "I bake when I'm nervous. I kind of overdid the baking today." Between thinking about Mack and worrying about meeting Imani and her friends, I'd baked up a storm. "What started as a plan to bring one dish turned into three." I wiped my sweaty palms against my thighs. "I'm not good at socializing."

June rubbed my arm. "Yes, you are. But I get it. This is new for you—being around shifters after avoiding them for so many years."

I nodded. "It feels like the first day of high school, wondering if I'll make friends or end up an outcast."

June kissed my cheek. "You'll be fine. Now go. Have fun."

I grabbed the handles for the three containers and headed toward the door. "Don't do anything I wouldn't do," I called out over my shoulder.

"I'm not making any promises," June said before I shut the door behind me.

* * *

The trees thinned as I drove alongside them, and soon the road opened out again into a valley with a long driveway bordered by streams and shadowy forest.

"Wow," I murmured, driving along the driveway until it curved past the edge of ranchland marked by a white stock fence. "Ain't this fancy." A huge ranch house stood perhaps a quarter-mile up the hill.

Several vehicles were already parked when I pulled up to the ranch. Getting out of my SUV, I reached into the back, pulling out my containers, and shut the door. I climbed the stairs and made it to the ranch house's sprawling front porch when the door flew open, revealing a stunning woman with rich, dark skin, bow-shaped full lips, and a cloud of thick, curly hair that puffed around her face. And as soon as I saw her smiling face, I was instantly at ease.

"Hey, Aurora. I'm Imani." She reached out to take one of the containers from me while ushering me inside.

"Hi," I replied, stepping into her home. "Thank you for inviting me."

"I'm glad I did." She smiled at me. "I can tell you and I are going to become friends. You have a good vibe. Come on, let's head to the kitchen."

My eyes roamed around, panning the bright area. The far side of this room had a full, large kitchen. On the north side was a larger dining room area, where a long table sat, overhung by an antler chandelier.

"Wow." I took in the stunning decor. Everything about this

place spoke of expensive high quality. Timber furniture, leather upholstery, log walls with rich fabrics, and a variety of forged-iron reliefs. "Your home is beautiful."

"Thank you. I wish I could say the decor was all me, but it was stunning before I moved in. The only new thing that I added was this." She pointed to the artwork above the fireplace—it was a forged relief of two wolves, one huge and the other smaller in comparison. "Quinn made it. It's a depiction of him and me in the woods."

Then it clicked. "He owns the forge. I was there the other night and saw several pieces similar to this one."

Her smile widened. "Yes, he does a lot of large commission pieces, but he sometimes works on projects together with Rhett, Mack, Brody, Jasper, and Emmett. Quinn's a full-time black-smith, but they all like smithing. Their sculptures are so popular that when they sell them, they make some extra money for the town."

The pack's philanthropy spoke volumes about their character. I wasn't used to hearing about shifters doing anything that wasn't selfish or self-serving.

"Let's head to the kitchen. The girls can't wait to meet you."

Walking farther into the house, I stared at the gourmet kitchen fit for a professional chef. The ceiling was made of exposed wood beams, and the kitchen boasted two cooking areas which could no doubt accommodate all manner of cooking styles.

*Damn! This is my dream kitchen.*

Imani placed my container on the huge L-shaped quartz island. I loved that Imani and Quinn believed that the heart of the home was the kitchen. This kitchen had lots of room for mingling, an ample island with comfortable stools for chatting with the cook, and plenty of extra seating for when the meal was ready, such as a cozy banquette.

My eyes widened at the plethora of platters of food lining the island. I glanced at my containers. "Seems like you have more than plenty of food."

"Never," Imani quipped, opening one of my containers. "Not when it comes to shifters. It never fails when I have girls' night here—the pack crashes the party and demolishes our food." Her mouth dropped open when she pulled out what was inside. "What in the world?" She looked at me, then the dish, then back at me.

I shifted on my feet, feeling self-conscious. June told me that Imani was a renowned executive chef. In comparison, I was a self-taught baker.

"They're chocolate-glazed Boston cream whoopie pies," I said.

Imani took a huge bite of one. "I know," she answered over a mouthful. "They're beautiful and…" She moaned. "…delicious." Her eyes were wide. "You made this?"

I nodded. "Yes, I made everything I brought tonight. I'm a home baker. Nothing professional." I pulled out the baked goods from the other containers.

"Nothing professional?" Imani squeaked, staring at my jumbo brownies, chocolate-cream squares, and double-dark-chocolate cupcakes with peanut butter filling. "I bake, but it's nowhere near as good as your baking."

Pride swelled within me. "Thanks."

Imani's eyes narrowed. "Did June tell you about the Ridge baking championship Piper and I are having next week?"

"Yes."

Imani pointed at me. "You, girlfriend, are participating."

I shrugged. "Sure. I can help with—"

Imani choked, and I patted her back.

"Help?" She looked at me like I was crazy. "No. I want you to become a contestant. The prizes are great. Money, a contract to provide baked goods for our B and B, a storefront on Main Square."

"Well… I…"

"Don't answer right now," Imani said. "Please think about it, Aurora." Her eyes pleaded with me.

"Okay. I'll think about it." Just the thought of making my secret dream of opening my own bakery finally come true filled me with both joy and trepidation.

"Good." Imani smiled. "Grab those bottles of sparkling water, and I'll take the charcuterie and cheese board."

I did as instructed and followed Imani out the back door of the kitchen and down the stairs into a rustic outdoor living space nestled in a picturesque forest setting with beautiful furnishings, flagstone flooring, and a tall, stone-clad fireplace. The lit candles created a magical ambiance.

"She's here," Imani announced in a singsong voice.

I recognized one—Nyx—of the four women who were seated in teak Adirondack chairs surrounding a low, round teak table.

"Hi," I said, placing the bottles of sparkling water on the table.

"That's Rose." Imani gestured to the beautiful, lanky woman with a pouf of reddish-brown hair with pristine white streaks. "She's a doe-shifter."

I extended my hand. She stood, pulling me up into a big hug. "I'm a hugger." When we broke apart, Rose gushed, "I'm so happy to meet you, finally."

"My turn," said the gorgeous woman with high cheekbones and a blond buzz cut. She hugged me, then stepped back. "I'm Izzy."

"She's a witch and the town's healer," said a woman with dark skin, hazel eyes, and thick, curly chestnut hair. "And I'm Nova, the town's midwife." She hugged me tightly. "Welcome to the hybrid club, Aurora."

"Nova's a hybrid like us," Imani informed me. "And Rhett's mate."

"Welcome to girls' night," Nyx said before hugging me.

I gave them all a genuine smile. These women felt authentic and welcoming.

"Sit, Aurora," Imani ordered. "Get comfortable."

"What would you like to drink, Aurora?" Nyx asked. "We have wine and also a pitcher of sangria."

"I'll stick with water." I filled my glass and sipped, enjoying the bubbles dancing across my tongue.

Izzy rubbed her hands together, staring at the charcuterie and cheese board loaded up with cheese, meats, fruit, nuts, and spreads. "I'm going in." She put a little of everything on her plate, then tore off a piece of baguette.

Everyone did the same.

I moaned when I bit into the brie. "I'm a cheese junkie."

"And I'm a pastry junkie," Imani replied. "I don't want to share the baked goodness you brought, but I guess I have to."

Rose eyed me. "You bake?"

I nodded. "Home baker."

Imani snorted. "Bullshit. I took one bite of her whoopie pie and nearly passed out from sheer pleasure."

"Where is it?" Nyx demanded. "You know pastry is my jam."

"In the kitchen." Imani wagged her finger. "I'll get it next. We have to eat before the men get here."

Rose leaned closer to me. "June told me that you just retired from the military. How are you adjusting to civilian life?"

I took a bite of prosciutto. "It's too new to assess. I retired earlier than I'd anticipated due to getting injured in Afghanistan, so I'm trying to figure out what's next."

"Switching gears midstream isn't easy," Nova said. "Before becoming the town's midwife, I worked as a volunteer midwife in Africa. Now I'm running a new clinic, something I'd dreamed about but never thought was a possibility."

"I asked Aurora to become a contestant in the baking championship," Imani said. "That's how good I think she is."

Nyx glanced over at me. "Are you going to do it?"

Everyone stared at me expectantly.

"How many contestants do you have?" I asked.

"So far…" Imani held up one finger. "One."

"Josie," they all said in unison.

Imani pursed her lips. "I'm actively working on recruiting more contestants, but it's been a challenge."

My eyes widened. "I don't get it. The prize is great."

"No one wants to go up against Josie," Nova said. "They just don't want the drama. But I say fuck her and her conniving father."

"In a nutshell," Izzy said. "Josie and her father are wealthy, prominent members of the community, and they don't like losing."

"And that's exactly what will happen if anyone with an iota of baking skill goes against her," Rose said.

I frowned. "She can bake, right?"

Imani shook her head. "Nope. She owns a bakery that specializes in biscuits."

"Horrible, dry biscuits," Nyx chimed in.

"Then how does she stay in business?" I asked.

"She's rich, and her father purchased the shop as a hobby until she finds her fated mate," Nova said. "But that woman is pure evil. Pretty on the outside but toxic sludge on the inside."

"Nova and Josie have a bad history," Imani said.

"She attacked me in her owl-shifter form," Nova replied.

"Holy shit," I replied. "What type of owl-shifter is she?"

"A great horned owl," Rosa answered.

"Wow, that's one of the dangerous ones," I said. "Why did she attack you?"

Nova sipped her sangria. "She wanted my mate, Rhett, and I was in the way of her having him."

"Crazy stuff," I said before taking a bite of cheese.

"To say the least," Imani said. "Especially since Rhett wasn't interested in Josie in the first place."

"High drama," Nyx said.

"It sounds like it." I shook my head. "June told me about all the trials and tribulations you both went through since coming to this town. Would you do it all over again if you had to?"

"Yes," Imani and Nova said in unison.

"Quinn is the best thing to ever happen to me," Imani said. "We started out rocky. My welcome to the Ridge experience was me being chased and almost mauled to death by a crazy shifter named Sam. Then the townsfolk rallied to kick my ass out of the Ridge. But I'm here, in love with a man who worships me like the goddess I am. And I have a pack and friends who show me every day that I'm wanted and loved. I can't say I ever experienced that out in the human world."

"I agree," Nova said. "Rhett is the love of my life. That man loves me in every single way. But when I came to the Ridge, I questioned whether I could weather the storm of crazy. Shit, I had a run-in with a nude horse-shifter named Henry, who insisted on showing me his dick. And a mob of townsfolk who wanted to skin me alive when I was accused of killing Henry."

"Don't forget Rhett wanted to kick you out of town day one because of your Hunter bloodline," Izzy said.

"Girl, I can't forget that," Nova retorted.

"Or that Sam killed Old Man Henry and framed you for the murder," Nyx added.

June had told me all this, but hearing it again from them was like a reality show.

"And I already mentioned that I was attacked by Josie, the deranged owl-shifter," Nova said, taking a bite of salami. "But here I am. In love and being loved by a man who is everything I wanted and more."

"In my honest opinion," Nyx said, "I think you hybrids waste way too much time fussing about things that are not relevant. You were called here by the mating spell. That's the automatic qualify for a good and true match."

"That's what I say," Rose interjected. "I've been waiting for my mate for years, and you best believe when he shows up, I'm not wasting time. If he's not an asshole and he treats me right, that man is mine. Deer-shifter or not."

Izzy scoffed. "Your mother would lose her shit if your mate isn't a deer-shifter."

Rose shrugged. "I'm already a big disappointment because I'm over forty without a mate. I used to care what she thought years ago, but now not so much. Look at Imani, Quinn, Nova, and Rhett. Love comes in all shades, and they are in love."

"I grew up in a fucked-up pride with full-blood lions who treated me like crap because I'm a hybrid," I divulged. "That's why I made a conscious decision not to interact with shifters when I left the pride. I just never felt welcomed by shifters because I smelled like a human and couldn't shift."

Imani touched my hand. "That was their insecurities, Aurora."

Everyone nodded.

"June's told me about all the crap you and Nova had to endure because of being a hybrid," I admitted.

"Sure, there are full-blood shifters in the Ridge who don't believe in fraternizing with hybrids," Nova said. "But Imani and I don't give a shit about what those people think. Our mates are full-blood but don't care that we're hybrids."

Imani nodded. "You, me, Nyx, and Nova are black women, so we're no strangers to prejudiced people. But does that stop us from existing? No. So why would we let being a hybrid prevent us from finding love?"

Now that she broke it down like that, I could see how my excuse not to get involved with Mack because I was a hybrid made no sense. But I still had the other issues, like my PTSD, to contend with.

"I feel stupid for even bringing that up as an excuse not to give Mack a chance," I admitted. "Even when he made it clear that he doesn't care that I'm a hybrid."

"Because he doesn't," Imani said. "None of the pack does. They just want to find love, Aurora. And I'm proud to say that they don't care what shape, color, size, or breed it comes in. In my opinion, that's a true sign of men who have a lot of love to give."

"True that," Nova said, and she gave Imani a high five.

"But it still breaks my heart that some townsfolk can't get past this hybrid versus full-blood shit," Izzy said.

"Yup," Nova chimed in. "Especially when the unmated males are getting the feral sickness."

"Which was why Quinn asked my mom to cast the mating spell in the first place," Nyx explained.

Rose clucked her tongue. "It's a shame, really. Did you hear that Mr. Johnson's two sons just upped and disappeared into the outer edge this week?"

"Yup," Imani said. "Quinn has been worried about the uptick in unmated males getting the feral sickness. And that encounter Mack and Aurora had with that feral wolf-shifter so close to town is worrisome."

"When I read the group text Quinn sent to the residents, I clutched my virtual pearls," Nyx said. "A feral shifter venturing outside the outer Ridge is not a good sign of things to come."

"Not at all," Rose agreed.

"It's not the best of news," Izzy admitted. "But if the townsfolk keep alert and report any sightings of feral shifters venturing onto their property or in Main Square, we can contain this problem."

Nova snorted. "Residents don't take anything seriously until it directly affects them. If they did, they wouldn't be so against hybrids coming to the Ridge."

"True that." Imani clinked her glass against Nova's.

"I mean, really," Nova continued. "I can't believe they're actually bitching now about hybrids taking their men."

Rose popped an olive into her mouth. "Lordy, some townsfolk are nasty business. I mean, the shit they're saying about Mack and Aurora making out in front of the forge is the worst."

"What are they saying?" I asked.

"I wouldn't worry about it," Nyx answered. "They're just

mad because another unmated man is off the 'hot and single' list."

"But I won't know if we're a true match until my inner animal awakens," I protested.

"That's just a formality," Imani said. "According to Mack, he and his inner animal know that you're his fated mate."

Nova grinned at me. "He's got it bad for you."

Rose batted her long eyelashes. "I think it's so romantic that after twenty-three years, you two have been reunited."

"I'm not a romance chick," Izzy chimed in. "But I have to admit that him still wearing the bracelet you gave him twenty-three years ago does make my heart go pitter-patter."

"Yup," Imani said. "Shit, if that isn't a hint about what he feels for you, then I don't know what is."

"I hate to break it to you guys," I said, "but our story is not a romance story. It's more of a mystery suspense."

"Boy meets girl. Boy saves girl. Boy and girl meet years later," Nyx explained. "Sounds like a romance story to me."

I bit my bottom lip. "It's a little bit more complicated."

They all leaned forward expectantly.

I sighed heavily. "I have some issues that I'm dealing with from my time in the military. I have a lot of emotional rebuilding to do, and I don't want Mack going through my chaos with me. He deserves a woman without issues."

"And knowing Mack, he didn't budge from his stance of wanting to be with you," Imani said.

"He didn't," I confirmed.

"No one is perfect, Aurora," Rosa said. "Everyone has baggage. It's how you deal with it that matters."

"Yup," Imani agreed. "I should know. I grew up in the foster care system. And as you can imagine, I had all kinds of trust issues that played a big part in my pushing Quinn away when we first met."

"Same here," Nova disclosed. "I'm the poster child for mother-daughter issues. My mother made my existence a living nightmare growing up, which wreaked havoc on my self-esteem and left me with a hell of a lot of trust issues. My emotional baggage made me push Rhett away."

"None of us is perfect," Nyx said, looking at me.

"For damn sure," Izzy confirmed.

"I want you to know," Imani said, "that all of us are with you. We're here. You're pack."

I blinked back the tears. I'd never had this type of support from anyone but Aunt June and Mack.

"You women are phenomenal," I admitted.

"Are you trying to make us ugly cry?" Imani asked with a grin.

"Please don't," Izzy begged. "I can barely deal with Rose and her annoying need for group hugs."

"Nope, we're not crying," Nyx said. "Or hugging."

Rose pouted.

Nyx continued, "We're going to drink, eat, and dance."

Imani whooped. "Let's get this party started." She jumped up and went to grab her tablet from a side table near the outdoor fireplace. The song "Calabria 2007" by Enur featuring Natasja & MIMS blasted.

"Yes!" Nova screamed with a fist pump.

Rose pulled me up and started dancing. Everyone else got up and danced too. Their fun and laughter were infectious. We danced and drank, then ate and danced some more. They filled me in on the town's gossip and antics, and I laughed so hard that my stomach cramped.

I hadn't had this much fun… ever.

"You've got to be kidding me." My eyes were tearing up from laughter. "The head librarian, Missy, got caught having sex in the bathroom in the children's section of the library after hours?"

"True story," Imani confessed. "She and Dusty—a bear-shifter and owner of a biker bar—were busted going at it."

"Busted by his on-again, off-again girlfriend, Pandora," Nyx chimed in.

"And a fight ensued between Missy and Pandora that ended up outside with them rolling around and fighting in front of the library," Izzy explained.

"Only to find out that they enjoyed the tussling a bit more than they anticipated and ended up making out on the ground," Imani added.

I doubled over with laughter.

"They're dating now," Rose announced. "I heard it's getting serious."

"And Dusty is salty about their coupledom," Izzy said. "Calling both of them cheaters—"

"On him," Imani interjected.

I nearly fell off the chair from laughter.

I glanced up when I heard a male voice say, "Hey, someone said that music is too loud and called us to issue a summons."

"Lies," Nova said. "You guys just wanted some of our food."

"Busted," said a tall, muscular man with a crew cut who strode over, carrying a plate filled with food. He walked right to Nova, giving her a scorching-hot kiss.

Izzy rolled her eyes. "Get a room, guys."

When they broke off their kiss, Nova dragged him over to me. "Aurora, this is Rhett." I had to blink because her man was so handsome.

"Hello, Aurora." Rhett greeted me. "Nice to finally meet you."

"Same here," I said.

Rhett sat down next to me, dragging Nova onto his lap before he proceeded to feed her.

"Who made this?" a man bellowed from the top of the stairs outside the kitchen door. He was holding up a plate filled with my double-dark-chocolate cupcakes.

I raised my hand as if I were in school. "I did."

"They're very good," he replied, shoving one into his mouth.

"Quinn!" Imani yelled. "Those are not for you."

He stomped down the stairs and headed straight for Imani. When he reached her, he held the other cupcake above her head. "Take it from me." He grinned.

Imani stepped closer and got on her toes. "Feed it to me, baby."

"Damn, that was hot," he growled before doing as she instructed.

"The pack is here," Nyx grumbled. "Girls' night is officially over."

My heart raced when I saw Mack walk out of the back door, followed by three men.

Mack walked over to me and leaned down, kissing me on the shoulder. "Hey, beautiful."

"Hey, sexy kitty," I replied.

A huge guy with a ponytail started dance-battling Rose. The two other men came over, plopping down in empty chairs. Each had a plate filled with cupcakes, brownies, and chocolate-cream squares.

"Seriously, who made this?" one of them asked.

Nyx pointed over to me.

"These are delicious," he complimented me. "By the way, my name is Jasper. Ponytail Man"—he pointed to the man dancing with Rose—"is Emmett."

"And I'm Brody," the other guy said.

"Hello," I said.

Mack tugged me up from my chair, sat down, and pulled me onto his lap. "Pass me a brownie, Jasper," Mack demanded.

"You ate two already," Jasper complained.

"Bro," Mack growled.

"Here, but if you want more, go get it yourself," Jasper said.

Mack moaned as he took a bite. "These are delicious, Ro. You entering the baking championship?"

I grinned. "Since you guys seem to love my baking so much, why not?"

"Quinn, Aurora said yes," Imani exclaimed, jumping up and down as if she'd won the lottery.

My cheeks heated. "You guys sure know how to make a girl feel good."

"Quinn, we need champagne to celebrate. Get a bottle from the fridge."

"Only if you come with me," he replied. "I love watching your sexy ass walk up the stairs."

Imani slapped his arm. "We have company."

Jasper rolled his eyes. "It's not like we haven't caught you two going at it the kitchen."

"And in the living room," Brody chimed in.

"And in the forge," Emmett called out.

"Shut it," Imani said, wagging a finger at them before dragging Quinn toward the kitchen.

Sitting sideways on Mack's lap, I asked, "How was your day?"

"Boring without you."

"Flattery will get you everywhere, Deputy," I replied.

"Hmm… I like that."

"Champagne for everyone," Imani called out from the top of the stairs, uncorking the champagne bottle.

All of a sudden, a loud, cracking sound pierced the air. I nearly dropped to the ground on pure instinct. I felt a tightness in my chest, and it was hard to breathe. I felt closed in and panicky. I bolted to my feet and away from Mack.

"Ro?" Mack called, but I ignored him.

When I made it to Imani and Quinn, I asked in a robotic voice, "Restroom?"

"What's wrong?" Imani asked.

"Nothing," I lied.

Quinn frowned but said, "Through the kitchen, make a left."

I brushed past them with my heart racing. Cold sweat trickled down to the small of my back. I shivered. The horrible memory of the feeling of the fire burning my skin came back in a rush. I brushed my trembling fingers against my hip, where the scar remained.

Hurrying inside the bathroom, I shut the door, pressing my back against it. A wave of panic hit me again. A fear of being closed off, claustrophobia, and pains in my chest nearly brought me to my knees.

I shut my eyes and saw myself picking up body parts of my soldiers. Another memory flashed, one of me holding my soldiers as they died in my arms on the battlefield. More memories consumed me, of seeing the blood of soldiers spattered all over my uniform. I slapped my palms against my ears to block out the echoes of my team's shouts in my head.

Closing my eyes, I forced myself to take deep, calming breaths.

*I'm having a bad reaction.*

*It's normal for things to remind me of that day.*

I breathed in through my nose and out through my mouth.

*One. Two. Three. Four. Five.*

*I am in a safe place.*

*The noise was champagne popping.*

After a few minutes, my heart started to slow down, and some adrenaline evaporated from my system.

Walking over to the mirror, I checked my face. My dark skin was dewy, and my eyes were a tad bit red.

"The pack must think I'm crazy," I murmured, knowing that because they were shifters, there was no way they hadn't smelled my fear. I felt weak and stupid and broken. There was no way Mack should and could want me. I couldn't even bear to hear the sound of popping champagne without losing my shit.

I wanted to break down and cry, but that would have to wait until I got home. Now the only thing going through my mind was escaping the ranch without being detected by the pack.

I heard knocking on the door, and I froze.

"Ro?" Mack called out. "Open the door."

"Not now, Mack."

"Aurora, I said open the door."

I turned to face the door but didn't open it. I knew that I was being childish, but I was mortified about what had just happened. I couldn't face him.

"Unless you plan on spending the night in there, I don't see the point of this," he said.

He was right. I had to come out sometime.

Taking another deep breath, I smoothed down my hair before unlocking the door.

Mack stepped inside but left the door open—the bathroom was too small for the both of us as it was, and shutting the door would be the equivalent of sardines in a can.

"What are you doing?" I asked, stepping back.

"PTSD episode?" he asked, cutting to the chase.

I licked my lips. "Yes. The champagne." I twisted my fingers nervously. "The popping." I threw my hands in the air. "It's not getting better, Mack."

He grabbed my face. "You have to be patient with yourself."

"I know… but I just want this PTSD thing to go away. And I don't want to hear that the only cure is time and therapy."

I squeaked when Mack turned me around to face the mirror with him against my back.

"Mack, what are you doing?"

"Look in the mirror, Ro. What do you see?"

"A woman who looks terrified."

"No," he snapped. "You're beautiful, strong, intelligent, and mine."

"Mack, you don't know what you're saying."

He turned me around. "Are you telling me that I don't know what I need?"

"No. I'm saying you deserve better. Not some broken woman who runs for cover at the sound of a car backfiring and champagne popping."

"You are my better, and I'm not going anywhere," he

growled. "You're stuck with me. I'm with you through thick and thin."

"Grrrr!" I screamed before storming out of the bathroom. I could hear Mack on my heels, but he didn't stop me or say anything.

Arriving in the kitchen, I dug around in my purse, pulling out my pill bottle.

His eyes were slits when he said, "You've got to get past the drugs, Ro."

"Fuck off," I snapped.

I knew full well the ramifications of the drug—opiates, a central nervous system depressant—that I used to treat my post-traumatic stress disorder. The drug could exacerbate depression and anxiety while also disrupting my sleep patterns. There was also a chance that I could develop long-term tolerance—needing more of the drugs to achieve the same effect. But I didn't care.

With shaking fingers, I popped the top, shook out one pill, and swallowed. I grabbed a bottle of sparkling water from the island and guzzled. Once done, I squared my shoulders and walked out the back door into the backyard.

I swallowed hard when I saw all eyes focused on me, but I wasn't backing down from this. "I apologize for my odd behavior. I'm going through some things right now, and I'm not adjusting too well to civilian life."

"There's nothing to apologize for, Aurora," Quinn said. "We're former military. We have plenty of experience with soldiers who have PTSD."

My stomach plummeted. Shame and anger coursed through my veins. I swung around like a madwoman to face Mack, who was now by my side.

"You fucking told them?" I hissed.

"What the hell are you talking about, Ro?" Mack demanded. "I would never betray your trust."

Ignoring the anger and hurt shining in his eyes, I jabbed a finger into his chest. "Liar."

"Calm down, Ro," he said as he reached for me.

I slapped his hands away. "Don't touch me," I screeched in a tone I'd never heard before. I was out of control with emotions that felt foreign and wrong. I had to leave. I was taking whatever was going on with me too far.

I bolted away, into the kitchen, through the house, and out to my SUV. I expected Mack to come after me—he didn't. Maybe he'd had enough of my crazy… Good, I didn't need him anyway. I'd relied on myself all my life and could continue going solo.

When I finally got inside my vehicle, my nerves were a wreck and I was shaking like a leaf. Starting the SUV, I pulled away from the ranch, racing off like I was being chased. I wasn't. Neither Mack nor his pack gave two shits about me.

I clenched my fingers around the steering wheel as my mind raced a mile a minute. I could feel myself spiraling, but I couldn't stop my downhill slide.

*How could he betray me like this?*

*Telling the pack about something I'd told him in confidence.*

*Is this why Imani invited me to her house tonight?*

*Because she and her friends think I'm some damn basket case desperate for friends?*

*Fuck!* I pounded on the steering wheel.

*Mack and his pack are probably still sitting around in the backyard, laughing and talking about me.*

I banged the steering wheel again. "Stupid. Stupid. Stupid."

*This is what I get for opening up to Mack.*

*Never again.*

# CHAPTER 18
## MACK

*What the hell? This shit can't be happening.*

I turned to go after Ro when I heard Rhett say, "Leave her be, Mack."

I whirled to face him and the pack. "Fuck that!" I tightened my hands into fists. "She's mine to protect. Didn't you smell her fear?"

"We all did," Rhett answered. "That's why you need to give her space."

"Her emotions are high," Jasper said. "And if you confront her right now, she'll lash out like a cornered animal."

They were all right, but I hated the hurt and fear I'd seen in her expression. Ro was spiraling. I recognized her behavioral signs—agitation, irritability, and hostility.

*Go after her,* my inner beast begged.

My chest tightened. I was flying high on adrenaline. The need to chase her down and protect her rode me hard. But I also knew that Ro was not in the emotional state to listen to me. She was in fight-or-flight mode.

*How in the hell could she think that I'd betray her?*

I strode over to the pack, taking the empty chair. Rubbing my hand over my chin, I tried to calm my nerves.

"Why was she so angry?" Imani asked, staring at Quinn with a concerned expression.

"It's hard to heal and place the war behind you when you get off the battlefield," Quinn explained.

"Quinn's right." I sighed. "Ro has a very deep-seated, painful belief that she's broken because of the traumas she experienced both growing up in a fucked-up pride and after the roadside bomb that nearly took her life in Afghanistan." I crossed my legs. "She's ashamed of her PTSD."

"Why would she feel ashamed?" Izzy asked. "We're"—she gestured to all of us—"not perfect. We're far from it. We would never judge her."

"Never," Rose added.

"We know that, but she doesn't," I replied.

"I've seen this before with soldiers," Emmett said. "Where the person feels responsible for what happened and views themselves as a bad person. And they're not. Shame is a common symptom for people with PTSD."

I nodded in agreement. "It's tearing me up inside to know that she won't open up and trust me. She can't deal with PTSD alone. If she tries, the emotional and day-to-day struggles will only get worse."

"But doesn't she understand that she's a part of our pack?" Nova asked.

"It's complicated for veterans," Brody explained. "PTSD is often associated with combat trauma. Witnessing a horrific event like a deadly roadside bombing or the killing of a child can take an emotional toll on you, causing you to relive the event and feel angry, depressed, or distant."

"We were lucky," Rhett said, gesturing to Quinn, Emmett, Brody, Jasper, and me. "We had one another. We served together, so we knew what the battlefield was like. We've all also witnessed fellow soldiers with PTSD."

"But she has you, Mack," Rose said. "You know what she's going through. You can help her."

"She doesn't want my help, Rose," I explained. "She thinks that her PTSD makes her weak, unlovable, but it doesn't. She's mine. My fated mate. And I don't need her animal to wake up to tell me that."

"Maybe that's part of the problem," Nyx said. "Having her animal awake and willing to help her heal would be an asset. Aurora might be struggling to trust her decisions about you and her. Without her animal confirming that you and she are fated mates, she'll continue to doubt she's the one for you."

"I agree with you, Nyx," Nova said. "But I know from personal experience that even with your animal cosigning the mate match, it's still not that cut-and-dried, especially when you have trust issues."

"Maybe she needs space," Imani replied.

I sat up. "I'm not letting her go."

"We don't blame you," Emmett said. "From what I've seen, she's a keeper."

"Exactly," Brody said. "What we're saying is that she needs space to come to you."

Rhett nodded. "Because if you push, she'll run and you'll lose her forever."

My heart tightened. Losing Ro would kill me.

Giving her space would be hard, but I knew it was the right thing to do. She had to truly know that I was the man who would have her back no matter what. For our relationship to work, Ro had to trust me, and no amount of pushing could force that to happen.

But Ro was a stubborn woman, and I had no idea how long it would take for her to come to me. I had to be patient because there was no time frame for building trust.

I had to have faith that she would come to me with her heart open and ready for me to love her forever. And until that day came, I'd wait—patiently—for my woman to come home to me.

# CHAPTER 19
## AURORA

I walked into June's bar and was greeted by the sounds of banging and sawing from Jasper's construction team.

I waved at Jasper, who was talking to his workers.

Jasper waved back before striding over to me. "Hey, Aurora, long time no see. The pack has been worried about you."

"I'm fine." I tried not to fidget uncomfortably but failed. "I've been busy helping Piper, Bonnie, and Freya with the arrangements for June's birthday party."

His eyes narrowed like he could see through my bullshit excuse. "Hmm, I see."

"Yeah, well, um…" I tugged on the bottom of my faded T-shirt. "You know where June is?"

"Straight back." He pointed. "And to the left."

"Thanks," I said, hustling away. "Nice to see you," I threw over my shoulder.

It really wasn't nice to see him. I was still embarrassed about my meltdown in front of him and the pack three days ago.

Following his directions, I landed in the kitchen and found June peering down at construction plans.

"Hey," I called out.

June inspected me. "You look like shit."

I shot daggers at her. "Gee. Why, thank you. Didn't you hear? Bloodshot eyes with dark circles are the new thing."

"Sarcasm doesn't look good on you, darling." June pursed her lips.

"What do you want from me? I'm exhausted from no sleep."

I cracked open one of the bottles of water sitting on the counter beside her before pulling out a pill from my pocket and washing it down with a swig of water.

"Then why are you taking those pills?" June pointed at me. "Didn't you tell me that they worsen your insomnia?"

"They do." I gulped more water. "But it's better than doing nothing."

"How about just talking about what you're feeling, Aurora?" She grabbed my hand. "I'm here for you. Hell, all of us are."

"All of us?" I snatched my hand away.

June sighed tiredly. "You've been avoiding Mack's calls and texts. You won't respond to Imani's or Nova's calls either. You're isolating yourself, and that's not good, Aurora."

"I'm not isolating myself. I've been busy helping with your birthday arrangements. It's also why I'm here. I'm on my way to the grocery store but decided to drop by on my way."

She gave me the stink eye. "Arrangements that you won't tell me anything about."

"Is this about you or me?" I asked, looking her up and down.

"You," she snapped. "Isolating yourself."

I crossed my arms.

"You won't talk to any of them, Aurora. They care about you."

"They don't even know me," I snarled.

"They know enough to care, and if you would just open up to them, then—"

"Can we change the subject?" I begged.

"No." June slammed her palms against the makeshift counter. "Look at you. You've been wearing those same sweatpants for three days. Your hair looks like a bird's nest of crazy."

She grabbed my chin and clucked. "And you have dark circles under your eyes." She released my face.

I stuck my fingers into my hair, self-consciously trying to finger-comb through my tangle of thick, tight curls, and I winced when my fingers snagged inside my "bird's nest of crazy."

*June's right. I've been letting my grooming habits slide a bit—okay, a lot.*

I barely had the emotional and mental energy to shower. And I'd been holding my sweatpants hostage for far too long.

June continued. "Hell, if I didn't force you to have breakfast and dinner with me every day, you wouldn't eat. What the fuck is going on with you?"

"I told you what happened at Imani's ranch."

June got up in my face, holding up three fingers. "That was three days ago."

"Don't yell at me," I barked.

"Someone has to," June replied. "This is not you." Her hand gestured to all of me. And she was right. "It's like an alien crawled up your ass and is invading your body. Have you given up on yourself?"

My lips quivered. Her words slammed into me. I was ashamed of the woman I'd transformed into. There were so many times that I came close to booking a flight to anywhere but here.

"Yes," I answered. "I have given up on myself." My shoulders sagged.

June touched my cheek. "Why?"

"Because I'm broken."

"You're letting what the pride called you when you were younger into your head?" June asked.

"Yes." I shook my head. "I thought I'd gotten over that years ago, but I haven't. I realize now that my emotional wounds haven't healed, they just scabbed over. And what happened to me in Afghanistan scratched off my scab, causing it to bleed and re-form. I feel scarred, June." I twirled my bottle of water in my fingers. "Now look at me. I'm what some in the Army culture would call a broken soldier."

"Aurora, you're not—"

"Listen to me." I placed a hand on hers. "I need to get this out, or I never will."

June nodded.

"My wound is invisible, but I see and feel it every day. It's a wound that feels as real as one that bleeds, and I'm ashamed of it."

"You need help, Aurora. I'm here for you, but I'm not military. Mack is, and he'll know exactly what you're going through. Why won't you accept his help? You know damn well that he wasn't gossiping about you to his pack. They're former military like you, Aurora. You think they can't see the signs of PTSD?"

What June said was true. Soldiers knew the telltale signs of PTSD, whether they wanted to admit it or not.

"I know Mack wasn't gossiping about me behind my back. I came to that conclusion days ago, which only added to my list of things to be ashamed about. June, I acted like a raving lunatic in front of them. None of my recent behavior is normal me. I feel like I'm on a roller coaster and I can't get off."

June leaned forward. "You can talk to me about it."

"Thank you, but it's not the same. Only a soldier understands that physically being home doesn't mean coming home."

"You can talk to Mack."

"I know that I can, but I'm not ready, June."

"But…"

"I need time."

"He's been by the bar asking for you," June offered. "He's hurting because you've pushed him away."

I swallowed hard. "Mack is a good man. I hate that I'm putting him through this bullshit. But I have serious trust issues. You know this. I don't trust him enough to stay if my PTSD gets worse. I feel like a broken mirror, June. I can see all the cracks, and I'm scared to death that Mack can see them too."

"Aurora, I see so much of myself in you. I had no trust in myself or others." She twirled the pen in her hand. "When we were young, your mother and I had a rough life. We partied hard together, got mixed up with the wrong men, did a lot of questionable things. I got out of that life, but your mom didn't, and that's how she met the Rossi brothers. When I moved to the Ridge, I trusted no one, lived like a loner because I was paranoid that I'd fall into the same trap from my old life. But I learned that no man or woman is an island. You need people you can trust in your life. You need people who will always have your back. People who will love you despite your cracks."

"Building trust isn't easy," I replied.

"No one said it was. Trust requires time, commitment, and vulnerability. You're holding out your heart in your hands, offering it to someone, and essentially saying, 'Here's my heart—please don't mess with it.'"

"It's the vulnerability that I struggle the most with," I admitted. "I learned the hard way—from the pride—that relying on anyone but yourself is a weakness. It's hard for me to open up to anyone. Remember how long it took for me to open up to you?"

"But you did, with time and our commitment to our relationship," June said.

She was right. It did take time for me to trust her, but I eventually did and never regretted it. But I was undecided about whether I was being a fool for trusting again.

*Will Mack hurt me?*

"I need time, June."

"There's nothing wrong with taking time, Aurora. But use it to strengthen the relationship in front of you, with Mack."

"I'll think about it," I said.

"Good." June nodded.

"June?" a man's voice that I recognized called out. It was Mack.

"What's he doing here?" I whispered to June.

June shrugged.

Mack appeared in the entryway, looking sexy and masculine, while I stood in the kitchen looking like death warmed over.

"Hi, Aurora," he said with no smile. "You're the woman I'm here to see."

I arched a brow. "How did you know I was here?"

"Jasper," he said simply. "Can we talk?" he asked.

I eyed June, who avoided my gaze. "We're busy," I started.

"No. We're done," June said, picking up the construction plans before walking away. I tried to grab her arm, but she evaded me. "I have things to discuss with Jasper."

June patted Mack's arm. "Good luck," she said before leaving the area.

An uncomfortable silence settled between us as my mind raced to remember whether I'd brushed my teeth this morning, then I recalled that I did.

He strode up to me. I took several steps back to put distance between us. His mouth tightened.

"So what do you want to talk about?" I asked, crossing my arms.

He mirrored my motion and crossed his beefy arms. "I really expected more from you, Aurora. But not answering my calls or texts? That shit is fucked up. I'd expected a fuck-off response, but instead, I got crickets."

"Fuck off," I replied, glaring up at him. "Does that make you feel better?"

"It does. At least I know you have some fight left," he replied with no heat in his tone. "You running away with your tail between your legs was disappointing, to say the least."

I slammed my palms against the makeshift counter. "Are you trying to pick a fight with me?"

He shrugged. "I'm just stating facts. You and I know that I didn't tell the pack shit about your PTSD, but you used that lame-ass excuse to push me away."

His words were like a stab to my heart. I saw the hurt in his eyes and heard it in his voice. He'd expected better from me but ended up hurt.

I swallowed around the emotions. *This is all for the best. He needs to move on from me and us.*

"What do you want, Deputy?"

"You know what I want, but I'm not getting into that shit with you right now. At this point in time, all I want to know is are you showing up to the baking championship, or are you going to chicken out?" he asked.

*Oh hell no… No, he didn't just say that.* My shoulders straightened. "Chicken out?"

"I'm surprised you haven't ghosted the Ridge by now," he said. "How many times have you packed your bags with the intention of leaving town?"

*Every night since the incident at the ranch.*

"That's none of your business," I answered.

"But it is my business." He stepped closer. I stepped back. "But I'm not going to belabor why. All I want to know is, are you competing or not?"

I lunged forward, poking him in the chest. "I don't answer to you, shifter."

"You're right, but you should answer to yourself." He grabbed my chin. I pushed his fingers away. "A soldier never walks away from a mission. If you can't commit to me, at least commit to yourself and stop disappointing yourself."

Without another word, he walked out of the kitchen.

*Disappointing yourself?*

*Who the fuck does he think he is, talking to me like that?*

I stormed out of the kitchen to finish our argument, only to see every head in the room turn in my direction.

Mack was gone.

All the construction workers plus June and Jasper were there.

"I'll see you later, June," I said while walking out of the bar. Thank goodness she didn't follow—I needed time to think.

I got into my SUV and pulled away, driving past the grocery store and away from Main Square with no destination in mind.

Sometime later—I didn't know how much time had passed or where I was—I pulled over to the side of the road.

A scream erupted from my mouth.

All my frustration, anger, sadness, and fear collided into the wail-scream. I sounded like a wounded beast.

I banged on my steering wheel over and over again as tears streamed down my cheeks.

I was sinking in emotional quicksand. I needed help.

I was so damn tired of being on the battlefield that I'd brought back with me.

It was time for me to put myself first.

It was time for me to come home.

Pulling out my cell, I called the one person who knew me better than I probably knew myself at this low point in my life.

"I need your help," I rushed out.

"I'll text you my address," Mack replied.

# CHAPTER 20
## AURORA

Following Mack's directions, I found myself driving through the forest for a while before pulling up next to his parked SUV. Getting out of my vehicle, I was surrounded by nothing but forest.

"Well, this is interesting," I said aloud while crossing the small bridge that spanned over a creek. Finally making it across the bridge, I traversed the winding gravel footpath through a forested canopy until a cabin concealed beneath the trees appeared.

I gasped at the exquisite cabin with a sprawling deck that appeared to wrap around the entire house. "Now this I wasn't expecting."

Standing on the magnificent deck was a bare-chested Mack. "Come inside. The door is open."

I walked up to the house, opening the door. The inside of his home was just as amazing as the outside. There were sweeping cathedral ceilings with exposed beams and lots of stunning stone details.

"Take the stairs to your right," he called out.

Doing as instructed, I found myself on the second landing, with glass doors wide open to the deck. Stepping outside, I found Mack lounging in a wooden Adirondack chair with a beer bottle in one hand.

"Hey," I called out, hovering behind him.

"Have a seat," he said.

I hesitated, then capitulated to his demand, taking a seat beside him.

"I'm not a coward," I announced.

Crickets were chirping.

"No. You're not."

I turned to stare at him, but he remained focused on the scenery before us. I settled back in my seat, stretching my legs in front of me, and found myself relaxing while watching the sun descending below the horizon and the light of the day slowly fading.

"This is serene and beautiful," I said, listening to the pulsating sounds of cicadas building up to a crescendo before abruptly ending.

"That's why I built my home here," he replied. "It's relaxing to immerse myself in nature every day and night." He took a sip of his beer and remained quiet.

I followed his lead, silently taking in the sounds and views of nature.

We just sat there in comfortable silence until the moonlight cascaded down and the lights automatically kicked on inside his home.

"What now?" I asked him.

He turned to look at me. "It's late. You can take my spare bedroom."

I didn't relish a ride back to the cottage right now. I was relaxed and wanted more time surrounded by this exquisite setting.

"Okay, I'll stay."

He nodded. "Good. I'll show you to your room. Then I'll make us dinner." He stood, and I followed him as he strode along the deck and around the corner.

"Did you design this house yourself?" I asked.

"With the help of Jasper." He stopped at a glass door. "I knew what I wanted, and he made it happen." He pushed open the door. "This is you." I stepped inside the room, and he turned on the lights, revealing a space with wood floors and walls. Rugs were scattered strategically on either side of the massive bed, which had a wooden headboard.

"Wow, this is really nice," I said. Between the door that led directly to the deck and the large window that took up a big section of the wall, nature was literally just a few inches away.

"You can keep the door and windows open. Between the night air and the sounds of nature, you should fall asleep easily." He walked over to the other side of the room, opening the door that led to the hallway. "I'll start cooking dinner. When you're ready, just take the stairs to your left, and you'll find the kitchen."

When he disappeared, I plopped down at the edge of the bed. "What are you doing, Aurora?" I asked myself. I was still angry with Mack, but there was a side of him that soothed my ragged nerves. I needed his help for my survival, and I was woman enough to admit that I couldn't do my healing alone.

Sighing heavily, I texted June, telling her where I'd be tonight, before getting to my feet and leaving the room to find Mack.

I'd made it down the stairs when I heard the clanging of pots, so I headed toward the sound.

I stood in the entryway of his kitchen, watching him bustle around while he chopped vegetables and stirred things around in the pan. There was something hot about watching him cook for me.

As if he could sense my thoughts, he froze, looking over his shoulder with a sexy smile. "Don't stand there, Ro. Come inside."

I strode in, peering around and admiring the stone walls,

ceiling beams, and a barnlike door that added rustic touches to his casual and inviting home.

I leaned my hip against the butcher-block center island, and my eyes widened as I watched him forming dough into sticks. "Are you making garlic breadsticks from scratch?"

"Uh-huh. It's a lot tastier than store-bought breadsticks, and they're so easy to make."

"I agree," I replied. "I also prefer making my own breadsticks." I grinned at him. "We have a lot in common."

He winked at me. "That we do." He put the sticks onto a baking sheet.

I walked over and opened the oven for him, and he popped the sticks inside to bake.

"How about I make dessert?" I offered.

"I'm not going to turn you down. Check out my refrigerator and cabinets to see if I have the ingredients you need. In the meanwhile, I'll make a green salad."

I checked the refrigerator, pulling out the ingredients I wanted, then rummaged through his cabinets. Once I had everything I needed, I got to work. Mack and I worked side by side in a comfortable silence, and I loved it. I stuck my cheesecake brownies into the oven, then cleaned off the counter.

We set out the plates, napkins, and utensils on the counter.

Standing with the refrigerator door open, I asked, "What do you want to drink?"

"I'm good with sparkling water," he replied, setting out glasses.

I pulled out one large bottle and set it on the counter while Mack put all the rest of the food down next to it. I took out my brownies to cool.

"Time to eat," Mack announced, pulling out one of the bar stool chairs nestled by the counter. "Here you go."

I sat down, and he took the seat next to me. I liked the informality of eating at the counter with the feast spread in front of us.

He dished out a large slice of lasagna for each of us, and I put a healthy serving of salad into each of our bowls. I dug into the lasagna, and my toes curled when the heavenly flavors burst in my mouth.

I moaned out loud. "This is really good, Mack."

"Thank you."

Bite after bite, I fell in lust over the layers upon layers of al dente pasta, tasty ground meat, creamy béchamel sauce, and rich, melted cheese. I cleaned my plate along with the breadsticks and salad.

I sat back and sighed. "This was the best meal I've had in a while."

"Good enough to make you forget how angry you are with me?" he asked.

I gave him the side-eye. "Almost."

He grinned. "Then my job is almost done." He rubbed his palms together. "Dessert time."

I served up two big pieces of brownies and was about to dig in when Mack said, "No. Let's take it out on the deck." We grabbed our plates and headed to the deck, sitting down in the Adirondack chairs.

The bright-green insects—katydids—fluttered under the moonlight, a high-pitched noise accompanying their quick and nimble flight.

Mack bit into his brownie and groaned. "I love your brownies."

"Thank you." I preened with pride before popping a piece of the brownie into my mouth, savoring the cheesecake flavors that complemented the deep, decadent brownie.

"I've enjoyed tonight," I said.

"I have too." He extended his hand to me, and I took it. I didn't know how much time went by with us sitting under the moonlight holding hands. My eyes started to droop from the combination of the cool night and good food.

Mack shook my hand gently before releasing it. "Time to go

to bed." He stood, collecting our plates before escorting me inside the kitchen.

"You get ready for bed," he said. "I'll take care of the dishes."

"Nope." I shook my head. "We'll get it done faster as a team."

We made quick work of putting away the leftovers and placing all the dirty dishes, glasses, and utensils into the dishwasher. Every surface was cleaned before I turned to him. "Now we can both sleep."

We headed upstairs, stopping in front of my room. "Do you have a T-shirt I can wear? I'd like to take a shower before bed."

"Sure," he replied. "I'll be right back."

I headed inside the bedroom, kicking off my sneakers. Padding over to the window, I opened it, allowing the cool night air inside.

"Here you go," Mack said.

I turned to find him standing at the threshold. He extended the T-shirt to me. I arched a brow before walking over to him. "Thank you." I took the shirt. "I had a good time tonight. It took my mind off my problems."

"That's the magic of the forest," he replied. "See you in the morning." He walked away, and I shut the door.

It was amazing how when I'd woken up that morning, I'd expected my day to go one way, but it ended up with me hanging out with Mack, enjoying a stress-free night.

He didn't ask me to talk or do anything but just be still and relax. Only Mack figured out the best way to comfort me when I was stressed was just staying calm and being kind.

# CHAPTER 21
## AURORA

I jumped up into a sitting position at the sound of Mack bellowing, "Up and at 'em!"

My heart thudded as I pushed my hair from my face only to see Mack standing on the bedroom threshold with a wooden spoon in one hand and a metal pot in the other.

"What the fuck, man!" I snapped.

"Wakey, wakey!" he chirped. "It's time for our morning run."

I yawned. "What time is it?" It was the first time in a long time that I'd slept straight through the night.

"Three in the morning."

I frowned. "Are you out of your mind? I'm going back to sleep." I slid back under the covers.

Bang! Bang! Bang!

I covered my head with the sheets.

Bang! Bang! Bang!

"Fine," I grumped, kicking off the sheets. "We're running."

"I thought you'd see it my way. Up and at 'em. I'll see you downstairs in fifteen minutes."

I sat up, giving him the evil eye.

He pointed to the dressing table. "I put some clean clothes

over there." He turned to leave, then stopped and glared at me. "Don't keep me waiting."

I gave him the one-finger salute.

Thirteen minutes later, I was dressed and downstairs, wearing his T-shirt and drawstring basketball shorts. My attire looked ridiculous—because everything was huge on my body.

"Where are you?" I called out.

"On the front porch."

I headed in that direction and found him outside, stretching and wearing all black—loose black track pants, fitted black T-shirt, and black sneakers.

"Do you always run this early?" I demanded.

"Yup," he replied while continuing to stretch. "Get to warming up, Ro. It's going to be a long, vigorous run."

I blew out a breath, fighting the urge to strangle him. I hadn't been running in ages, but I did as he instructed, warming up my muscles.

"Let's go." He took off running without another word, leaving me scrambling to keep up. My heart thudded fast, and my lungs burned.

"Slow your pace," he said. "You're running way too fast. Listen to the rhythm of my feet and follow. Relax and just listen."

I relaxed, listening to the rhythm of his feet softly pounding against the ground. Instinctively matching his pace, I made my breathing slow.

We ran in complete silence. It was just us and the woods. Mack veered off the path, through a rugged section of the woods that required us to dodge tree limbs. As we approached a muddy path filled with huge puddles of water, he jumped over the water with not even a drop of it touching his sneakers while I stomped through it clumsily.

I was a mess, with muddy water splashing all over my sneakers and legs, and to add to the drama, I nearly tripped but caught myself.

I ran up to Mack with arms pumping. "You okay?" he asked.

"Peachy," I grumped, barely keeping up with him.

"You should be faster than this," he said. "If you smelled that feral shifter, then your inner animal is awakening."

"If she is, then I clearly haven't gotten the memo." I was huffing and puffing from the sheer effort to keep pace with him.

"Apparently not. You can't even make it through this light jog." He picked up his speed, forcing me to push my lungs to their absolute capacity. My legs were begging me to stop the torture.

I looked at him like he'd lost his ever-loving mind. *Light jog? Is he serious?* I was dying here.

"Come on, Ro. You're breathing like you're about to pass out. Slow down your breathing," he barked. "Inhale slowly. Let the air fill your lungs. And stop trying so hard."

My body sputtered like an old car, revolting against the effort.

He slowed his pace. "Take it easy. Just tune out the burning in your lungs and muscles. Your mind is in control of your body, not the other way around."

I tried to quiet my mind, pushing through the burning and pain, concentrating on moving through the forest. And it was actually working. My breathing slowed down, and my body glided effortlessly beside him.

"Okay, now listen to what the forest is telling you. Your ability to focus on your surroundings is very important." His voice was very melodic and calming. It pushed me to engage all my senses. I inhaled the cool, crisp forest air, hearing the rustling of leaves as birds moved from branch to branch. It was as if my feet grew wings. I became lightning fast.

Mack's pace quickened, and I kept in step with him.

"Now what do you hear?" he asked.

I heard the very distinct sounds of the wings of birds flapping in the distance, the popping sounds of water hitting rocks, and animals nervously scurrying across the forest ground.

My eyes widened. "Everything!"

Mack laughed. "Your animal is definitely coming awake, and when she's fully awakened, you'll be able to hear things you couldn't even imagine existed."

The thought was exciting. I'd always wanted to truly be a shifter.

We ran in comfortable silence until we reached a thrashing river and Mack stopped. I slowed my pace.

"That was the fastest I've ever run," I said.

Mack nodded approvingly. "In time, you'll run faster." He touched my cheek. "How do you feel?"

"Exhilarated." I jumped up and down, pumping my fists in the air. "Did you see how fast I was going?"

"I'm talking about your mind." He paused. "What's going on in there?"

I instantly sobered and kicked a rock with the tip of my sneaker. "I'm starting to feel calmer, which is progress, given how I've felt since that night at the ranch."

"How did you feel then?"

"Unglued," I said. "Totally clueless." Don't ask me how I transitioned from feeling like he was my total enemy to this awkward conversation of spilling my true feelings out to him. "I've been trapped in my own memories for days, and honestly, I couldn't stop questioning my self-worth and abilities." I bit my bottom lip. "Then when you came into June's, questioning if I was going to follow through with the championship, I wanted to slit your throat because you'd gotten too close to the truth. I'd given up on myself and wasn't going to go to the baking competition." I sighed. "I felt angry at myself. Angry at you and the world. After I left June's, I drove off to nowhere in particular until I pulled over and literally wept like a damn baby. Something I've never done."

He cupped my face. "Then you called me."

I nodded. "Because as angry as I was at you, I knew you were the only person I needed to be around while I brushed myself off and figured out where things went off the damn rails."

"I'm honored that you turned to me, Ro."

"And I'm honored that you welcomed me with open arms," I whispered.

He nodded. "I'd like you to stay here this week."

My eyes widened. "I can't just squat at your place."

"I'm inviting you to stay, Ro. I think you'll find your way, surrounded by the peace and quiet my home can provide."

I grabbed his arm. "What about work?"

"I'm due for some time off."

"Mack…"

"Listen to me, Ro. You need this, and so do I. I feel in my gut that this is a turning point in our relationship."

I stared at him with no words.

"Give me four days," he demanded.

I nibbled on my bottom lip. "Sex would just complicate things between us."

"This is not about sex. It's about strengthening our emotional connection," he explained.

I arched a brow. "Do you really think we can spend that much time together without you ending up between my legs?"

"As much as I want to make love to you, I don't think you're ready. So I agree sex would definitely complicate things."

I was shocked that he clearly understood where I was coming from.

"Exactly," I answered.

"You need to heal on your own terms. So do it here, with me by your side."

I reached up, cupping his cheek. "God. How can a man like you not be taken by some lucky woman?"

"I am taken… by you." He winked at me. "Let's head back." He looked at me mischievously. "Last one back has to cook breakfast."

"You're on," I answered.

Without warning, he took off, running at top speed.

I sputtered, "You asshole," then sprinted after him until I caught up to him.

He glanced at me briefly. "Damn, you're slow. I think June can run faster than you."

"I'll show you slow." I picked up speed, dodging branches and jumping over fallen trees. Mack kept pace, not breaking a sweat. Sometimes he'd speed up, and other times he slowed to a crawl. He was deliberately toying with me. He could have left me in the dust, but he didn't—at least not yet.

"Oh, look at my lioness go," he said.

I laughed and shoved him, trying to make him trip over the fallen, gnarled tree in our path.

"Hey, that's cheating," he complained.

"Tomato. Tomahto," I replied while barely keeping pace with him.

In a blur, he did a crazy somersault before landing a few paces in front of me.

"Show-off," I grumbled.

"See you at the house, lioness," he called over his shoulder before speeding through the forest and disappearing.

"You're lucky that I make a damn good breakfast!" I yelled.

# CHAPTER 22
## AURORA

After a big breakfast made by me—the loser of our race—Mack gave me a tour of his beautiful backyard oasis. In addition to areas for outdoor dining and entertaining, there were secluded spots for lounging, like his hammock strung between two trees and a large chaise piled with plenty of outdoor pillows that was ideal for sunbathing or lounging with a book.

After my tour, I took a long, hot shower to ease my aching muscles. Pulling my hair into a ponytail, I slipped into another one of Mack's T-shirts. I was heading downstairs when I saw a note from Mack on my bed.

**My lion is pretty antsy for me to shift and stretch our legs. I'll be back by lunch. Relax, take a nap, and enjoy my home.**

Grabbing my cell, I sent June a text about my plans to stay with Mack for a few days. Then I headed downstairs, grabbed a bottle of water from the refrigerator and a book that I found interesting from his coffee table. I headed outside to the backyard, deciding to lounge on the hammock.

I breathed deeply while sprawling on the hammock. "Damn, this is the life." I could see myself spending lots of time at Mack's house. He and I had the same design sensibility, making this place somewhere I could enjoy.

*Nope, Aurora,* I chastised myself. *No dreaming of a future with him, and keep this solidly grounded in the here and now.*

A warm breeze swept across my skin, carrying the scent of jasmine. My eyelids slid closed, and I was pulled into a peaceful sleep.

* * *

My eyes snapped open when I felt splashes of water against my skin. Grabbing everything I'd brought outside with me, I dashed inside the house. It felt late, yet there was no sign that Mack was back. I glanced down at my cell and noticed I'd missed a text from Imani and Nova, checking in with me, and another from June, saying she'd dropped by with my bag of clothes and toiletries, leaving them on the porch because we didn't answer the bell.

It was way past lunchtime, and Mack hadn't returned, which was unlike him not to keep his promise. But knowing shifters, when they transformed into their animal, they just went with the flow.

Picking up the large overnight bag June had packed for me, I brought it to the bedroom and unpacked, happy to have my own clothes to wear.

Slipping into black leggings and a T-shirt, I went to the kitchen and started making a hearty lunch for Mack and me. Shifting took a lot out of the body and expended a ton of calories. Mack would be starving when he transformed back into his human form.

I started with crispy, gooey, creamy, and salty Monte Cristo sandwiches, rolled-up roast beef, cheddar, and tangy horseradish in a tortilla, and finished with Parmesan shavings on the large turkey-and-avocado salad. Mack had devoured all the cheesecake brownies I'd made last night, so I'd have to bake more treats after lunch.

I set dishes and utensils on the butcher-block counter, then grabbed a glass of water before I went out on the deck to wait for his return.

Hours later, he still hadn't come back, so I ate a late lunch and packed everything into the refrigerator. I frowned, standing on the deck as I peered into the forest, only seeing birds frolicking. I traversed the long deck that wrapped around his house and saw no signs of Mack.

*Ro, don't panic. He just lost track of time.*

I wasn't one of those possessive, you-need-to-be-with-me-at-all-times women, but something about Mack not showing up as planned needled me.

I called his cell and heard it ringing in his bedroom—he'd obviously left it behind.

"Ro. Stop it. He's a big boy." And a huge lion who was at the top of the food chain. Against another animal, Mack's lion would win, hands down.

I walked into the living room, drifting from photo to photo of Mack with his pack. In every one of the photos, he was either grinning or mirth was reflected in his eyes. I could tell the pack was his family, and that made him very happy.

I headed into the kitchen and started baking. Hours later, with everything cooling on wire racks, I went into the living room and turned on the television. Curling my feet under me, I decided to binge-watch a series that had very good reviews.

After watching several episodes, I had a quick dinner of salad with chocolate chip cookies for dessert. The automatic lights switched on throughout the house. It was now late into the evening, and still no Mack.

I picked up my cell with the intention of calling Imani but stopped. *He's a shifter, for fuck's sake. That's what they do—shift into their animal and roam the land.* And Mack had lots of terrain.

I went upstairs, taking a quick shower before donning comfy sleep pants and a top. I left my bedroom door open so that I'd hear when he came back. Sitting up in bed, I made sure to charge my cell as I read in bed. But it wasn't too long after that my eyes started to droop, and I fell asleep with Mack on my mind.

# CHAPTER 23
## AURORA

I woke up the next morning to the sound of my cell's alarm ringing. Jumping off the bed, I marched out of the room and headed to Mack's bedroom. The door was open like he'd left it, but there was no sign of him having come back.

Going back to my room, I brushed my teeth, took a shower, dressed, and headed to the kitchen to start coffee. While it was brewing, I went out to the deck, my eyes searching the terrain.

It'd been twenty-four hours that he'd been gone. It wasn't healthy for shifters to spend more than a day in their shifter form.

Maybe he'd encountered a feral shifter and gotten bitten or scratched. *Is he hurt?*

I bit my bottom lip.

Or maybe his feral sickness was flaring up, and his animal had taken control of his mind and body.

The last possibility—of him losing touch with his human side —chilled me to the bone.

Maybe I was making a big deal out of nothing.

Mack could be perfectly fine.

I had a light breakfast before deciding to head out to see if his SUV was still parked next to mine.

Taking the winding gravel footpath through the forested canopy, I reached and crossed the small bridge that hovered over the creek.

I found Mack's SUV still parked next to mine.

Turning around, I headed back to his home, all the while contemplating calling June. But if I did that, something told me that she'd turn my concern into a fiasco, with everyone in town showing up to search for Mack as if he were a missing child. I didn't want Mack being MIA to turn into a circus. More importantly, I couldn't betray his trust by telling anyone that he was in the first stage of the feral sickness.

Back at the house, instinctively, I started stress baking. There was nothing I could do but wait for his return, which was frustrating as hell.

"Fuck!" I slammed my palms against the butcher block.

When Mack got home, I was going to kick his ass for making me worry about him.

After baking up a storm, I made a quick lunch, ate, and started early on dinner. Steaks, mashed potatoes, biscuits, salad, grilled vegetables. But nothing distracted me from the time ticking and Mack being a no-show.

My stomach was such a nervous wreck that I skipped dinner. It was eight at night, and I sat in the living room with the television on and my cell in hand.

Everything in my gut told me that Mack was in trouble.

I called Imani.

"Aurora, finally. Don't ever ignore my calls and texts again."

"I know, it was a real fucked-up thing to do, but my head wasn't right. I promise you I'm not normally a bitch, but I'm calling about something that's bothering me. I'm at Mack's, spending time with him, and he shifted and went for a run yesterday morning, but he hasn't been back." I nibbled on my bottom lip. "I'm worried."

"Oh shit," Imani replied. "Quinn's here. Let me put you on speakerphone."

"What's going on, Aurora?" Quinn asked.

I repeated what I'd just told Imani.

"Maybe I'm making a big deal out of nothing," I said.

"No. You're not," Quinn replied. "Look, we'd come over there right now, but it's night, and having a pack of alpha males traipsing on another alpha's territory—especially a five-hundred-pound-plus alpha lion—is a recipe for trouble and blood being spilled."

"You're right." Lions were territorial and marked their territories by roaring and scent marking with urine. If Quinn and his pack came onto Mack's territory while he was still in lion form, he'd attack them just on primal instinct.

"If he's not back by morning, give me a call, and we'll head over there," Quinn said.

"Okay." Now I was more concerned. Morning was hours away, and the more time Mack spent in his animal form, the harder it could be for him to find the mental strength to return to his human self.

"Aurora, listen to me. It will be all right," Quinn said with a calm voice. "But under no circumstances should you go out there and look for him. He's been in his lion form for too long, and he might not recognize you and could attack and hurt you. You don't want that in Mack's head when he shifts back. It would devastate him to hurt his female."

"I hear you, Quinn. I'm hoping he'll show up tonight. If not, I'll call you first thing in the morning."

"Good. Get some sleep," he said before ending our call.

But sleep was the last thing on my mind. I sat for a while with my stomach churning with worry. When nine hit, I'd had enough and went upstairs to put on a sweatshirt and my sneakers. I strode downstairs and rummaged through Mack's kitchen drawers until I found a flashlight. Sticking my cell in my back pocket, I headed outside. I had plenty of experience, both from the military and growing up in the pride, with tracking people and animals. It was a skill set that I excelled at.

I found Mack's lion paw prints, following them until they disappeared.

I shined the flashlight around, looking for broken branches, bushes, or anything to lead me in the direction he went. Using the light, I raised it to the trees to see if he was hanging out on a limb. He wasn't.

I should have known this would happen. Mack was Special Ops like me. If he didn't want to be found, he was skilled enough to camouflage himself from detection.

I had two options—continue walking aimlessly through the forest, or head back to his home. Neither of the options was high on my to-do list.

I panned the area again and stilled when I heard a faint, unfamiliar female voice in my head say, *Left*. Then there was silence. I knew I hadn't imagined the voice. It had to be my inner animal.

She was awake. Excitement and confusion flooded me. One, because my inner beast was finally awake, but why was she so faint? It was as if she was tired and weak. But I didn't have time to stand in the middle of the forest at night contemplating what was going on with my animal. I had to keep moving.

I headed in the direction she instructed me to—left—but that eventually led me to a dead end.

*Right*, my animal instructed.

"But there's no path right?" I asked aloud.

*I said, right!* she snapped.

"Well, ain't you a bossy bitch," I grumbled while pushing through the thick forest, nearly getting slapped in the face by a heavy branch. Heading straight, I found myself in a large clearing with no Mack in sight.

"What now?" I said aloud. "He's not here."

*He is here*, my inner animal said.

Shining my flashlight around, I saw no lion. I wasn't going to argue with my animal, but so far, her tracking skills sucked.

My nose twitched when I picked up a faint sour smell that I

recognized—feral sickness. I waved my flashlight around quickly, hoping to catch the animal before it reached me.

Another scent wafted up my nostrils. It was Mack. Then I knew that he was watching me. I could smell and sense it.

"Come out, Mack," I demanded.

There was utter silence, which was eerie for a forest filled with creatures of the night.

"I know you're there," I tried again.

Leaves fluttered to the earth, and I pointed my flashlight up into the tree. Mack's lion was lying on a branch, surrounded by leaves, something I'd thought was impossible because large adult males were just too big and heavy. They were better known for lazing about under trees, especially in the heat of the day.

"Get down," I ordered.

He roared.

"I'm not scared of you, Mack. Get down. It's late, and I want to go home."

He didn't budge.

I stamped my foot. "Don't make me come up there," I threatened. I had no intention of climbing the tree, but the threat sounded badass to me.

A few beats later, he actually got to his feet. I gulped when I heard the creaking of the branch that seemed to be struggling to hold his weight.

The lion jumped down with ease a few feet from me.

"Come on." I beckoned with my hand. "Start marching, young man. You've got some explaining to do."

He roared at me, then charged, stopping just short of me.

I didn't move. I wasn't scared. This was Mack, but not totally. I could tell from the look in his eyes that his animal had taken over completely. There was no humanity in his gaze, just pure animal. But I also knew this lion could have killed me already if that was his intention.

"Look, kitty. I know you're upset with me because I haven't

let Mack claim me, but you won't get your way by acting like an ass."

He roared again.

"Yeah, yeah, you're mad."

He lay down and glared at me.

"Good news," I said to him. "My inner animal is awake and led me to you." I gave him two thumbs-up. The lion yawned, clearly not impressed by my revelation.

"Mack is mine," I declared. "Now be a good kitty and let him shift."

The lion stared at me.

"I'm going back to Mack's place. You better be there in fifteen minutes, or that's your ass, lion." I pointed a finger at him.

I backed away, facing him until he was no longer in sight.

I took a deep breath. "That was crazy as hell," I said aloud, and it was. That whole thing could have gone sideways and ended with me getting hurt, but Mack was mine and he needed me.

It didn't take me long to arrive back at the house. I stood outside and waited, but there was no lion and no Mack.

I meant it. If he didn't show up, I was going back to try again. And I'd continue trying to lure him home all night if that was what it took. I was stubborn like that.

I sat on the steps and waited some more.

"Come on, Mack. Don't make me have to drag your ass home."

I blew out a breath. I was thirsty, so I decided to grab a bottle of water before heading back out. "This is going to be a long night," I murmured, heading to the kitchen.

I skirted to a stop. Mack was standing in the kitchen, naked and devouring a smorgasbord of food that littered the counter.

He glanced over at me but continued eating.

I sat down on the bar stool and stared at him silently.

He opened a bottle of water and guzzled it, then another and another. All the while, no words were exchanged.

Mack was home, and that was all that mattered right now. We could talk about what happened later. Right now we both were too emotionally raw.

He continued eating, and I could smell the light wisp of the feral sickness on his skin.

I stood and walked out of the kitchen, heading upstairs. I sent Imani a text, letting her know he was back, then I took a quick shower and dressed for bed. I left the door open to the bedroom before hopping into bed. I wanted to make sure I heard him heading to bed. I couldn't deal with another shifting-into-his-animal-and-dashing-away incident. Not tonight… not for a long while.

I lay in the darkness with the moonlight shining across the bed. I yawned, completely exhausted. I was determined to stay awake, but the exhaustion won and I fell asleep.

I didn't know how much time passed before I was awakened by the sound of an owl hooting. I reached for my cell on the nightstand. It was a little after midnight. Kicking off the sheets, I got out of bed and strode down the hall to Mack's bedroom. The door was open, and he was on the bed. My shoulders sagged with relief.

"You okay?" he asked, not moving.

"No." I swallowed hard. "You?"

"No," he replied gruffly.

I strode into his bedroom, lifted the sheets, and climbed into bed with him. I scooted my back against his chest, and he wrapped a heavy arm around my waist and nuzzled my neck.

"Good night," I whispered.

"Good night," he said.

# CHAPTER 24
## AURORA

I woke up with sun streaming on my face and an empty bed. Rolling over, I pressed my face into his pillow, picking up his familiar scent of warm cinnamon and mint citrus notes entwined with patchouli, and none of the sour feral-sickness smell from yesterday—thank goodness.

Leaving his room, I brushed my teeth and pulled on sweatpants and a T-shirt before heading downstairs and following the scent of freshly brewing coffee. Mack was standing by the counter with a cup in hand. I didn't even say good morning and strode up behind him, pressing my chest against his back and wrapping my arms around his waist. Last night was one of my top sleeping moments. I had no nightmares. No insomnia. And no attempt by either of us to do anything but cuddle before falling asleep.

I released him and headed over to fill a cup with coffee.

"You slept well," he remarked.

I turned to face him. "I did." I took a sip of coffee while examining his face. He looked well rested, given the past couple of days. "So what are we doing today?" I wanted to make today fun, given that I'd be leaving tomorrow because it was baking championship day.

"How about we try our picnic again?" he asked.

"I'm down for that. But I'm starving right now, so what's for breakfast?"

He arched a brow. "Is it my turn or your turn to make breakfast?"

"Yes, it's your turn." I softly punched him. "Don't try to get over on me."

He kissed the top of my head. "Would I do that?"

"Yes," I quipped. "So get to making my breakfast, kind sir." I plopped down on the bar stool and drank my coffee.

"You're a bossy female," he remarked before leaning across the counter, kissing my lips softly. "And I love it."

Leaning back in my chair, I said, "Less talking, more cooking. Time for me to be the queen for the day."

"You're my queen every day," he said gruffly before turning to the refrigerator and getting out ingredients.

Effortlessly, he prepared our breakfast. I would have helped, but I suspected he needed to keep busy after his ordeal.

"Are you ready to talk about it?" I asked him.

I wanted our discussion about what happened to be on his terms because I knew how frustrating it could be to be prodded about shit you just weren't ready to discuss.

He placed huge omelets on each plate, putting them on the counter. "After our breakfast while you were in the shower, my animal was nagging me to shift and stretch our legs." He shrugged. "I left you a note, and it was business as usual when I shifted." He poured orange juice into two glasses. "I remember running into the forest but nothing else until you stood in front of me, telling me to get my ass home in fifteen minutes." He sat down next to me. "I remember running home and shifting into my human form before walking into the house." He took a bite of omelet. "I knew something was wrong as soon as I walked into the kitchen and saw the calendar—it was almost two days later."

I chewed and swallowed my mouthful of eggs. "Your animal took over your mind." It was a statement, not a question.

He nodded. "Yes, which is fucking embarrassing." He grabbed my hand, kissing each finger. "I apologize for leaving you for so long. You had to be worried for you to come out to the forest that late at night." He released my hand, giving me a stern glare. "By the way, don't do that shit again. There are dangerous animals out there at night."

I lightly tapped his cheek. "Well, don't fucking scare me like that ever again." I swallowed hard. "Mack, I was terrified for you. First, I thought that you might have been attacked by a feral animal. Then I started having thoughts about your animal taking over your mind. I called Imani and Quinn because I didn't know what to do. And Quinn didn't want to come out here late at night because he didn't want you to mistake your pack for enemies and attack."

"I spoke to Quinn and my pack this morning. They told me you were worried about me."

"I had to call them, Mack."

Mack sighed heavily. "That was a good decision. I wasn't in my right mind. My lion is pissed at me for not claiming you and angry at you for not claiming us." He ran a hand through his hair. "I can feel my feral sickness progressing. I don't want you to get hurt."

"You listen to me, Mack. I'm not afraid of you."

"Ro…"

I pressed a finger to his lips. "You heard me." I poked a finger against his chest. "So pass on the message to that asshole lion-shifter inside you that's pouting like a damn child."

Mack laughed. "He respects you. Whatever you did last night, you now have his respect. You must have given him a good tongue-lashing."

"Something like that." I grabbed his face. "I'm not walking away from us, Mack. I need you to understand that. My time with you has cemented that you are mine as I am yours. I know that it might not be easy… our relationship. There's no perfection in either of us. But my time with you has awakened not only my inner beast but the woman that I can and want to be."

He smiled. "Does that mean she talked to you?"

"Yes. That's how I found you. The bossy female led me to you when I lost your trail." I sighed heavily. "Which is really annoying because I pride myself on being an excellent tracker."

"I guess she's better."

"Shut it, sexy kitty." I held up a finger. "The last thing I need is my kitty thinking that she's the boss of me."

"So are you excited about the possibility of shifting?" he asked with a gleam in his eyes.

"Yes," I said softly. "It's also frightening to be so close to getting the one thing that I wanted all my life. Self-happiness. My inner animal. And a man who makes me smile."

He cupped my cheek. "I'm going to love and protect you so hard, darling."

My heart thudded. "Ditto." I pulled away from him. "Now stop distracting me and let me eat my breakfast."

"Yes, ma'am."

* * *

It was a perfect, peaceful day as we sat on the lush grass shaded by a tall tree and the most incredible mountain backdrop.

After our delicious picnic spread, including prosciutto, figs, fresh bread, cheeses, olives, salami, and crumbly key lime cupcakes, we enjoyed lounging in the grass with our stomachs full, just talking and laughing.

"Tell me what you love most about living in the Ridge?" I asked with my head in Mack's lap.

"Everything." He lifted my hand, kissing the inside of my wrist. My stomach flipped from the sensual contact. I wasn't used to being touched on my wrist—especially not the inside. It was intimate.

"Be more specific, kitty."

"My pack. The peace and quiet. The fresh air and no traffic. The slower pace." His eyes remained on mine. "Do you think you can handle living in a small town like the Ridge?"

I ran my palm along his thigh. "I've never been a city girl, so living in a small town wouldn't be hard. It's the being around Others that will take time to adjust to."

"Most Others in this town are caring," he said, placing my hand back on my belly. "The rest are just ornery fuckers who will never be happy."

"I know that," I said. "I'm not a people pleaser anyway."

He chuckled. "Good. You'll fit right into the pack."

Suddenly, the clouds were black and low.

"It's going to rain," Mack pointed out. "We better head back."

We gathered all our picnic stuff and headed back to his home. We barely made it inside before the rain came down in sheets.

I walked over to his big windows, watching the rain. "From here, you can see the tree canopy, and it feels like I'm in a rain forest. It's so beautiful."

Mack came to stand behind me. "Talking about beautiful." He started kissing the side of my neck. His lips against my neck were quite a turn-on.

"Sexy kitty, there will be no sex."

"Oh, there'll be sex," he said against my neck. "Just not today."

Turning around, I gently brushed my fingers against his neck.

"So what would you like to do on my last night here?" I inquired.

He arched a brow. "Is that a trick question?"

"Do you think about anything but sex?" I asked, running my fingers through his hair.

"Around you… no." He nipped my bottom lip.

"I see." I licked his lips. "How about popcorn?"

He ran his hands over my ass. "Never tried it, but I'm down with eating popcorn off your delicious body."

"No." I shoved him playfully. "Get your mind out of the gutter. I'm talking about making popcorn and watching a movie."

"I'm not going to lie. I'm a little disappointed that I'm not getting to eat popcorn off your body."

I laughed. "Come on, freaky kitty." I grabbed his hand, tugging him toward the kitchen.

"All right. All right."

Once we made it into the kitchen, I went for the cabinet where I'd seen the popcorn, pulling it out.

When I turned around, Mack was holding out a white teacup with veins of gold running around it as if it was held together by those gold threads.

"I made this for you," he said, shoving it into my hand.

The fact that it was handcrafted by him made the cup even more special to me. "It's beautiful." I turned it around, examining the teacup. "Was it broken and glued together using gold glue?"

He tilted his head and studied me. "It's kintsugi—golden repair—the Japanese art of putting broken pottery pieces back together with gold, emphasizing not hiding the break."

I arched a brow, still not getting his point.

He continued. "It's a metaphor for embracing your flaws and imperfections. By doing that, you can create a stronger, more beautiful you." He cupped my cheek, watching me closely, a look in his eyes that made me feel precious and beautiful. "I don't expect you to be perfect. In fact, I appreciate the fact that you trusted me enough to show me your old wounds. I'm not perfect, Ro. We are both imperfect, but we can heal, grow, and survive blows that life hands to us, and live to tell the tale."

Swallowing hard, I felt my pulse pick up. To have a man so strong and good who cared about my well-being was over-whelming.

I placed the cup on the counter before reaching up and trapping him with my hands around his face. "Thank you, Mack. For this precious time with you. For your gift. And for being you."

Dragging his face down, I kissed him, and he deepened the kiss, sliding his tongue into my mouth. I moaned, pressing myself to him and moving one hand to slide through the back of his hair. This man was mine, but I wasn't going to rush into sex with him, even though my pussy was pulsating with the need to have his cock inside me. I broke the kiss, and his eyes were dilated and he was breathing heavy.

His voice was a velvet whisper against my ear when he said, "Mine."

"Always," I replied.

* * *

After our movie night, both of us went our separate ways to get ready for bed. I stood under the hot spray of the shower, contemplating my time with Mack. Who would have thought that me walking onto his property, feeling like a raged-out bitch with one goal—to punch him in the face—could have ended with me being offered an olive branch and an opportunity to find myself again?

The truth of the matter was that for so long, I'd been trapped in a turbulent sea of my own memories. His life preserver helped me to stop questioning my self-worth and abilities. I'd started the process of brushing myself off and taking a good long, hard look at myself.

Stepping out of the shower, I pulled off my shower cap. Massaging several drops of my citrus, ginger, and lemongrass body oil into my damp skin, I paid special attention to the scarred skin on my hip.

After putting on my lingerie, I stared at my reflection while smoothing on moisturizer. My dark skin glowed. There were no dark circles under my eyes from insomnia. The almost-manic gleam that used to be there was gone. I was learning to turn off my inner critic with self-love, talking to Mack, yoga, running, and/or baking. Now I had effective methods to ease my anxiety attacks, and as a result, I'd stopped taking my psychotropic medication. But I wasn't under any illusion that I was cured; it would take time for me to feel completely whole again, and every day would be a work in progress. But I was getting stronger, and that was the most important thing.

I quickly combed through my naturally textured hair before putting on an open turban head wrap that was essential for protecting my hair at night.

Striding into the bedroom, I stared at the bed. I didn't want to sleep alone. I'd gotten spoiled last night by sleeping with Mack. I wanted Mack emotionally and physically, but I was hesitant about having sex with him so soon.

*Claim him,* my inner beast demanded in a weak voice. *He's yours.*

I shivered at the wispiness of her voice.

I closed my eyes and focused on communicating with her mentally.

*Why do you sound so—?*

My beast cut me off, *Like a plant without sunlight and water, I'm wilting from your neglect of yourself and, therefore, me. But you are healing, mending, growing, transforming into a new, stronger version of yourself. Continue along this path, and we both will prosper. But remember, part of our journey is claiming our fated mate.*

In the past, sex was number one on my priority list when it came to men. If a man sucked in bed, I knew that relationship wasn't going to work for me. But since meeting Mack and spending time with him alone, I knew that I'd been wrong. It wasn't about sex being boring or a man not living up to my sexual standards. It was about what else our relationship was offering. And I found the answers during my stay with Mack. Other men had fallen short because I knew that if I took sex out of the equation, there would be nothing else. Now I understood that finding a man who knew how to treat me with love, caring, and acceptance was more important than sex.

*We need more time together before we have sex,* I told my beast.

*A claiming is more than sex,* my beast answered. *It's assuring your mate that you want him and you will not run away. You have not made a vow to both man and beast that you are theirs and they are ours.*

I frowned. *Didn't I make that clear to Mack already?*

*Not directly,* my beast said. *Tell them, and that will settle his beast and cure his feral sickness. It will also start my healing, making me stronger.*

Well, that wouldn't do. I had to rectify this problem immediately.

# CHAPTER 25
## MACK

With the rain still pouring, I sat up in bed, thinking about Ro instead of reading the book I held in my hand.

Ro and I had come a long way since she'd arrived in the Ridge. I felt our relationship strengthening and our bond growing, but that did not reassure my inner beast. I could feel him prowling within me. He wanted me to claim her, and nothing short of that would do. I suspected that was why my inner animal had taken over my mind and body for almost two days. It was also why my feral sickness was progressing despite the fact that my fated mate was in the room next door.

*Just do it!* my beast roared.

*No! I will not claim her without her consent,* I barked.

No matter how much I loved her—and I did—I would never force her into a relationship she did not want. I too needed to be loved and claimed, but this couldn't be forced on Ro.

The light in my room was on when Ro stood on my threshold wearing sheer, boy-cut panties that accentuated her voluptuous curves and a black tank top that displayed the fullness of her breasts. My eyes traced the scar on her hip that took nothing away from her beauty.

"What took you so long?" I growled, tossing the book onto

my nightstand.

She climbed onto my bed, straddling me. Her closeness surprised me, and I treasured it.

"You're an impatient man," she complained. "You know that, right?"

"Only when it comes to you, lioness," I said, wrapping my arm around her waist, dragging her closer so that our chests were mere inches from each other.

She was absolutely gorgeous, her thick hair pulled away from her face by a head wrap and her face freshly scrubbed.

"I'm not going anywhere, Mack," she whispered against my neck before leaning back to stare at me.

I nearly jumped for joy but instead nipped the juncture between her neck and shoulder—a sign of my possession.

"I'm a hard woman to understand, so I always doubted if there was a man who would ever accept me for who and what I am."

"Me. I know who you are, Ro. You're not alone. I see you. I need you."

I reached up, wiping away the teardrop at the corner of her eye.

"And I need you," she whispered. "I'd been trapped in my own memories for so long. I sometimes try to ignore them, but oftentimes I can't. I didn't realize that I had never left the battle-field. I brought the war home, and it took a toll on me. And for so long, I felt that something important had been stolen from me, and I had nobody I could talk about it with." She cupped my cheek. "Until I found you."

My heart thumped hard in my chest. Her trust and faith in me, in us, humbled me.

"We found each other," I said, reaching over and brushing my hand down her back.

She nodded. "These few days with you have made me realize what was fueling my angst. I was angry at myself because I wasn't back to 'normal'—the woman I was before the roadside bomb. But you've shown me that there is no going back, that woman is the old me. Who I am today is the 2.0 me, the stronger me."

"Ro, I've never met an interesting person who didn't have a past and/or wounds. Perfection is a fucking myth." I placed her hand over my heart. "This is real."

She kissed my jaw, down the column of my throat, and to my collarbone. She put so much tenderness, passion, and meaning into those precious, gentle kisses, and they claimed me like no words ever could.

"I belong to you, and you belong to me," Ro declared. "So tell your crazy cat to stop acting like an asshole and get right."

My inner cat purred, and I knew that our turbulent struggle was over. Ro's gesture and words were the balm for our wounds.

I chuckled. "He's purring, so he's got the message loud and clear."

"Good, because I'm not going to be a happy camper if I have to traipse through the forest again to find your ass." She pursed her lips.

"I think my cat and I are back on speaking terms because of your declaration."

"And let him know that our official claiming will not happen until my inner beast is healthy. I've put her through the wringer, and she's on the mend." She paused. "Which brings me to another important topic—sex. I want you on every level, emotionally and physically, but we need a little more time to learn about each other."

"I've been celibate for over five years, Ro. I can wait for you."

Her eyes widened. "That's a long time."

I shrugged. "Before coming to the Ridge, I was that guy who fucked around, but that shit got real old. I made up my mind when I started living here that I wanted more. I wanted my fated mate. And until I found her… you… again, I wasn't going fill my time with meaningless sex."

"I took a break from sex a little while before Afghanistan," she confessed. "In my last relationship, I started questioning what I would have left if I took sex away from our relationship, and the answer was that we, indeed, had nothing between us. Just simply sex." She sighed. "That was a big wake-up call for me." She stared at me. "I know what our relationship is offering—love, trust, and acceptance—but I want us to wait until my beast is healed. My gut tells me it's important for both our animals to be healed and on the same page."

"I agree. We both do still have healing to do." Her animal needed healing from her trauma, and so did mine—from the feral sickness. Besides, I'd waited all my life to find Ro again; I could wait a little bit longer to consummate our mating.

She leaned forward, trapping my face with her hands before planting her luscious lips on mine. I deepened our kiss, stroking my tongue into her mouth. Ro inched closer, wrapping her arms and legs tightly around my waist as I devoured her mouth. She sucked at my tongue, and I growled low in my chest. This woman, without a doubt, was the missing piece in my life.

"We need to stop," she whispered. "Before we start something we shouldn't finish."

I broke our kiss, pressing my forehead against hers. I didn't want our first time to be something she'd regret.

"Sleepy time," she said.

I leaned back with a smile playing on one side of my mouth. "It's going to be the first time I've had to sleep with a hard-on." I winked at her. "Every night since you've been in the Ridge, I've gone to sleep with the vision of your face in my head and the memory of your scent lingering in my memories."

"And now I'm here." She kissed my neck and the top of my chest before sliding off me onto the bed. "Hug me, sexy kitty."

I reached over to the nightstand, turning off the lamp, before sliding down onto the bed and pulling her back against my chest.

"Good night, lioness."

"Good night, sexy kitty."

# CHAPTER 26
## AURORA

When June pulled up to Bane's Bed & Breakfast, she turned to smile at me. "Wow, my animal and I are really loving your new calm vibe." She grabbed my hand. "I couldn't be prouder of you."

"Thank you. I feel better." I did. I hated leaving Mack's oasis this morning, but I couldn't stay in his wonderful bubble forever. Before I'd left, we had a long breakfast together on the deck, taking in the sounds and views of his lush forest. And the kiss we shared after he'd walked me to my SUV was deep, passionate, and lingered in my mind during my journey back to June's cottage, where I got ready for my big day.

June sniffed loudly. "So no sex, huh?"

I laughed. "It's impolite to smell me for signs of sex."

She shrugged. "We're all wondering when the big event is going to happen."

"Well, you and your cougar crew can stop wondering. It will happen when it's time and not before."

June rolled her eyes. "I don't know why younglings are so uptight about sex. Just have sex already."

I arched a brow. "If my inner beast is okay with me holding

off on having sex with Mack, I think you can relax about it." I'd told June about the awakening of my inner beast, and June nearly threw a "Hey, everybody. Her lioness is awake!" party.

"Fine," June grumped.

"So can we go now?" I asked. "I have baking to do."

"Are you sure about this?" June asked, gesturing to the B and B. "Don't walk through that door if you're not going to make the Ridge your new home."

I nodded. "I'm sure. I never would have come to the B and B if I wasn't. Win or lose, I'm giving life in the Ridge a shot."

"But why now?"

"Hey!" I arched a brow. "You don't want me here anymore?" I joked.

"Oh hush." June fanned me. "I've been begging you to come here for years. I would love it if you stayed, but I want you to be sure of what you're committing to. There're a hell of a lot of people in there who will be disappointed—including Mack and me—if you hightail it out of town without giving life in the Ridge an honest try."

I locked eyes with her. "I've thought about this decision long and hard. It's not just about the competition, because there's no guarantee I'll win. It's about me doing something that scares the shit out of me." I pointed to the door. "And walking in there and possibly failing terrifies me. And I'm not just talking about the competition, but with Mack." I sighed deeply. "But I've realized that my not trying is failure. So whether I win or lose—with the competition and Mack—I'm a winner in here." I tapped my head. "And here." I touched my heart.

June squeezed my hand. "I've been waiting for so long for you to come to that conclusion." She pinched my cheek. "Now let's go and win this championship."

We got out of the SUV and walked up to the B and B.

"This is beautiful," I said, staring at the absolutely stunning historical-looking gem.

"It is," June agreed. "It was built in 1924 and sat unoccupied for years until Piper turned it into a B and B."

Pushing the iron fence open, we strode past the gardens, sauntered up the front stairs, and opened the unlocked door.

"Do we have time to look around?" I asked June.

She glanced at her watch. "Yes, but let's be quick."

We walked around the large rooms filled with ornate furniture and flooded with natural daylight. The architectural details blew my mind, from Italian marble mantles, crystal chandeliers, crown moldings, massive windows, and spectacular wood floors.

"June?" Piper called out. "Where are you? I saw your SUV parked outside."

"I'm in the grand ballroom," June answered.

I heard the rapid clicking of heels before Piper entered the room.

"I'm happy you're here, Aurora," Piper exclaimed, rushing up to me and giving me a hug, then June. "Imani was freaking out." She looped her arm through mine, tugging me out of the room. June followed.

"Why?" I asked.

"Because she didn't think you'd show," June answered for Piper. "She's been texting me all day, asking me to make sure you showed up."

I frowned. "I would never not show up. My word is my bond."

"Well, you haven't been answering anyone's texts or calls, dear," Piper pointed out. "How could she know?"

I gave Piper the side-eye. "I was busy with Mack."

Piper perked up. "I heard about you spending time with him. How did it go?" She stopped to sniff me.

I leaned away from her. "Uh, Piper, sniffing for signs of sex is not cool," I protested.

"I can't just turn my shifter inclinations off and on, sweetie," Piper protested with a saucy grin.

"Can we go now?" I asked. Totally weirded out by women old enough to be my mother prying into my lack of a sex life.

"Sure," Piper said, dragging me along as we continued to walk.

Heads swiveled when we strode into the room.

My mouth fell open. "Where did all these people come from?" There weren't many vehicles outside, yet the massive space was packed with at least forty people.

"Most people walked over here," Piper informed me.

I waved at Bonnie and Freya. And I laughed when Nyx, Izzy, and Rose held up their hands for a high five from me—which I gave each of them. I recognized some of the people from my frequent visits to the grocery store and waved.

"Wow," I whispered, glancing around.

One section of the room had rows of chairs like a concert. Another section had a massive gourmet kitchen with four U-shaped workstations. Each had a large sign at the bottom with a name, designating the contestant's assigned station.

The stations were equipped with a stove, mixer, and two glass canisters, one marked SUGAR and another FLOUR.

Imani ran up to me, giving me a big hug. "I'm so happy you're here, Aurora."

I hugged her back. "I wouldn't miss it for the world."

We pulled apart and just smiled at each other.

"Hey, wait a minute!" Josie yelled. "Imani, it's not fair to have your friend in this competition."

Imani jammed her hands on her hips. "I'm not a judge, Josie, so shut it."

Josie sneered before turning to address the crowd. "Anyone else besides me sick and tired of these hybrids?" She tapped her foot like an impatient child. "First, they take our men. Now they're taking over this baking competition."

"Who is they?" I whispered to Imani. "Are there more hybrids in this competition?"

"No. Josie's doing what she does best, being a drama queen." Imani said the last two words loudly.

Josie shot her a dirty glare.

"I agree with Josie," a short man with blond hair bellowed.

"Of course you do, Milton," Bonnie said. "She's your daughter."

Milton's face flushed red. "That doesn't mean I'm not entitled to my opinion, Bonnie."

"Hey, wait a minute," said a tall, thin man with black eyes, a potbelly, and a brown cowlick. "I thought this competition was only for residents."

Freya pointed at the man. "Shut it, Weasel."

Bonnie chimed in, "Chester, how many times do we have to explain that hybrids become citizens automatically once they arrive in the Ridge?"

Chester, the weasel, scratched his head. "I keep forgetting."

June rolled her eyes. "It's so amazing that you have amnesia at the most convenient times."

"Like when he wants to stir the shit pot," Piper pointed out.

"Well, I don't think it's fair that the hybrid gets to compete at the last minute," Josie complained.

Imani looked Josie up and down. "I'm going to say this once. You either get over to your assigned workstation, or you forfeit your right to participate in this competition."

Josie threw her hands in the air, then flounced over to her assigned station, mumbling, "Damn hybrids."

Josie's tirade stirred the crowd, who started bickering among themselves.

Piper whistled loudly, and the audience went silent. "If you don't shut it, sit down, and act right, I'm going to throw you troublemakers out." Everyone took a seat. "Good." She nodded. "Let's get this competition started."

"Aurora, you're over there." Imani pointed to the station right next to Josie.

I took my spot. Josie wrinkled her nose at me. I returned the gesture by scratching my nose with my middle finger.

Imani and Piper stood before the audience.

"I'd like to officially welcome everyone to our first Ridge baking championship, hosted by me, Imani Bane, and Piper Bane," Imani announced. "We have four contestants who get the chance to take home a grand prize that includes $2500, an exclusive one-year contract to provide baked goods to Bane's Bed & Breakfast, and a free storefront location on Main Square."

The crowd clapped and whistled.

"Let's introduce our talented contestants," Piper announced. "We have Aurora, our newest resident and home baker. Josie, the owner of Yonder Biscuits. Missy, our very own head librarian. She's a home baker as well. And Skipper, the owner of Skipper's Locksmith. He's also a home baker."

The audience clapped, whistled, and stomped.

"The judges for this competition are"—Imani pointed to the only three people sitting in the front row—"Donovan and Sinner McDermott, owners of the renowned Sinner + Do Smokehouse, and their sister Odessa McDermott, who helps run their business."

The crowd whistled.

My heart sped up with excitement. I'd heard of Sinner + Do. They had several locations in the human world, and their restaurants were so popular and beloved that their smokehouse had made appearances on lots of popular food shows. The two brothers were huge, muscular men with black hair and looked like they could be MMA fighters. Their sister was a voluptuous brunette.

The judges rose to their feet and waved to the audience before striding out of the room.

"The judges will be back to judge the bakers' creations," Piper told the audience.

"Okay, let's get to the rules," Imani announced. "This is a one-day competition with three rounds of baking in which the contestants will create a confection that's centered around a specific theme. The winner of each round advances to the next round while the baker with the worst dish is eliminated. Each round will be timed." She pointed to the large digital clock on the wall. "You only get judged on what is plated before the timer is up, so manage your time well. For each round, the bakers must balance decoration and flavor. Even if the cake is beautiful, it must also be delicious. So in essence, flavor always trumps appearance."

Imani turned to look at us pointedly. "Because this competition features baking, we've allowed contestants to bring written recipes they can refer to during the competition."

I was grateful for the allowance to bring written recipes. I certainly couldn't compete without my recipes because, for baking, the measurements needed to be precise, and no one could store that much information in their head. I pulled out my binder of recipes from my messenger bag, placing it on my workstation.

"There's an oven for each contestant." Piper pointed to the long wall with a row of ovens and three large stainless steel refrigerators. "The refrigerators are well stocked. And you have access to plenty of pantry items, pans, pots, platters, and dishes." She indicated a wall of shelves packed with items. "Also, each contestant's workstation has a mixer, cooktop, and their own canisters of sugar and flour." She paused. "The rule is that before the timer is up, your baked item must be plated and placed in the middle of your workstation, and your hands must be in the air. So that means no touching." She gave us each a stern stare. "If your item is not in the designated location, you're disqualified. If you try to add something to your dish after time, you're disqualified. And if we find out that you've cheated, you're disqualified. Now please put on your aprons."

I put on my apron and rubbed my sweaty palms against it.

*This is it. No turning back now.*

A small commotion arose at the entrance. It was Quinn and

Mack walking in. Now I was even more nervous. Mack stood at the back of the room, scanning the crowd before his eyes locked on mine, giving me a wink. I waggled my eyebrows.

"For the first round, the bakers have ninety minutes to make a dessert that features honey and walnuts," Imani announced. "Honey and walnuts are on the pantry shelf." She cued Piper. "And your time starts… now."

I blew out a calming breath before leafing through my binder, finding my recipe for honey-walnut bars. I ran over to the pantry, getting all my ingredients. I placed everything on my workstation, then preheated the oven before getting more stuff out of the refrigerator.

In order to win this round, I had to manage my time well. I started my honey-walnut bars that I'd made a zillion times successfully. Once done, the bar would be buttery, crisp on the bottom, and gooey and nutty on the top.

I couldn't go wrong with this recipe. I was in the zone and didn't bother checking out my competitors while I put all my ingredients for my shortbread into the bowl of the stand mixer. Once done, I pressed the dough into a pan before placing it in the oven.

While my shortbread was baking, I got to work on the topping for my walnut caramel. I melted butter, whisked in honey, sugar, salt, and vanilla, and cooked it for a few minutes, waiting for it to come together, but it didn't. My stomach plummeted at the gloppy mess in my pot. I glanced up at the clock. I was running out of time. I rechecked my measurements, only to confirm that I had measured everything correctly.

Taking a deep breath. I threw out the hot mess of a topping and started the caramel over again and got the same results—it didn't look right. I dipped my spoon into the caramel and tasted it. It was bitter without a trace of sweetness. *What happened to the sugar?* I checked the labels on the canisters—salt and sugar—and dipped my spoon into the sugar. It wasn't sugar; it was salt.

*What the hell!*

"Dammit," I exclaimed.

*Was the sugar mislabeled?*

*Or is this something else, like sabotage?*

But the clock was running out. I didn't have time to ponder the mystery of this clusterfuck. I had to regroup. I'd used what I'd thought was sugar for my shortbread dough, so I'd have to redo the dough along with my caramel.

I could do this. The military had taught me to remain calm under all circumstances and to think quickly.

I ran over to the pantry and grabbed an unopened bag of sugar, reworked my shortbread dough, and got it into the oven. I restarted my caramel, which worked this time. Combining honey and two types of salt in my rich caramel topping, I glanced up at the timer. It was going to be tight getting everything finished.

"Five minutes," Piper called out.

It took everything in me not to lose my shit as I got my shortbread out of the oven, pouring the walnut caramel over the top, even though I didn't have time to cool it completely. I didn't bother to remove the bars from the pan in order to cut it into pieces and just pushed the pan to the middle of my workstation.

"Fuck," I grumbled under my breath. I wasn't even sure if the shortbread was cooked all the way through.

I glanced over at Josie, who was posing left and right while her father took photos of her. Missy, the librarian, was waving at Pandora, who was waving back enthusiastically. Skipper, the locksmith, was grinning at his dish like he wanted to ask it out on a date. Meanwhile, I was seething that my dish was a disaster. My eyes narrowed on all the contestants who were suspects in my salt incident, and I planned on getting to the bottom of exactly what happened after the first round was judged.

The judges strode into the room, taking their seats.

"Great first round," Imani said, and the crowd clapped. "Skipper, please place your dish over on the presentation table." She gestured to the round platform mere inches in front of the judges. Once he did that, Imani said, "Please tell the judges what you made."

Skipper puffed out his chest. "I made honey-walnut baklava."

"Go ahead and serve each judge a slice," Piper ordered.

Skipper did as instructed, and each judge examined and smelled the offering before digging in.

Odessa took a sip of water before saying, "I love that it's drenched in hot honey, which allows the layers of phyllo pastry to stay crisp, unlike the sugar syrup-coated version of baklava."

"I agree," Sinner said. "I was impressed by how the pastry stayed crispy. I also love the honey flavor, and the addition of cinnamon is great. But there aren't enough walnuts, and that was one of the major ingredients."

Donovan nodded. "I agree with Sinner, but overall, this is good."

Skipper beamed while rocking back and forth on his heels.

"Thank you, Skipper," Imani said. "Bring your dessert back to your station." She glanced over at me. "Aurora, your turn."

It took everything in me not to run out of the room. I'd never been as unsure of my dessert as I was right now. With my head held high, I brought my dessert, which was still in the pan, over to the presentation table.

"I made honey-walnut bars," I said.

"Sounds delicious. Serve it up," Sinner demanded.

I nodded before using the parchment paper to lift my baked item out. When I tried to cut it into bars, the caramel oozed everywhere—this was not how it was supposed to look. Caramel was all over the plates as I brought it up to the judges—who looked at me, then their plates, and then back to me.

I was embarrassed by the disaster of a dish that I'd presented, but it wasn't the end of the world. If I made it to the next round, I'd just do a lot better.

"Yeah, I know it looks like a hot mess, but I'm hoping it tastes better than it appears," I explained.

The judges each ate my dessert.

Sinner held up a forkful of my shortbread. "Your dough is underbaked. What happened?"

I shrugged. "Ran out of time. I had to restart my dough after realizing that my canister of sugar was mislabeled—it contained salt instead of sugar." The audience gasped. "As you can imagine, my caramel had to be restarted too due to that mishap." I crossed my arms. "I'm not making excuses. I'm just stating facts."

"That's unfortunate," Donovan said. "Because from what I tasted, your dessert would have been an absolute winner if you'd had the opportunity to properly execute it."

Odessa nodded. "Yup, I agree with my brother." She glanced over at Piper and Imani. "I hope you get to the bottom of what happened with Aurora's sugar-salt conundrum."

Imani's eyes tightened. "You best believe we will."

I removed my dessert from the presentation table, going back to my workstation.

The judges tasted and critiqued Josie's and Missy's desserts, and both received mixed reviews. Josie's dessert was tough and chewy. Missy's dessert did not have enough honey or walnuts and had a soggy bottom. The judges left the room to deliberate.

Imani clapped her hands loudly, and the crowd turned to look at her. "The results of the first round will be delayed. Everyone, please clear the room. We'll call everyone back when we're ready to announce the results."

Pandora walked over to us. "What's…"

"Pandora," Piper started, "only contestants are allowed in this area. Please step back."

Pandora held up her hands. "I just wanted to help."

"Thank you, but no," Imani said. "Clear the room."

Pandora rolled her eyes before stomping away.

Imani turned to all the contestants. "Take a break. We have your numbers, so we'll call you when we're ready to resume."

"What's going on?" Josie asked.

"Clear the room," June demanded in a hard voice.

Josie rolled her eyes before flouncing out of the room with Missy and Skipper on her heels.

"We'll keep them out," Bonnie said before she, Freya, Rose, Izzy, and Nyx shooed the last of the audience from the room, then headed out.

Quinn and Mack came over while Imani grabbed the canister that was clearly labeled Sugar off my workstation and tasted the contents. "What the hell? It's salt!" She eyed me. "I swear to you, I put sugar in here."

"Sabotage?" Quinn asked.

"Yes," Imani said. "That's why I'm so happy you convinced me to put hidden cameras in here."

I leaned into Mack when he wrapped an arm around my waist. "You okay?" he asked.

"Pissed off, but I'll survive," I replied.

"That's my lioness." He kissed the top of my head. "We'll get to the bottom of this," he promised before releasing me to stand by Quinn's side. June wrapped an arm around my waist.

"We'll run the footage right now," Mack said. "See if we find anything."

"Imani, you should probably tell the judges what we're doing and to hold on for a few minutes until Mack and I can review the video," Quinn said before pulling out his cell.

I arched a brow. "What's going on?"

"The video is stored in the cloud," Mack answered.

Giving them time to work their magic, June and I walked over to Imani and Piper.

"I knew something was wrong the minute I saw your face," June said. "You had that 'oh shit' expression."

"I can't believe someone would sabotage me," I added. "It makes no sense. I haven't baked for anyone outside the pack and June, so why would they perceive me as a threat?"

Piper shook her head. "That's a good question. But whoever it is will get their ass handed to them."

"Yup," Imani chimed in. "No one messes with my pack." She patted my shoulder. "No one."

I smiled, loving that despite me ghosting her, she still had my back.

"I'll be back. I've got to tell the judges what's going on." Imani hustled out of the room while we waited for Mack and Quinn to tell us who the shady fucker was who had sabotaged me.

# CHAPTER 27
## AURORA

It took longer than anticipated for Mack and Quinn to review the video, but when they found the saboteurs, I was shocked.

Missy and Pandora were caught red-handed swapping my sugar for salt.

"This makes no sense," I said. "They were so nice to me at yoga class. Besides, they never tasted…" I stopped short. "Wait, the granola I made for Nyx. They have tasted my baking." I tightened my fists. "But to sabotage me? That's a real bitchy thing to do."

"It is," Imani said. "Honestly, I suspected Josie, but apparently I was wrong."

"So what now?" I asked.

"Missy is disqualified. And after I told the judges what she did, their recommendation is that all the remaining contestants go forward to the second round," Imani explained. "And I agree. What do you think, Piper?"

"Yes, it's only fair," Piper answered. "June, can you tell Bonnie to let the contestants and audience back inside so that we can resume?"

June nodded and walked toward the entrance.

Imani rubbed her hands together. "I can't wait to publicly

disqualify Missy. Her actions, along with Pandora's, were unseemly."

Mack pulled me to the side. "Are you good?"

I blew out a breath. "Golden. I'm more determined than ever to win."

He grabbed my chin before leaning down to kiss me quickly before backing away. "Give them hell," he said.

I winked at him. "I plan to."

Mack and Quinn went to the back of the room as the audience filed into the space. All the contestants, including me, took our spots at our workstations. I didn't glance at Missy, not wanting to give her any hints that we knew what she and Pandora had done.

Imani and Piper stood at the front of the room.

"Everyone, take your seat," Piper ordered.

"One of the rules was broken by Missy," Imani explained. "She tampered with Aurora's canister of sugar, swapping it for salt."

The crowd gasped.

"That's a lie!" Missy yelled.

Pandora stood and said, "She would never do that."

"Wouldn't she?" Imani asked suspiciously. "How about you, Pandora? Would you do such an ugly thing?"

Pandora shifted from one foot to the other.

Imani continued. "Because I have video of you helping Missy tamper with Aurora's canister."

Pandora's face turned beet red.

"I'm sorry," Missy said. "I..."

The audience booed Missy and glared at Pandora.

"No excuses," Piper barked. "You. Are. Disqualified. Give me your apron." She wiggled her fingers impatiently.

Missy moved away from her workstation, her steps slowing as she passed my workstation. We eyed each other, and there were so many things I wanted to say about her unscrupulous behavior, but I decided to keep it classy by remaining silent.

Missy nodded with resignation as she took off her apron, handing it to Piper before bustling out of the room with Pandora at her side. I had a feeling the townsfolk would never let either of them live down their dirty deeds—shifters despised cheaters.

Skipper clucked his tongue while shaking his head.

Josie's eyes narrowed on me with an accusatory gleam in her eyes.

"What?" I snapped at her.

"You hybrids are always causing trouble," she responded.

"Yes, you're right," I replied with a saccharine tone. "I made Missy and Pandora tamper with my stuff so that I can lose this baking competition," I snarked. "Girl, get a life," I finished, totally dismissing her.

Josie huffed but didn't say another word.

"Now that we've dealt with that nasty business," Imani said to the audience, "the judges, Piper, and I have decided that none of the remaining contestants will be eliminated this round. Therefore, Skipper, Josie, and Aurora will move on to round two." She turned to look at us. "I will not waste my time repeating the rules. But know this: I will not tolerate shenanigans." She wagged her finger. "You've been warned."

"For the second round," Piper announced, "the bakers have two hours to make two different pies." She cued Imani. "And your time starts... now."

Pies were not my thing, but I had to knock out this round with my best baking or I was sure to be eliminated. I started on my mini frozen key lime pies, whizzing through the recipe. I ended by lining the muffin pan and piping the key lime batter evenly into the tins, topping each with my cracker-crumb mixture, and popping the entire pan into the blast freezer to set. Then I moved on to my banana pudding custard pie that had a secret layer of vanilla wafer cookies between the banana-topped custard and the meringue topping. I was in a baking rhythm now, and my focus was only on what was completed and what I had left to finish.

I peeked up at the clock. I had plenty of time to get my pies completed and plated. I removed my key lime pies from the pan, turned them upside down on the large platter, and removed the paper liners. I breathed a sigh of relief that they were set. Spreading reserved cream over the pies and topping them with key lime zest, I was practically dancing when I saw how delicious they looked. My banana pudding custard pie was already on a platter in the middle of my workstation. Now my key lime pies joined the custard pie.

"Time is up," Piper announced.

For the second round, I was proud to present my pies to the judges, who absolutely loved them and gave me glowing feedback. Josie's pies had crusts that were pale and underbaked, and for Skipper's pies, one had a crust that was too tough, and the other had a soggy pie bottom.

I was on pins and needles waiting for Piper and Imani to announce the results of the judges' deliberation.

"The winner of the second round is…" Piper unfolded the paper and scanned it. "Aurora."

The audience clapped. I jumped up and down while pumping my fist.

Josie snorted. Skipper's forehead broke out in a sweat.

Piper turned to me. "Congratulations, Aurora. You move on to the third and final round. Josie and Skipper, please step forward." They both did as instructed. "Unfortunately, one of you will be eliminated. The other will move on to the third round, joining Aurora." She paused dramatically. "The contestant eliminated is…" She stared at the crowd, then back to Skipper and Josie. "Sorry, Josie. You have been eliminated. Please hand me your apron."

"No!" Milton wailed, grabbing his head.

"This is bullshit!" Josie stamped her feet like a child whose bike had just been stolen. "Everyone knows that I'm the best baker in town."

The audience outright laughed at her statement.

"Apparently, they don't think so," I said under my breath, but Josie heard and rounded on me like an enraged bull.

"What did you say, hybrid?" Josie snarled, marching over to my workstation. Piper blocked her path. But I was ready for Josie. If she swung on me, I was going to wipe the floor with her ass.

"Apron," Piper demanded.

"But I need to win," Josie blubbered.

"The judges' decision is final," Imani confirmed.

Josie snatched off her apron, but instead of handing it to Piper, she tossed it on the floor before stomping away into her father's waiting arms.

"Yeah, that was so classy!" Piper shouted while picking up the apron off the floor and putting it on Josie's workstation.

Milton patted Josie's back as she sobbed. "You have not heard the last of us," he threatened with eyes locked on me. "Come on, baby," he cooed to Josie. "I'll buy you that car you've been wanting."

Josie wiped her nose and nodded while Milton escorted her out of the room.

"Wow, that was high drama," I said.

"Welcome to the Ridge," Skipper replied. "You haven't seen anything yet."

Imani clapped her hands to get the audience's attention. "Please settle down. We have one more round before we announce the winner of the Ridge Baking Competition." The crowd quieted and took their seats. "For the third round, the bakers have two hours to make a birthday cake." She cued Piper. "And your time starts... now."

I took a deep breath to gather my thoughts and plans. I couldn't play it safe this round if I wanted to win. I decided to make a coconut layer cake and started on enough batter for four cakes.

"How you doing over there, Aurora?" Skipper asked.

"Nervous," I admitted.

"I've seen your stuff. You have nothing to worry about," Skipper replied.

I looked over at him with a genuine smile. "Thank you. You're not bad yourself. What are you making?"

"Chocolate cake with vanilla buttercream. You?"

"Coconut layer cake," I answered.

"Sounds delicious," he said.

"Good luck, Skipper."

"You too." He winked at me.

We both wanted to win, but it didn't mean we couldn't respect each other.

Dividing my batter among four nine-inch metal cake pans, I smoothed the tops with a spatula then, placed coconut chips in a single layer on a baking sheet. I put everything into the oven. The cake would only take twenty-seven minutes, so I was making good time. Wiping my hands against my apron, I moved on to my frosting, and I alternated my work by getting my cakes out of the oven, taking them out of the pans to cool on wire racks while finishing my frosting.

I glanced up at the clock. Time was winding down. I put my cakes into the refrigerator to cool faster. My eyes drifted over to Skipper's workstation, where he was already assembling his cake. He was fast, but I didn't let what he was doing worry me. Taking my cake out of the refrigerator, I cut each cake in half horizontally, placing one layer onto a cake stand before spreading frosting over it and repeating that for the next seven layers. I put my cake back in the refrigerator to chill.

I looked up to find Mack smiling at me. I winked at him.

Nyx stood up and whistled. I laughed. Honestly, it felt great to have so much support.

Taking the chilled cake out of the refrigerator, I covered it with frosting, then gently patted handfuls of toasted coconut chips over the sides and top of the cake. I didn't have time to chill the cake anymore, so I pushed it to the middle of my workstation. I peered over at Skipper's cake, and it was gorgeous.

"Time is up," Imani announced.

The audience erupted with clapping and whistling.

The judges strode into the room, taking their seats.

"Skipper, please place your cake over on the presentation table," Imani ordered. Once he did as instructed, she said, "Please tell the judges what you made."

"I made a chocolate cake with vanilla buttercream," he explained. "Instead of covering it in white frosting, which, in my opinion, would be too sweet, I added chocolate glaze drips down the sides." He cut a slice for each judge and served it.

The judges examined and smelled the offering before eating it.

"I'm super impressed by your dessert, but unfortunately, the taste doesn't pay off," Sinner said. "There wasn't enough chocolate. Did you add coffee?"

"No," Skipper replied.

"Yes, that's the problem," Sinner explained. "Coffee brings out the taste in chocolate."

"Yes, I agree with Sinner," Odessa replied. "Also, there was an imbalance in the layering. Too much frosting."

Donovan nodded. "And the vanilla buttercream was too sweet. But overall, Skipper, great job. And if I were you, I'd keep working on perfecting this recipe. It's going to be killer once you work out the kinks."

I thought their comments weren't too harsh.

"Thank you, judges," Skipper said before bringing his dessert back to his station. Everyone clapped, including me.

I brought my cake up to the presentation table.

"I made a coconut layer cake," I announced. "I toasted the coconut to give it a knockout garnish." I cut a slice for each judge and brought it to them.

The judges sniffed my cake, then examined it before digging their forks into their slices.

Donovan sat back and stared at me, making me fidget.

"Well, your coconut cake is a coconut lover's dream,"

Donovan commented. "Great comeback from round one, Aurora."

"Thank you. I love to bake." I grinned.

"I can tell," Donovan replied, a speculative gleam in his eyes. "Your cake was supremely moist with a soft, fluffy crumb and an intense coconut flavor."

"It's intensely flavorful," Odessa agreed. "And your cake crumb is soft as silk."

"I agree with everything Donovan and Odessa said," Sinner chimed in. "However, I can see from here"—he pointed to my cake still on the presentation table—"your cake is crooked, which means your frosting is too soft, causing your cake to lean. Make sure to chill your cake in the refrigerator longer. Otherwise, I wouldn't stress about that. Even a crooked cake is still delicious." He grinned at me.

I nodded. "Noted." It was true, but on the whole, the judges seemed to love my cake. I brought my dessert back to my station while the judges left the room to deliberate.

"Can I taste your cake?" Skipper asked.

"Sure. Only if you give me a slice of yours."

"Deal," he answered.

We swapped slices, and when I tasted his cake, I knew I was in trouble. Skipper was an excellent baker.

"Very good, Skipper."

"Not as good as yours," he said. "Wow. Great cake, Aurora."

Imani and Piper walked over to us with a huge stack of mini paper plates. "Would you two mind slicing up your cakes for the audience to taste?" Imani asked.

"No problem," I replied as Skipper also nodded and did as directed.

Piper, Imani, Skipper, and I handed out cake to the audience. When I got to Mack, who was alone at the far corner of the room, I asked, "So how did I do?"

He turned me around, nudging me into the corner, his broad

back blocking me from view. "I'm proud of you," he said while tracing a hand down my back.

My lips curled up into a smile. "Thank you. So." I held up a plate. "Would you like to taste?"

His eyes roamed over me. "Yes, I'd love to taste every inch of you."

My nipples throbbed and pebbled from his words, and I had to fight not to cover them. "You'll have to settle for cake right now."

"Feed me," he demanded in a husky voice.

Breaking off a piece with my fingers, I brought it to his lips. His mouth closed around the cake along with my fingers, his warm tongue flicking the tips of my fingers sensually.

I nearly moaned aloud, just imagining his tongue licking me everywhere. I squeezed my thighs tight.

He leaned down and said in my ear, "Your sexy kitty can't wait to lick your sweet pussy."

My cunt pulsed. *Jesus, he's sexy.* His gaze raked over me, heating every inch of my skin. "Behave, sexy kitty. We're in a room full of shifters who can smell what your touch and words are doing to my body."

He pulled back. "I'll behave… for now." Wicked intent shone in his eyes.

"Everyone, take your seat," Piper demanded. "The judges have given me the final result."

"Got to go, sexy kitty," I said before giving him a quick kiss. I could feel his heated gaze on my ass, so I swayed even more, giving him a show. When I arrived at my workstation, I gave Skipper a thumbs-up. I wanted to win, but if I lost, I'd rather it be to him.

Piper opened the paper with the results. "The winner of the Ridge baking championship is…" She paused. "I feel like I need a drumroll or something."

"For goodness' sake, just tell us!" June shouted.

The crowd laughed.

"Oh, hush your mouth, June," Piper grumped. "Anyway, the winner is Aurora."

My eyes widened, and my heart thumped faster. I didn't move and just stood there, not believing that I'd heard my name.

"Aurora, darling," Piper said. "You won!"

I shook myself out of my stupor when Skipper came over and shook my hand. "Congratulations! I knew you'd won the moment I tasted your cake."

"Thank you," I responded, shaking his hand in a daze. "I couldn't ask for a better competitor."

"Aurora," Imani called out. "Get your butt over here."

The audience was clapping and stomping their feet. Izzy, Rose, Freya, Bonnie, Nyx, and June were now in front, joining Piper and Imani. They all hugged me one by one while congratulating me.

"Speech!" someone from the audience shouted.

Nyx nudged me. "Give your fans what they're asking for."

"I, uh, wow." I scratched my neck. "This is major for me." June nodded at me encouragingly. "I want to thank the Bane pack, June, Freya, Nyx, Izzy, and Rose for all having my back." Emotions clogged my throat. I eyed Mack, who was still in the corner. I beckoned him, but he didn't move. "And a special shout-out to the deputy." I blew an air kiss to him. He grinned. "Winning today is special to me. I didn't think that coming here would start a new life." I shrugged. "But here I am, the winner of a freaking bakery."

Rose and Izzy shouted, "Woo-hoo!"

"Anyway, thank you," I continued. "And don't forget to visit my shop when I get it up and running."

I stared around at the pack, Mack, my new friends, June, and the crowd, and all I saw were smiling faces. This was fucking amazing.

# CHAPTER 28
## AURORA

Hours later, after the championship ended, I was sitting on my bed in June's guest cottage, reviewing the checklist Freya, Piper, and Bonnie had created for June's birthday party. We'd taken care of everything so far except for her birthday cake, which I was personally going to bake.

I grinned, still not believing that I'd won the baking championship. I had no clue how to run a bakery, but I wasn't afraid to learn. I glanced over at my cell, nibbling on my bottom lip. It was getting late, and I wanted to talk to Mack before I went to sleep.

"Fuck it." Like a junkie waiting for my next hit, I grabbed my cell and called him.

"I thought you might not call." His voice was raspy, as if he'd just woken up.

"Did you fall asleep?" I asked.

He laughed. "Caught. I nodded off after I got out of the shower. My lioness wore my ass out, trying to keep up with her over the past few days."

"It's the other way around. You wore me out." Stretching out my legs, I leaned back against my stack of pillows. "I hope that means that tonight I get a good night's sleep." I hadn't had insomnia or nightmares for a while now, and I hoped to maintain my winning streak.

"Hmm." I heard the noise of movement in the background. "I might be able to help with that."

"Do tell, sexy kitty."

"Turn off all the lights," he commanded.

His order aroused my interest. "Hold on." Reaching over to the nightstand, I placed my tablet on it before turning off the lamp.

"Don't forget to open the windows," he instructed. "The fresh air in the Ridge will do you good."

"You're a bossy alpha," I grumped playfully before getting off the bed and opening the windows, allowing the night air inside. "Okay. I'm in bed." I inhaled deeply, easily picking up the forest smells—damp moss, wet tree trunks, flowers—in the air. "Wow, still can't believe how sharp my sense of smell is now that my inner beast is awake."

"It's nice, huh?" Mack said.

"That's putting it mildly." My breathing became easier and deeper at the same time. I started to feel better and stronger with every inhalation. "It feels like I'm actually breathing for the first time in my life."

"This is your first step, lioness. Wait until you shift for the first time."

I sighed, not believing that what I'd thought was impossible might soon become possible.

"Put me on speakerphone," Mack ordered. "You're going to need both hands for this."

I arched a brow. "What is my sexy kitty up to? Is this a phone-sex situation?"

"Yes. Are you interested?"

"Hmm… I've never had phone sex before. I'm intrigued."

He chuckled, the sound of it sending my heart racing and making my palms sweaty. "I'm glad that I'm your first and last. Do I have your permission to make you come?"

My skin tingled as if he'd actually stroked me. "Yes."

"Now take off your panties."

"I'm pushing them off my hips," I informed him. "They're sliding down my legs. I've just tossed them on the floor."

"Good girl," he said.

I lay on the bed, bathed by the moonlight, in only my T-shirt.

"Spread your legs wide," he ordered.

I moaned at the huskiness in his voice combined with the command. I'd never been into being dominated by a man, but with Mack, I trusted him not to take advantage of my submission in the bedroom.

"I'm spreading them."

"Good lioness. Now touch your pussy."

I'd masturbated before, but never with anyone being present.

"If you want to stop, tell me, Ro, and that's what we'll do."

"I want to continue." I spread my legs wider. "I'm rubbing my finger up and down my clit."

He growled. "Faster."

"I'm going faster." I moaned as my back arched, feeling the tightening deep in my belly.

"Harder," he ordered.

"I'm…" I flung my head back. "Going faster… harder." I experimented with lengthening my strokes.

His growl was low and deep in his throat, and every erogenous zone in my body tingled with awareness as I panted and moaned.

"I'm getting hard just thinking about my lips touching your skin, licking your pussy, making you mine."

"Oh my goodness. I'm coming." My back arched off the bed. A warm, fuzzy feeling zinged through my body, and I shuddered. My clit pulsed, and my cheeks felt hot.

"Holy hell," I gasped out when I finally came down from my orgasmic hill. "That was intense." Pulling my sheets over me, I stretched my arms above my head, feeling relaxed and sleepy. "Thank you."

"It's my job to please you, lioness. Now sleep."

"What about you?" I licked my bottom lip. "Do you need…"

"I need to have my cock inside you, and nothing else will do. But I've learned to be a patient man, Ro. Good night, lioness."

"Good night, sexy kitty."

When our call ended, I curled up on my side and fell blissfully asleep.

# CHAPTER 29
## AURORA

I strolled into the posh-looking Rebellious Rose boutique and stared at the packed establishment. Eclectic music floated through the air, matching the relaxed but upscale ambiance of the shop. The space was small but sleek and very glam. The walls were painted black, which allowed the rich, vibrant colors of the clothing on display to pop against the beautiful darkness.

"About time," Rose cooed, swaying over to me wearing a tight cream dress that fit her lanky body like a glove. Her reddish-brown hair with pristine white streaks was pulled back into a ponytail. "You were supposed to be here by one thirty," she admonished me before wrapping her arms around me.

I patted her back. "Last-minute group meeting with Piper, Freya, and Bonnie." I stepped back. "They're making me nuts with their need to check and recheck every little detail for June's birthday party."

She laughed. "Well, aren't you happy that June's birthday party is tomorrow?" She looped her arm through mine, escorting me through her boutique.

I sighed heavily. "Yes." I glanced around the crowded space. "What's going on here? Your shoppers seem a bit... frantic and manic." I watched two women playing tug-of-war with a leather top. In another area of the boutique, three women were bickering over some blood-red top while playing a grown-up version of the keep-away game.

She shrugged. "It's a typical Friday. But never mind that. We need to focus on your primary mission for being here. You need to find something sexy to wear to June's party."

I nodded, my eyes scanning the store, and honestly, all the clothing I saw looked expensive. I would have worn something I already owned, but this was a very special occasion, so I wanted something new. "This is a fabulous boutique."

She gave me an impish smile. "Thank you. It's my little piece of glam paradise." She continued walking by all the racks of clothing and stopped at the long line of fitting rooms, nudging one door open. "I have an outfit that will look hot on you. I'll be right back."

"Damn, you're bossy," I grumbled good-naturedly, stepping inside and shutting the door. I stripped and waited for Rose to come back. When she finally did, she handed me a dress over the door.

"That's it? I need more options," I said, scrutinizing the pink dress.

"Nope." I could hear Rose's lips pop over the *p*. "This dress is the one. It's not leather, but I love it."

I pursed my lips. "But it has thin spaghetti straps. There's no way I'll be able to wear a bra."

"Exactly. Your breasts are spectacular. There's nothing better than sexy cleavage. Besides, you need to live a little. Remember the theme of June's party is hedonism."

I sighed. Rose was right. Between the subtly sheer material and hip-baring leg slit, this dress was the be-all and end-all of sexy looks.

"Put it on, Aurora."

"Fine," I grumbled.

I took off my bra because it would stick out like a sore thumb in this slinky number. I slid the dress over my head, and it glided down my body like silk. Giving myself a once-over in the mirror, I fell in love with the garment. The bodice was designed to pull up the voluptuous swell of my breasts, similar to the support of a bra. It was sexy and naughty, and it embodied the persona of a seductress on the prowl. The one thing I didn't like was that the high slit showed my burn scar that ran from my hip to midthigh.

"Get out here," Rose demanded. "I want to see it."

Opening the door, I strutted out. "What do you think?" I turned left and right like I was posing on a fashion show runway.

"Hot." Rose touched my shoulder and made a sizzling sound. "Admit it."

"Admit what?"

"That I'm a fabulous designer, and this dress is the one."

I laughed. "Are you fishing for compliments?"

Rose shrugged. "Yes. I need my damn ego stroked."

"You're wonderful. Yippee!" I pumped my fists in the air. "You did it. I'm wearing the dress of all dresses."

"Now that just sounds sarcastic, but I forgive you." She smiled.

I sighed. "Really, Rose, you're a talented designer. I'm just a little nervous about debuting all this." I gestured to my scar.

Rose grabbed my hands. "No one cares. You are still beautiful."

"I know, but I'm not interested in making my scar a conversation starter at the party."

Rose released my hands and fluffed up my hair. "You need to spend more time around Others, Aurora. We believe scars are a mark of a warrior, and we respect that badassery. So flaunt it like the warrior lioness you are."

I smiled. I'd never had friends until coming to the Ridge. Now I was learning that having people in my life—besides June—who honestly cared about me was a gift to be cherished.

"Okay, I'll take it," I replied.

"You had no choice, lioness. I designed it for you." She nudged me gently toward the dressing room.

# CHAPTER 30
## AURORA

After leaving Rose's boutique, I decided to stop by the police station to invite Mack out for a late lunch. Other than his good morning text, I hadn't had time to talk to him all day.

Walking into the station, I wanted to turn back around when I saw Josie facing off with two women.

"Take your basket of rocks and get the hell out," a willowy woman with light-blue hair demanded while shoving the basket in her hand at Josie.

Josie snatched the basket. "Well, I never."

A petite woman with long brown hair replied, "And you never will. Now go on and get. The deputy doesn't want your baked goods." She looked Josie up and down.

I arched a brow. Now I was really interested in what was happening.

"Don't you think that he should be the judge of that, Heidi?" Josie snapped.

Blue Hair snorted. "He's told you several times that he's not interested in your goodies."

"To hell with you, Sally. I'm leaving it." Josie slammed the basket onto the counter before turning to head out. Her nose flared when she saw me. "Hybrid."

"What about it?" I asked with my hands on my hips. Josie was one of those women who was beautiful on the outside—with blond hair, Cupid's-bow lips, and baby-doll eyes—but ugly on the inside, given her nasty attitude and mean, toothy grin.

"Get out of my way," Josie hissed.

I arched a brow. "Make me." I was done with Josie's bullying tactics.

Josie glared at me. I didn't budge. I guess she sensed I wasn't the chick to fuck around with, and she flounced around me, making a beeline for the door before exiting.

I clucked my tongue. "That woman is a whirlwind of crazy."

"That's what happens when you're a spoiled, rich brat," Blue Hair replied while unceremoniously dumping Josie's basket into the trash can. She held out her hand to me. "Nice to meet you, Aurora. I'm Sally, the sheriff's analyst."

I shook her hand.

The brown-haired woman strode up to me with a wide smile. "And I'm Heidi, his administrative assistant." She grabbed my hand. "Everyone is talking about you."

I frowned.

Heidi laughed. "In a real good way. The gossip is that you did a really great job at the championship yesterday."

Sally nodded. "They said you can bake your ass off. I can't wait until you open your shop."

"Wow, that's a lot of praise and expectation," I said.

"Do you know what types of baked goods you'll be selling?" Sally asked.

"I'm so fresh off my win that, honestly, I haven't given it much thought," I answered. "I'm meeting Imani later today to see my location, so I'm hoping once I get inside, I'll have a spark of ideas."

"Well, I'm happy for you," Heidi announced. "We need new blood in this town, despite what the naysayers think."

"Yup," Sally chimed in. "And I'm happy that conceited owl-shifter got taken down by you. Josie had been telling townsfolk for months that the championship was hers."

"Yeah, well now Josie and Milton are going around telling people that the championship was fixed by Imani and Piper. Of course Josie thinks she should have won," Heidi revealed.

My eyebrows shot up. "That's a lie. It wasn't fixed."

"Don't worry," Sally said. "Most people don't believe that shit. Josie and Milton have sour grapes. They're like children. If they don't get what they want, they stomp and yell until they do."

Heidi touched my arm. "Watch out for them. They have a tendency to get real nasty."

"Thank you for the heads-up," I said. "So I came here to see Mack. Is he here?"

They both shook their heads.

"He's over at the fountain," Heidi said.

"You can't miss it," Sally added. "Once you step out of the station, turn left and keep walking."

"Thank you," I said. "Nice meeting both of you."

They both grinned. "We'll be seeing you tomorrow," Heidi said. "We've both been invited to the party of the year."

I waved at them before walking out of the station and following their directions to the fountain. It didn't take me long to find the enormous stone fountain with water cascading over the edges of the shell into the basin. Four massive carved wolf heads around the pedestal and four shells around the basin spilled water, creating a spectacular display.

"Oh, this is definitely going to be entertaining," I said aloud at the sight of several naked men yelling and goading two men who were on their feet, wrestling each other while Mack stood on the side, drinking from the large paper cup in his hand.

"Hey, Mack," I said when I reached his side.

His face lit up before he gave me a quick kiss. "Hello, gorgeous. I wasn't expecting to see you."

"I had errands in Main Square today, so I thought you and I

could have lunch. I stopped by the police station. Heidi and Sally told me where to find you."

One of the men puffed out his chest with his dick on full display. "Hi, Aurora. Nice to meet you. My name is—"

Mack growled at him. "Eric, tend to the fight and stop trying to flirt with my woman."

Eric scowled but did as instructed.

"What's going on?" I pointed to the ongoing scuffle between the two men.

"It's the otters-versus-the-penguins battle. It happens every day like clockwork. I'm just here to keep the fight from getting bloody."

"Why are they fighting?"

"To see who gets to swim in the fountain," Mack explained. "They've worked out a system. Each group picks someone from their side to fight. The two battle until someone's knee hits the ground, and that person is the loser."

My eyes widened. "That sounds insane."

Mack shrugged. "I know, but it works."

"But why don't they just swim at Bogbeast Lake?" I asked.

Mack shook his head. "Nah, that won't work. That's the selkies' and mermen's territory."

"What?" I replied. "That doesn't make a bit of sense."

"We're shifters. None of what we do makes sense."

I just waved my hand in the international gesture of "I give up." "Anyhoo, let's move on from this insane topic. You up for having lunch?"

He ran a finger across my cheek. "Hell yes. But I have to wait until they have a victor." Then Mack shouted over to the men, "Will you two hurry up? I don't have all day."

One of the tussling men shouted, "I almost have him!"

The other man snapped, "Bullshit!"

Both sides whistled and shouted like they were at a concert.

"Wow, this is insane," I muttered before saying to Mack, "I have one more errand. I'm meeting Imani at my new shop. She's handing over the keys. Why don't you meet me there after"—I gestured to the two men—"they're finished doing whatever that is."

"Will do," he replied, then gave me a loud, smacking kiss.

Turning, I started walking away, when all the men said, "Bye, Aurora."

I laughed when I heard Mack growl, "Keep your eyes off my woman's ass."

# CHAPTER 31
## AURORA

After following the directions that Imani sent me via text, I drove along the one-block stretch of vacant shops before parking in front of the shop that was now mine.

Getting out of my vehicle, I walked up to the store that looked as if it was taken straight out of a Norman Rockwell painting.

Imani was already standing outside with a huge grin on her face. And after hugging each other, I pointed out, "It's awfully deserted around here." There was no foot traffic, and all the storefronts across the street and on the same side of my corner shop were vacant.

"I know, but trust me, these storefronts are the best spots in Main Square because they're near Bogbeast." She gestured grandly. "This section of Main Square used to be all the hot spots when Quinn was growing up, but the shifters who rented these spots either passed away, retired, or got exiled from the Ridge."

My brows furrowed. "Why did they get exiled?"

"Put it this way, they did not believe in friendly business competition. Some of the former owners of these storefronts"— Imani pointed to the vacant spots—"were killed and buried in the backyards of those that were exiled."

"I know shifters are mean like rattlesnakes, but..." I shuddered. "Damn."

"Yeah, damn," Imani agreed. "But that was back in the day when this town was first created. Quinn says it was like the Wild West back then. Now things are a lot more civil. So are you ready to see inside?" Imani asked, jingling keys in the air.

"More than ready."

Opening the wood-framed glass door, Imani pushed it in grandly. "Step inside your new business."

The sun streamed into the shop, highlighting the large space with one entire wall with a built-in bookcase.

"This used to be a bookstore," Imani explained. "But there's a hidden room somewhere in here that leads to a secret speakeasy. Quinn told me that during the 1920s, his great-grandfather made the consumption of liquor illegal in the Ridge, but this spot was one of many speakeasies that continued to serve alcohol."

My interest was definitely piqued because I remembered reading that during the Prohibition era, speakeasies—illicit establishments that sold alcohol—became prominent.

"That's intriguing," I said before walking up to the dust-covered bookshelf, wondering if there was a hidden door behind it that led to the clandestine venue.

"I know. Have fun finding the secret entrance." She gestured to the large space. "So what do you think?"

"I love it. It's a blank slate," I said, heading to the back with Imani beside me. "After I come up with a niche, I'll have to renovate, but I can work with this." The back area was also empty.

"The electricity is on," Imani pointed out. "Plus this place has good bones."

"Yes, it does." I turned to face her. "I can't thank you enough for this, Imani. This"—I spun with arms wide—"is a dream come true."

"What are you thanking me for? You won the championship. This is all your doing. Here you go." She handed me the keys.

"This is your baby now. Quinn will be handing over the deed to this property shortly."

I clutched the cold keys as the excitement bubbled in my stomach. "I can't believe I'm a business owner."

"I'm so excited for you," Imani said. "If you want, contact Jasper about any renovations you need. You've seen the work he's done on June's place and also on the B and B, so I think he'll be able to hook you up."

I loved everything I'd seen in both locations, not to mention his help with Mack's place, so I'd have no hesitation in contacting Jasper for help with my renovations.

We walked away from the back, heading toward the front door.

Imani turned around and hugged me. "Welcome to the Ridge, Aurora."

I returned her hug. I'd never had close friends because, frankly, I thought I sucked at connecting with women and forming friendships.

When we pulled back, I said, "Thank you, Imani."

She winked at me. "We hybrids have to stick together. Also it doesn't hurt that you and Mack are a thing."

I laughed. "We are indeed a thing."

Imani placed a hand on my shoulder. "He's a great guy."

"Yes, he is." And I sincerely meant it.

Imani glanced down at her watch. "Damn. I've got to go. I have so much food left to make for June's birthday party tomorrow night." She opened the door. "Call me," she said before walking out, closing the door behind her.

I spun around in the center of the floor, feeling like a giddy kid.

*This is all mine.*

"Okay, let's get to planning, Aurora," I said aloud.

I pulled out my cell phone from my messenger bag. I needed to jot down ideas for my shop while I perused the space. After inspecting the front, I moved to the back, then my cell pinged with a text from Mack.

MACK (TEXT): *Are you still at your shop?*

ME (TEXT): *Yes. Are you still refereeing the otters-versus-penguins battle?*

MACK (TEXT): *Unfortunately. Hopefully I'll be there soon.*

ME (TEXT): *Okay. See you soon.*

Striding over to the back door, I unlocked it and turned the knob, but it didn't open. I yanked again, but it didn't budge. I put the broken door on my list of things that needed to be repaired. Having a back door that couldn't open was a safety hazard.

Scanning the space, I happened to look down at the dust-covered, tea-stained oak floor and spotted a large hatch cut into the planks. Making my way over, I saw that it was a trap door in the floor.

"I have to check this out." Grabbing the metal ring handle attached to the hatch, I yanked it, and the door sprang open easily.

Fumbling with my cell, I turned on the flashlight, shining it down into the inky darkness. There were spiral stairs that appeared to be sturdy. When I reached the bottom landing, I found the light switch on the wall and turned it on, illuminating the space.

I was shocked at what I saw. Whoever owned this speakeasy had not skimped when it came to the design. It was a cozy hide-away that boasted sofas, glittering chandeliers, and mood light-ing. I ran my fingers over the long bar with a hand-carved shelf behind, filled with lots of liquor bottles.

I picked up one of the dust-covered bottles, wiping off the label. "This looks expensive." My head snapped in the direction of the hatch door when I heard it slam shut.

"What the hell!"

Placing the bottle on the bar, I stormed up the stairs, pushing at the hatch. It wouldn't budge. There was no lock on the inside, and I didn't remember seeing any lock on the outside. Then how was it being held shut?

Bending my knees, I pushed up at the door again.

Nothing happened.

Pulling out my cell, I saw I had no signal.

"Fuck." I stomped down the stairs and tried standing in different spots in the room to find a signal. After multiple frustrating tries, I still had nothing.

I refused to panic as I sat down on a dusty bar stool. Mack was planning on meeting me here. All I had to do was wait, and he'd find me. My SUV was still parked outside, and with his being a shifter, he'd be able to pick up my scent.

I held my cell over my head toward the tin ceiling, hoping by some miracle I'd get a signal, but I didn't. "Well, that was a waste of time," I grumbled.

I rubbed my forehead, feeling a migraine coming on.

"Okay, Aurora. Just chill the fuck out. It will be all right," I said aloud, but something in my gut suspected that it wouldn't.

I sat there quietly for a few minutes, listening for signs of life above me. But I heard nothing. My nose twitched when I picked up a faint scent. I sniffed, trying to discern what the smell was. And then it came to me because I'd know that scent anywhere. It was smoke.

Getting to my feet, I charged up the stairs, banging on the trap door. "Help! Anyone up there?"

There was silence.

I banged harder. "Help!"

My heart thudded faster when the scent of smoke became stronger.

My hands started trembling as I started having shortness of breath. "Fuck. This is Afghanistan all over again. I'm going to burn to death." I nearly tumbled down the stairs in my haste to get a bar stool. Dragging it up the stairs, I started using it as a battering ram. "Mack? Someone? Help!" I brought the stool up against the hatch, banging the shit out of it.

*I'm going to die.*

Dragging the stool down the stairs, I shoved it aside before pacing back and forth, feeling like I was losing my mind. I was having a full-blown panic attack. *I'm going to die.*

I clutched my chest, and the room started spinning as my mind drifted back to being pinned inside the Humvee. The smell of burning flesh. The pain of metal digging into my skin from the vehicle caved in around me.

*I'm going to pass out and not wake up while I burn alive.*

My inner beast roared in what sounded like an honest-to-goodness "get your shit together" command.

Stopping in my tracks, I took a deep breath through my nose. I started breathing out slowly and deeply through my mouth.

My mind kicked into gear, and my panic started to subside.

*This is not Afghanistan.*

I started counting while closing my eyes and focusing on my breathing.

*One.*

I breathed in and out.

*Two.*

*Three.*

I breathed in and out.

*Four.*

*Five.*

My breathing was now calm. My heart rate even. I checked my cell again, and this time, I had one bar. I called Mack, and he answered.

"Hey, Ro, I'm almost—"

I cut him off because I didn't know how long my signal would last. "Fire. I'm in the back of the shop. Trap door. Hurry." My cell went dead, but I didn't panic again. I could handle this situation without losing my shit. I'd been through worse than this in the military. If I could survive combat, I could survive this.

I scanned the room for exits. There were none.

I had so much to live for—myself, my new life, my pack, June, Mack. But if I died, at least I knew I'd overcome so many obstacles in my life and I'd found Mack.

I smiled, feeling truly at peace but not ready to give up on life. I had way too much to live for.

I stomped back up the stairs and shoved and banged on the trap door, even though I wasn't expecting a new development. But the act of doing something made me feel better, and I was fighting for my life instead of waiting to die.

*I'm a fucking fighter.*

And I swore to myself when—not if—I got out of this alive, I wasn't waiting on life to happen to me.

"I'm going to grab life by the balls and ride the fuck out of it."

# CHAPTER 32
## MACK

*Ro's in danger.*

My heart thudded hard as I raced across Main Square on foot after receiving her call. *There's no way I'm losing her.*

A low growl rumbled in my chest. My lion battered and clawed inside my skin with the primal need for release.

I could have driven, but I was faster running.

Townsfolk dashed out of my way as I ran like a madman.

Still racing, I called Quinn, not giving him time to talk. "911," I barked. "Fire at Ro's shop." Then I ended our call. Quinn would know what to do.

When I finally reached Ro's shop, my heart raced when I saw heavy flames shooting into the air.

I stood, feeling as if I had been punched in the gut while I watched as the flames licked the air with ferocious intensity. The stench of burning rubble seared my nose. My heart raced as my body combated the need to shift so I could tear into the shop like a savage beast.

My heart plummeted. She could not be dead.

Ro was mine, branded by the bond tethering us together, and no one was going to snatch that away.

"No!" I yelled with despair. I could see the fire in the front of the shop, so getting in that way wouldn't work. There had to be a back entrance. Running around to the back of the shop, I roared when I saw Milton standing at the back door with a long metal bar in his hand.

His head whipped around, and his eyes were wild. "I've got to wait. If she gets out, I have to kill her. She has to die. That's why I set the fire."

Roaring, I lifted his ass up into the air by his shirt. "You did this?"

I heard feet running and smelled Quinn and Rhett coming up behind me.

"What the hell is going on?" Quinn yelled.

"I set the fire," Milton whimpered. "I'd do anything for my baby girl."

My canines extended. I saw red. The need to kill him raced through my veins. He'd set my mate on fire.

My claws extended from my fingers.

*Kill,* my inner beast urged. *Rip him to shreds.*

"Mack, no," Rhett begged.

Ignoring him, I dug my claws into Milton's skin.

"Help me!" Milton wailed. "He's going to kill me."

"Mack!" Quinn yelled. "The firefighters are on their way."

I blinked. All I wanted was to kill Milton, and then I smelled it. The whiff of a familiar scent. Ro. I dropped Milton onto the ground like trash. There was a vent near the foundation. Marching over to the vent, I sniffed.

"She's down there," I roared, walking back over to the rear door, yanking on it. "I smell her."

"Mack, what are you doing?" Quinn barked.

I didn't care what he was saying; my woman was in there. I yanked and yanked until the door gave way, cracking open. Prying my fingers into the gap, I tugged, ripping the door open. As I jumped inside, the smoke was thick, and fire was creeping closer to the rear.

I scanned the floor, looking for the trap door Ro had told me about, but I didn't see anything but two cinder blocks lying on the floor.

"That fucker," I yelled, feeling Rhett by my side as I threw the blocks off and yanked the trap door up. Running down the stairs, I found Ro sitting on the floor. She jumped up, rushing over to me.

I clutched her to me. "Oh, baby. You're all right, but we've got to go."

"Mack!" Rhett yelled. "This place is about to collapse. Get your ass out of there."

I pushed Ro ahead of me, and we climbed up the stairs and out the back door. Once outside, Ro collapsed onto the ground, coughing and gasping.

"No!" Milton screamed, surging toward Ro, but Rhett caught him. "Why is she alive?"

I tightened my fists as pure rage raced through my blood. "You committed arson with the intention of killing my mate."

"She's a fucking hybrid!" Milton screamed, spittle flying out of his mouth. "She took what belonged to my daughter. I set that fire, and I wanted to kill her." He laughed like a deranged man.

"Well, you're going to jail, and in the morning, you'll stand in front of the town council for judgment," Quinn said, glaring at Milton.

Milton laughed. "They'll never charge me. I've done too much for this town. Besides, I did a service to this town by trying to kill that"—he pointed at Ro—"thing."

I leaped forward to rip his head off, but Quinn jumped between us. Ro stood, tugging on my arm.

"No," Ro said hoarsely. "Let justice prevail."

Her plea released the tension from my body. I wrapped my arms around her protectively. My body shuddered at the thought of how close I came to losing her.

"Let's go, Milton," Rhett growled, dragging him away.

Quinn patted Ro's back before saying, "I'm heading to the front to see how the firefighters are doing."

Ro and I were alone, and she was cocooned in my arms.

"Thank you," she whispered.

"I'll always be here for you, baby." I swallowed hard. "I almost lost you."

She looked up at me, tightening her arms around my neck. "Almost, but I'm here, and I'm not going anywhere."

"Neither am I," I growled before pushing my fingers through her hair, fisting her thick strands as I kissed my woman deeply and thoroughly.

# CHAPTER 33
## AURORA

With Mack by my side, I stood with a gray blanket wrapped around my shoulders, finishing my statement to Rhett, relaying everything that had happened before, during, and after the fire.

I was stunned that Milton had tried to kill me over the fact that I'd won the baking championship and his daughter Josie didn't.

Rhett patted my shoulder. "I've got all the information I need, Aurora. If there's anything else, I'll be in contact with you." He nodded to Mack before heading over to their pack—Quinn, Brody, Emmett, Jasper—who were talking to the firefighters who had taken care of the fire.

I stared at the charred mess of my shop. "Well, there goes my dream of opening a bakery."

Mack turned me to face him. "We'll rebuild. Besides, I'd rather have you than a damn shop."

I leaned my cheek against his chest. "This town is insane. Milton trying to kill me over losing a damn baking championship is cuckoo for Cocoa Puffs."

He tightened his arms around me. "Milton is in jail, and he'll remain there until the morning, when he'll go before the town council for punishment."

I backed away from Mack when I heard June exclaim, "Where's my niece?"

"I'll be back," Mack said. "I want to hear the firefighters' assessment of the damage." He gave me a quick kiss before walking over to Quinn and the pack.

June ran up to me, hugging me so tight that I could barely breathe.

"Aunt June, too tight," I complained.

She released me. "Sorry. Are you okay?"

"Yes, I…" I didn't have time to finish my sentence because Imani, Rose, Izzy, Nyx, Bonnie, Nova, and Freya came up to me, each taking turns pulling me into a hug.

"Quinn called June and the pack," Imani explained. "And I called everyone, and we rolled over here gangsta-style."

"Milton did all this?" June asked.

I nodded, then explained everything that I knew.

"This 'let's kill the hybrids' shit is getting real old," Nova snapped.

Imani crossed her arms. "Yes, it is."

"The town council will deal with him first thing in the morning," Bonnie replied.

"We sure will," Freya said. "And I'm pushing for nothing less than expulsion from the Ridge."

"A hard line has to be drawn," Nyx said. "Or townsfolk are going to think victimizing hybrids is okay, and it's not." She wrapped an arm around me.

"Izzy and I need to perform a medical checkup on you," Nova said, eyeing me. "We need to be sure you don't have any injuries."

"I'm fine," I protested.

"Let us be the judge of that," Izzy said as she and Nova ushered me away and toward a large SUV.

* * *

After Nova and Izzy finished giving me a thorough examination and gave me the thumbs-up to go home, Mack whisked me away.

Inside the guest cottage, I was exhausted and just wanted a hot shower and sleep.

"Mack, I'm okay."

"Humor me," he said, escorting me all the way to my bedroom.

I sat on the edge of the bed, and he crouched down, pulling off my shoes. "You need a hot bath." He stood. "I'll run it for you. Where's the—"

Getting to my feet, I grabbed his hand. "No bath. I'm taking a shower. You sit down." I pushed him onto the bed. "I'll be right back."

I grabbed my lingerie from the dressing table and headed to the bathroom, shutting the door.

Not that I didn't appreciate Mack, but his coddling was making me nervous. Besides, I needed time by myself to decompress and fully take in the trauma I'd just experienced.

I could have been burned alive, but I survived.

Stripping out of my clothes, I put on a shower cap and turned on the shower before hopping inside, allowing the hot spray to beat against my skin as my thoughts settled. My near-death experience today had given me a greater appreciation for being alive. I essentially got another chance at life, and I planned on living it more purposefully than I'd done before. No more hiding from life. I planned on experiencing it to the fullest.

After getting out of the shower, I pulled off my shower cap, dried off my body, and took my time moisturizing my skin before pulling on my T-shirt and panties.

Opening the bathroom door, I spotted Mack lying on my bed with the windows wide open and the lights off. But even in the dark room, with my superheightened shifter senses, I could clearly make out his features and that his eyes were wide open.

Padding over to the bed, I climbed onto him, straddling him. "Are you spending the night, sexy kitty?"

He traced his fingers across my thighs. "I can't leave until my beast and I are sure you're all right."

"Mack, I already—"

"I almost lost you, and the thought is killing me inside."

I grabbed his face. "You're not getting rid of me that easy."

"If you hadn't stopped me, I would have killed Milton," he said with a harsh voice.

"He's not worth it, Mack. It's over."

"It won't be over until he's punished," Mack replied.

I trailed my fingers down to his chest. "No more talking about him. And promise me that there'll be no revenge plots. I need you."

He grumbled.

"Promise me, Mack."

Seconds ticked by before he said, "Promise."

"Good." Satisfied, I slid off him onto the bed, turning to toss my leg over him as I curled up into his side. "Feel free to ogle my sexy body while I'm sleeping."

He chuckled. "Why, thank you." He rubbed my back in slow circles until I felt the slow slide of sleep consume me.

# CHAPTER 34
## AURORA

Reaching over, I squeezed June's hand. "Are you excited?" I asked her.

"You all have been planning my birthday shindig for a while. Of course I am," June replied with a smile.

We both got out of my SUV that I'd parked in front of Freya's massive estate. Lots of vehicles were already parked outside. Freya had requested that all the guests get there before June's arrival because we'd planned something special for my aunt.

June adjusted her breasts in the plunging neckline of her skintight gold shimmer dress while I sent Freya a text letting her know we'd arrived.

"Goodness, it's quieter than a church," June noted while glancing over at me. "I hope they're not planning on jumping out of the bushes and screaming happy birthday, because I don't do well with people sneaking up on me. That's just going to get a lot of people knocked the fuck out."

I laughed, putting my cell into my clutch before looping an arm through hers. "Thank goodness we're not planning a sneak attack. Come on, lioness." I ushered her around to the back of Freya's palatial estate.

The surrounding trees were draped in twinkling lights. "This is beautiful," June said, taking in the tall, spiral fire torches stuck into the grass pathway that led the way to her outdoor night party.

"You haven't seen anything yet," I informed her. "Your friends love you, woman." And they did. Freya, Piper, and Bonnie had worked tirelessly to make June's birthday party spectacular.

June beamed. "And I love them." She squeezed my arm. "And you. I'm so happy you're staying in the Ridge. I want you to have the kind of love and friendship that I have."

"Now I understand why you love the Ridge the way you do," I said.

This morning, everyone—the Bane pack, Izzy, Nyx, Rose, Freya, and Bonnie—had called to check up on me to make sure I was okay. Mack had disappeared before I got up, but we'd spoken several times today, even though he was busy with the whole bringing-Milton-before-the-town-council debacle.

When we reached the end of the pathway and stepped into the expansive backyard, the crowd screamed, "Happy birthday!" cueing the live band that began playing the song "Outstanding" by the Gap Band.

June's face split into a wide grin before everyone gathered around her to give her a hug. I grinned, glancing around at the transformation of Freya's backyard. There was seating with cozy, colorful floor cushions scattered around the grass. Impressive tents faced the seaside views. The checkerboard dance floor was gold and black, giving the guests something solid to dance on. Fire jugglers undulated to the music.

I walked over to the cake table that held two cakes and platters filled with gold-dusted cupcakes. The first cake was dramatically wrapped in black, and sugar made to look like broken shards of glass brought some sparkle to the cake. As a bonus, the cake had both a gold bottom tier and a silver cake plateau, serving as the base to the moody confection. The second cake was a piece of gold art that literally took the cake. The three-tier confection was covered in gold—perfectly fitting for June's birthday celebration. The cake was adorned with spun-sugar flowers and embossed with an image of a lioness on the front.

I felt a soft tap on my shoulder. Peeping over it, I saw Imani smiling at me.

"Hey, Imani."

She gave me a quick kiss on the cheek. "Hey, Aurora." She gave me a once-over. "Damn, that's a hot dress. Rose has been holding out on me. I'm wearing this." She gestured to the patterned cutout leather dress she wore. "And you're wearing sex on a platter." She pouted playfully. "Not fair."

I laughed. "At least you have underwear on." I placed my hands on my hips. "I'm nude under this dress."

Imani arched a brow. "Lingerie is overrated. Shit, I keep having to buy panties because Quinn is so impatient that he tends to rip them off me, caveman-style."

"Well, that's too much information," I replied with a grin.

She looped her arm through mine. "It's just real talk, girl. When Nyx told me how much shifters love to fuck, I was all 'Yay! Me too.'"

I burst out laughing at her statement.

Imani continued. "But damn, I didn't realize that I'd spend so much time with Quinn between my legs or with me on my knees." She grinned. "Good times."

"Doesn't seem like it's an issue," I countered. "Shit, I haven't had sex in years."

Imani winked at me. "I have a feeling your sex drought is about to be over."

I waggled my eyebrows. "That's the plan once this party is over." I hadn't discussed sex with Mack today, but I was ready to give myself to him completely. However, I'd been out of the dating game so long that I had no clue how to finesse the subject of sex. My gut-level plan was just pointing to my pussy and bluntly ordering Mack to "Insert your cock here."

"You outdid yourself," Imani said, pointing to my cake

creations. "You're very talented." She wrapped her arm around my waist, a gesture of affection that would have made me uncomfortable before coming here and getting to know my new family.

"Thank you, Imani. But it was winning the baking championship that unlocked my creativity. I know now that I can do anything. Before coming to the Ridge, I had no plans for my future. Shit, my mind was struggling to imagine a future outside the military. But here I am, on the verge of opening my own bakery shop." I paused. "Well, almost opening my own shop. I have to deal with the fire damage, but nothing is going to stop me, especially now that Milton is exiled from the Ridge."

When June had told me about the council's decision, my first reaction of sympathy—instead of happiness—had been surprising. Exiling Milton was the right decision, but it also had to be a fate worse than death for him. I'd heard that he'd lived in the Ridge all his life. Now he had to live in the human world. If that wasn't a slow death, I didn't know what was.

"The council got it right this time. Even though the vote wasn't unanimous—two Council members, Gertrude and Shane, voted no to exiling Milton," Imani added.

I frowned at Imani's revelation.

She continued. "But majority won, and their decision will be a warning that this town will not stand for victimizing hybrids. Change will happen in the Ridge, and those assholes hiding in the shadows causing trouble have now been warned. They know there are consequences for their actions. As we speak, Quinn, Mack, Jasper, Brody, Emmett, and Rhett are escorting Milton out of town."

"But why the whole pack?" I asked. "Were they expecting trouble?"

"Yes," Imani said. "The owl-shifters are hotter than fish grease about his punishment. And there is a small group of townsfolk who think the council's decision to boot him out of town was unjustified."

"Unjustified?" I argued. "Milton stalked and trapped me in the basement and set fire to my shop, then stood outside waiting for the storefront to burn down with me in it because he wanted to make sure the hybrid bitch was dead." Those were his hateful words from his documented confession to Quinn, Rhett, and Mack.

"You're preaching to the choir, Aurora. But believe it or not, some residents are complaining that the council should have been lenient because he didn't succeed in killing you."

My eyes widened. "Are you kidding me?"

She shook her head. "Unfortunately, I'm not. I love my mate, pack, and friends. The Ridge is now my home. The people here, for the most part, are welcoming, loving, peaceful people, but there's a dark undercurrent in the Ridge that worries me. Quinn said the dark underbelly has always been here, but I guess us hybrids coming to the Ridge is like poking the sleeping dragon."

"But we are"—I gestured from her to me—"the solution to the feral-sickness problem. Would they prefer their unmated males to go feral?"

"Sadly, yes. There are some who don't give a shit about the feral sickness. In fact, they think it's a rite of passage."

I shook my head. "They don't give a shit about the survival of shifters."

"But I do," Imani said.

I squeezed her hand. "I do too. When I saw that feral wolf, I realized this wasn't a problem to be ignored. That wolf was a man trapped inside his animal's body. He's someone's son. I'm on your team now, Imani. I want to help in any way I can."

"Thank you, Aurora. We need all the help we can get, because I have a suspicion that our problem with the hybrid haters and the issue of feral shifters venturing outside the outer Ridge is going to collide into a major clusterfuck."

"Well, sign me up. And as far as Milton goes, justice has been served, and I'm moving on now."

"Good. He's one shifter we don't have to worry about

anymore. Freya's adjusted the spell around the veil not to permit him to set foot in this town again." She squeezed my waist. "You're safe."

I nodded. "Enough about Milton. It's June's party." I gestured to our girl crew—Nova, Izzy, Rose, Nyx, Piper, Freya, Bonnie, and June—dancing in the middle of the floor.

Imani grinned. "Welcome to the family, Aurora."

The band started playing "Bidi Bidi Bom Bom" by Selena. Imani made a whooping sound while throwing her hands up in the air and gyrating her body. "That's my song." She dragged me onto the floor, joining in on the dancing, leaving the drama of the Ridge behind—at least for tonight.

# CHAPTER 35
## AURORA

Several songs and lots of drinks later, the guests were gathered around the cake table after June had blown out her candle. All the guests launched the gold metallic confetti cannon in their hands, sending a shower of gold confetti over June.

The guests clapped and laughed at the sight of the hired stripper feeding June her birthday cake. I doubled over with laughter at the hilarious instructions Freya, Bonnie, and Piper were yelling out to June about how to eat her cake.

"More tongue, June," Freya ordered.

"Flick that tongue," Bonnie directed while demonstrating the action.

"She's not doing it right," Piper complained.

"Oh, shut it," June exclaimed. "I know how to use my tongue." To prove her point, she proceeded to lick the stripper's fingers in a salacious manner while moaning indecently.

"Jesus, this is a porno movie waiting to happen," I predicted before walking over to the bar and beckoning the bartender. "Water. No ice."

Opening a bottle of water, he poured it into a glass, then slid it across to me.

Picking up my drink, I pressed my back against the bar. I

didn't want to miss a single thing. Sipping my water, I sighed as the strange fizzy combination of bitter and sweet rolled over my tongue. June had told me that the water came from the town's hot springs and was thought to be an elixir and was touted for having medicinal properties for both bathing and drinking. I wasn't sold on the water's elixir status, but I was told that the residents loved the water so much that they had hot springs water fountains at various spots in the Ridge.

Glancing around the party, I stopped my gaze on the dance floor crowded with gyrating bodies. Scantily dressed servers flittered around the edges of the dance floor, holding trays of champagne mixed with BF Home Brew—a special concoction crafted by Brody Thornbern's brewstillery that Others loved because it was the only thing that could get them drunk. I watched some guests heading inside the harem-like tented booths draped with luxurious heavy silk fabric that dotted the perimeter of the backyard.

And then I spotted him—Mack.

My body pulsed with arousal when I found him standing at the edge of the dance floor. Biting my bottom lip, I gave him a slow once-over, from his black tailored slacks that molded over his sculpted thighs to the crisp black shirt that fit across his magnificent, broad chest. With my heightened eyesight, I could see the dampness of his hair as if he'd just stepped out of the shower.

I waved at him. He winked at me.

"Damn, he sure knows how to make my pussy wet without even trying," I murmured.

Butterflies fluttered in my stomach. I waited for his approach, but he didn't move. He stood staring at me with a blatant challenge in his eyes. I knew then that Mack was daring me to make a move on him.

My heart was beating like I'd just run fifty miles in thirty seconds while Mack observed me.

*Damn, I want to lick every inch of him.*

*Well, game on.* Draining the contents of my glass and placing it on the bar, I swayed over to him. Once I reached him, I inhaled deeply, taking in his masculine scent of cinnamon and mint entwined with patchouli that was pulling me to him.

"Hi, sexy kitty," I purred.

"Hey, beautiful." He traced my face with his eyes. "I've been thinking about you all day."

His simple words made me hot.

"Ditto." I pressed my palm against his heart.

The live band started playing "Is This Love" by Bob Marley.

Taking his hand, I demanded, "Dance with me." Not waiting for his answer, I tugged him onto the dance floor. Pressing my back against his chest, I shivered with delight when he placed his huge hands on my hips. The heat from his fingers spread, warming me all over.

"I'm not a dancer," he said against my ear.

"Let me show you," I replied, swaying my hips from left to right, my ass pressed against his hard cock.

He growled. The sound sent a rush of pleasure to my pussy. My head fell against his chest, and I felt the slow slide of something inside me unfurling like a flower. My senses sharpened even more. I could hear conversations way across the backyard. The sounds of the clinking ice in glasses.

Mack tightened his fingers on my hip.

*I am ready,* my inner animal announced.

*Ready for what?* I asked her.

*For you to claim him,* my lioness answered.

I could hardly breathe. *This is it. My time to show Mack how much I need him.*

My skin felt hypersensitive. The sultry air around me seemed to shimmer. And God… his scent had intensified. I closed my eyes, breathing deeply, taking in the most provocative, alluring, magnetic scent I'd ever experienced. It was making me weak in the knees.

The scent of my mate brought my beast to the surface, and I

wasn't surprised when a low growl erupted from my throat. Turning to face him, I was stunned when I saw that his eyes had been transformed.

"Mack? Your eyes are amber."

"As are yours. Do you need more proof that you're mine and I'm yours?"

"No. Claim me," I demanded in an animalistic voice I barely recognized.

"About time." He lowered his lips to mine, hungrily kissing my mouth, tilting my head back, and deepening his kiss. He tasted like coffee and chocolate, my two favorite things. He repeatedly swept his tongue through my mouth, pausing only to nibble at my lips before sinking into me again, the passion and heat in his kiss bringing every erogenous zone to life. He tugged on my lip before leaving a trail of hot kisses down my jaw all the way to the hollow of my throat. I wrapped my arms around his neck and clung to him.

"I want to taste your pussy." His voice was a velvet whisper against my ear.

I whimpered at his request.

"Yes," I answered before glancing around to the partiers who didn't even glance in our direction. For shifters, displays of affection were nothing new. But as much as I wanted to leave June's party, this was a special night for her. "But can we wait…"

"Nope." He grabbed my hand, ushering me through the partiers and toward a tent that was empty. Closing the flap, he turned to face me.

"Chair," he grunted.

Backing up, I pushed the hem of my dress up under my breasts before sitting on the low-seated, cushioned armchair.

"Fuck! You're killing me," he growled. "Why aren't you wearing panties?"

"Better for you to eat me, sexy kitty."

My heart thumped hard in my chest when he knelt before me, then draped my legs over the sides of the chair.

"So fucking beautiful," he murmured with approval, pressing his mouth against my stomach, nibbling and kissing until all I wanted to do was burst into flames.

My nerve endings stirred and tingled. His touch and our physical connection felt intense, like a slow, smoldering fire. It was so different. So much more because of the way we had both just opened up, baring our souls to each other during our conversations. It was as if we both wanted to slow down, savor the moment, linger in the essence of the significant corner we'd turned together in our relationship.

Raising his head, he looked at me hungrily before pushing my legs out a little. Now I was even more exposed and vulnerable before his gaze. As he slid his fingers between the wet folds of my heat, I dug my fingers in his hair, wiggling closer when he slipped his fingers inside. His thumb circled and played with my clit.

I was dying for more, even though I was on the cusp of my first orgasm. As I stared down at him, my mind went numb. I needed more, but I was helpless. He stroked my pussy. I shivered, on the verge of exploding.

"Give it to me, lioness," he demanded huskily.

Finally, I'd found a highly skilled lover with whom I didn't have to orchestrate every touch and stroke.

And the way his eyes bored into me as if I were his goddess and he were worshipping me at my altar... It was humbling, sensual, exciting, and intense.

"Please," I whispered. "Lick me," I finished because I knew he had no intention of pushing me over the edge until I offered what he needed to hear.

"With pleasure."

He curled his huge hands around my thighs, spreading my legs wider. He thrust his tongue into my heat. That one abrasive lick sent my mind and body spiraling over the edge, and I whimpered.

He pulled his head back, watching as his fingers continued to stretch my greedy slit.

I was writhing and panting as my hips bucked wildly. He thrust his fingers harder. I moaned louder when his thumb found my clit again and played with it. I screamed and came again, feeling light-headed from the passion.

He nipped my inner thigh. "I love the taste of your cunt."

His lustful words made my toes curl. I wanted Mack more than my next breath.

The next swipe of his tongue against my pussy was like an electric current setting my skin aflame. I sank my fingers into his silky hair, shamelessly aching for more and not giving a shit that he was eating me like a champ while shifters were right outside.

He purred against my cunt, and the vibration against my pussy was my undoing. I moaned aloud, gripping his head for dear life. When I came down from my sensual high, Mack lowered my legs and wedged his torso between my thighs. Pressing his mouth to mine, he rammed his tongue into my mouth, allowing me to taste myself.

"Mine," he growled against my lips.

"Yes," I whispered.

# CHAPTER 36
## AURORA

At the end of the party, June had the live band play "Untitled (How Does It Feel)" by D'Angelo while the pack, June, Bonnie, Freya, Izzy, and Rose paraded Mack and me to his SUV in celebration of our eyes turning amber.

The whole fiasco would have been embarrassing if it weren't for the genuine happiness emanating from all of them.

"Jeez," I murmured, waving goodbye as Mack pulled away. "It's like they hadn't seen a mating in a while."

Mack laughed. "Cut them some slack. Matings are far and few between these days."

His words sobered me a little. He was right. Our being fated mates was a celebration. There were so many unmated males—including some of his pack members—who waited a lifetime for what we'd found. Reaching over, I grabbed his hand. "I wasted so much time. Can you forgive me?"

"Stop being so hard on yourself. There's nothing to forgive. You needed time to heal, and there's nothing wrong with that."

When we reached his place, Mack escorted me out of his SUV and to his home. Seeing his house in the distance felt like a homecoming. When we got inside, the lights were on, and I kicked off my heels, sighing at the coolness against the bottom of my feet.

"Come here," Mack said quietly before pulling me toward him and putting his hand on the small of my back.

For some reason, I found those two words to be the sexiest thing ever.

I leaned in closer, staring into his eyes. He cradled the back of my head before his mouth brushed against my lips ever so lightly before slowly increasing the pressure of our kiss. Slightly parting my lips, I touched the tip of my tongue to his lip. He growled, offering me his tongue. He plundered, possessed, and nipped, storming through my defenses, demanding my surrender—and I did. I moaned as the passion built slowly, stoking the embers of lust and need unfurling inside me. Erasing everything from my mind except for this kiss. I touched his ass, cupping it with my fingers.

We mirrored each other's movements, and our kiss became a seductive, erotic dance as he ran his fingers through my hair before fisting it, angling my head back, granting him deeper access.

He growled, a sound that rumbled down in his chest as he yanked up the hem of my dress before effortlessly hoisting me up. Instinctively, I wrapped my legs around his waist while he kneaded my ass with two hands. I became completely lost in the sensation of Mack.

He strode through the house and up into his bedroom. With his hand on my back, he lowered me onto the bed. Scrambling to sit at the edge of the bed, I waited for him to turn on the lights, illuminating his massive room.

My eyes feasted on him when he stripped out of his clothing. I shivered deliciously. He was gorgeous, fit, and muscular, with his thick cock jutting out in front of him.

"Dress off," he demanded.

I stood, slipping the spaghetti straps off my shoulders and allowing the dress to slide down. Stepping away from the material pooled at my feet, I allowed his eyes to fully take in my body.

"So this is me." I gestured to the scars that marred my skin.

He walked over to me, his eyes locked on mine. "You are beautiful, Ro. Your scars are a sign of your strength, courage, and bravery." His lips brushed my collarbone. "Let me show you how much I love every part of who and what you are."

My heart thudded faster. Emotions—Joy. Fear. Happiness. Love.—welled up inside me. I'd never felt anything close to this with any man.

I nodded.

"On the bed, my love," he ordered.

Easing onto the bed, I lay on my back.

"Tell me if any of this feels uncomfortable," he insisted, "and I'll stop." He stroked my chest with his fingers. My nipples pebbled. Expanding his touch, he traced across my shoulders and down my arms.

He played with the area inside the hollow of my elbow, then between my fingers. My back arched from the sensual pleasure his touch was wreaking on my body.

I flinched when he touched my scarred hip. "Easy, love," he cooed as he delicately and slowly swept his fingers across the puckered skin. Gradually, my body relaxed and my breathing evened out.

He continued playing with the curves, hollows, and angles of my scarred hip, giving the area his sensual, healing attention.

His touch was light, exquisite, and continuous.

He was taking his time, treating every part of my bare skin with loving care and attention, rather than focusing on the usual erogenous zones.

He explored my legs and behind my knees. He kneaded the soles of my feet before kissing them and my toes one by one.

He moved up to my breasts, using his breath and blowing about an inch away from my nipple. The sensual caress was erotic.

He released my body, then strode over to the large mirror in the corner of his room. Picking it up easily, he stationed it along the side of his bed.

"Are we going to have sex in front of the mirror?" I asked.

"Yes. I want you to see yourself in the mirror. So you understand how beautiful you are."

I'd never had sex in front of a mirror, but I wasn't opposed to expanding my résumé in the bedroom.

He got onto the bed, lying flat on his back. "Come here," he demanded. "Sit on my face."

I'd never done this position before, but I wasn't shy about trying something new. Facing him, I straddled his face with one leg on either side of his head. He curled his huge hands around my thighs, spreading my legs wider. And the second his lips and tongue touched my pussy, I was a goner. His tongue felt amazing on me, and when I caught a glimpse of myself in the mirror, I loved the view of Mack's undivided attention on my cunt. My mind and body started spiraling over the edge, and I screamed his name over and over like a prayer.

His mouth and tongue moved faster.

With my hands pressed against the headboard for support, I was writhing and panting as my hips bucked wildly. I moaned louder when his tongue flicked my clit and played with it mercilessly. I screamed and came again, feeling light-headed from the passion. Rolling over onto the bed, I panted after the hands-down hottest oral sex position possible.

He nipped my shoulder. "I love the taste of your cunt."

His lustful words made my toes curl.

"I want you now," I growled.

"Your wish is my command." Mack rolled off the bed, grabbing condoms from his nightstand and sheathing his enormous cock.

"On your knees," he ordered with an expression of burning lust on his face.

Getting on my knees, I felt the cool air brush against the backs of my thighs.

He lightly slapped an ass cheek. "Damn, I love your sexy ass." I watched in the mirror as he traced his fingers across the curve of my butt before parting my cheeks and burying himself so far inside me that my hips bucked and my pussy burned from the width of his big, thick manhood. With his fingers digging into the flesh at my hips, he held me still.

"Lie flat on your stomach," Mack said.

Being directed in bed was new and exciting for me. I was used to orchestrating all my sexual encounters, dominating men in bed. My being submissive was new and would never have worked for me with any other man but Mack. I trusted him to respect and take care of my body. When I did as instructed, we were both lying on the bed with him on top of me.

"Oh fuck!" I cried out as his cock slid in farther, stretching me ruthlessly. This position was like a modified doggy style, only with more body contact and amazingly tight friction.

I started to move, but he grabbed my hip. "Easy. You're tight. I don't want to hurt you." I took a deep breath, forcing my rebellious muscles to loosen.

He pushed forward slowly; then he increased his speed from a sensuous slide to hard, forceful pumping.

He curled his hand in my hair, snapping my head back. "You're mine," he growled into my ear. "Look at me."

When I glanced into the mirror, our eyes locked in really hot eye contact before his cock sank deeper between my sensitive folds and his balls slapped against my womanhood, sending tiny shocks through my body and bringing me closer and closer to the edge.

I peeped at the mirror and was shocked at how beautiful my body looked at this angle, with my back arched back so my butt was in the reflection too. Lifting up in a slight cobra position gave me a great view of my breasts bouncing.

"Mack," I groaned as the pressure tightened inside my core,

and I came hard while gasping and moaning as my pussy convulsed around him.

But Mack was still hard and fucking me like a stallion while his fingers squeezed my hips. He pulled out and plunged back inside me again and again, building another orgasm that swirled inside my belly like a hurricane.

I absolutely loved the way he looked at me while we were having sex. It was real and intense. And now I understood the purpose of the mirror and what Mack meant by wanting me to see how beautiful I was. The mirror showed us in our rawest states. It wasn't about being beautiful; it was about seeing the pleasure we brought each other.

"I am yours, Mack," I said while staring into the mirror.

With eyes locked on mine in the glass, he reared back and pushed forward. Every inch of him was sheathed in me. My body shook, my legs quivered, and my core pulsed, racing toward blissful release.

"Do you accept me as your mate?" he demanded roughly, thrusting faster.

"Yes," I moaned.

"You're mine. My mate. And what I claim, I keep, cherish, love, and protect."

His thrusts grew stronger as his body slapped against me. I clenched the sheets as I rocked back into his body. My body was burning for a sweet release. A strangled shout escaped his lips before he bit the spot between my neck and shoulder.

"Mate," he growled. "Mine."

I came so hard I screamed his name at the top of my lungs. My inner muscles contracted, milking him. He roared, shooting his seed as both of us crested.

He kissed me on my shoulder before pulling me up farther onto the bed. Clutching me against his body, he kissed me, and I kissed him back.

"Let me take care of the condom." He got off the bed, entering the bathroom. It wasn't long until he was back, holding a washcloth. I wasn't shy when he passed the warm cloth between my legs before getting back into bed with me.

I sighed, content, as we held on to each other, lips melding over and over as our sensual tremors passed.

"So this is what mating feels like," I murmured. "Now I understand what all the hoopla is about."

He nuzzled my neck. "And do you like it?"

"No. I love it."

"Me too," he replied, gently licking the mark he'd left on my shoulder, causing a shiver of lust and want to race through my body.

"Guess you're stuck with me, sexy kitty."

"I wouldn't have it any other way, my sexy lioness," he replied while nuzzling my neck. "You're mine," he said, raising his head to look at me. "And I love you."

I blinked back the happy tears. This big, tough man had a heart of gold.

"I love you, Mack." I leaned forward, softly kissing him before biting his lower lip and tracing my tongue along it.

His mouth trailed to my neck, biting over his mark of possession. He wrapped his arms around my waist and squeezed.

I grinned when I felt the brush of a hard cock. "Well, look who's ready for round two."

He kissed me long and hard before growling, "Get on your knees... now."

# CHAPTER 37
## AURORA

I awoke to the sun streaming through the windows and my body draped across Mack's like a blanket. I was completely exhausted from our all-night sex marathon.

Mack was a stallion in bed. I was amazed at how he'd kept pulling orgasms out of me when I was absolutely sure I was too tired to come. But exhaustion hadn't stopped me from screaming out from pleasure when he expertly pushed me over the edge again and again.

He slapped my ass, rolling me over onto my back. "Wake up, darling," he growled.

"I'm not done sleeping," I complained as a slow heat crawled all over my naked body like ants. "Open the window. I'm hot."

He kissed me lustfully before jumping up and heading for the bathroom. I listened to the water running, too exhausted to move, when the earthy scent of sandalwood and rosewood floated into the room. I groaned. Every muscle in my body was blissfully sore because my mate never seemed to get enough. His cock hadn't gone down for more than a few minutes last night.

Lifting my head, I pulled my thick hair away from my neck, hoping to relieve the suffocating heat racing through my body.

Minutes later, he came back into the bedroom, hauling me up and over his shoulder.

"Put me down," I grumped. "No bath. I'm too hot."

"I know. I can smell the change in your scent. You're going into mating heat."

He placed me in the oversized, deep soaking tub, climbing in behind me, pulling me against his chest. I sighed as the combination of the hot water and the heady scent of sandalwood and rosewood bath salts cocooned us. I felt the slow loosening of my muscles, and my brain started kicking into gear as the words *mating heat* echoed in my head.

"What the hell is mating heat, Mack?" I asked.

"Finally. I was waiting for you to catch on to what I just said." He laughed. "It's when a mated female becomes highly sexually receptive to her fated mate."

I sat up, sloshing water everywhere. "What?" I squeaked.

"No one from your former pride ever went into heat?"

"No. The brothers weren't fated mates with any of the lionesses." It was amazing, all the things I was still learning about shifters. "So mating heat is the equivalent of marathon fucking?"

"Yup."

"How is that different from what we've been doing all night?" I demanded.

"This marathon lasts for days."

I shook my head. "I love you, baby, but you wore me out last night. I'm going to need more sleep and lots of stretching to deal with this mating heat situation."

"This is not a negotiation, baby. You can't bargain with the heat. The mating heat starts and stops when it wants."

I snorted. "We'll see about that," I replied, even as a wave of heat washed over my body.

He chuckled. "There's no fighting the heat, Ro. Both Nova and Imani tried, and both failed. This constant state of arousal is something only I can satisfy."

"Don't worry." I patted his arm. "I've got this. Meditation is the key."

"Is it now?" he drawled.

"Yup. That and—" My speech was shortened when his delicious scent wafted through the air like freshly baked chocolate chip cookies. My mouth watered, and my pussy convulsed with need.

He licked over my mating bite. "You were saying?"

Closing my eyes, I took a deep breath. "Think calming thoughts, Aurora," I chanted.

I thought it was working until another wave of heat made my back arch.

"The battle is over, darling." Mack stepped out of the tub then, reached down to lift me. He made quick work of drying us off, then picked me up and marched me back to his bed, placing me on top as if I were precious cargo.

Spreading my legs wide open before getting onto the bed, he knelt between my legs. His gaze burned into me. "The mating heat is not punishment." His cock was hard and stretched taut, almost past his navel. The thick, round crown glistened with a small drop of moisture. His balls were tight with arousal. "It's a part of the pleasure of being mated. The mating heat is new to me too, but together we will learn and explore everything it offers." He leaned over, caging my head with his hands before kissing me hard and deep.

Breaking off our kiss, I murmured against his lips, "Let's explore."

He grinned. "That's my fearless lioness."

Reaching over to the nightstand, he grabbed a condom, sheathing his thick erection. Inching down my body, he pressed his mouth against my stomach, nibbling and kissing until all I wanted to do was burst into flames. Arching my back, I moaned as he cupped my pussy.

"Spread your legs, darling," he demanded.

I did it without hesitation and was rewarded when he slid his fingers between my wet folds. "Do you know what it does to me to see you this way?" Cupping a breast, he stroked the underside before tapping my nipple.

I wanted him more than I'd ever wanted anything, wanted his cock deep inside me. I wiggled closer, and he slipped his fingers inside my womanhood, allowing his thumb to circle and play with my clit.

"You are mine," he growled, stroking my pussy and making me shiver with need.

"Please," I whispered. "Lick me." My body quivered with a fire I'd never felt before.

He curled his huge hands around my thighs, spreading me wider, and his tongue thrust into my heat, sending me spiraling over the edge. Raising his head to look at me, he continued to stretch me with his fingers. I was writhing and panting as he thrust his fingers harder. I moaned louder when his finger found my clit again and played with it relentlessly.

*I am his.*

*I belong to him… and he to me.*

"Mack." I breathed his name and whimpered, all the fight going out of me.

As if it was the sign he'd been waiting for, he lifted his head, his smile gentle. "Nothing is sweeter than my strong lioness's surrender."

Wasting no time, Mack positioned himself above me, his weight on his knees between my thighs. He directed his condom-sheathed cock into position, smoothly slipping in, looking at me with burning possession all over his face.

"So tight," he whispered.

I struggled to breathe as his cock stretched me.

He gave me a slow smile. "I've never wanted anyone more than I want you right now," he grunted, fully seated, his balls bumping against my ass.

The tender affection in his words and in his eyes washed over me, making me feel cherished and desired.

He kissed my lips, my jaw, and my eyelids. I basked in his tenderness and love. He pulled out and sank back in, hitting my G-spot with precision.

I wrapped my legs around his waist as he continued to stroke me just right, making my legs quiver. My pussy sucked him in farther as he pumped deeper. I tilted my hips forward, and he adjusted his movements, so with each stroke, he brushed deliciously against my clit.

The deeper he pumped, the more I wanted him.

My head snapped back as he slid in and out. I writhed beneath him, meeting him thrust for thrust. I was trembling, moaning low and deep. He stilled my hips so I felt every inch of his pulsing cock.

He swooped down, taking a nipple into his mouth. He lifted his head, his eyes boring into mine. "Take me, Ro. All of me."

Instinctively, I knew that he meant more than just taking his cock, that he was asking me to take him the way he was—flawed and dominant.

Tears pricked my eyelids as I raked my nails across his back.

I sucked in a breath as he withdrew and plunged deep again. "I accept everything that you are," I declared.

"From you, I'll accept nothing less." Mack raked his eyes over me.

Dropping my head on his shoulder, I felt so connected to him.

Wrapping my arms around his wide shoulders, nails digging into him like a wild woman, I buried my face in his neck and breathed deeply, the scent of him somehow reassuring me. He continued pumping, hard and controlled. I was going insane from the building heat.

My breathing was fast and shallow with periods of whimpers intermixed. "Please… harder." I grabbed his head, pulling him closer, biting his lower lip. "Please?"

He let himself go, moving faster, pushing me into another

orgasm. Arching, I screamed as my pussy clenched around him, my body collapsing right after, worn out and sweaty.

His face was harsh and controlled as he pulled himself from my pussy, flipping me over onto my belly. He drew me up onto my knees. I moaned when he kissed my neck and shoulders and then rained kisses along my spine.

Nudging me forward onto my hands, he gripped my waist with his strong hands as his cock thrust into me smoothly. I cried out with pleasure when he gripped my hair with one hand and wrapped the other around my waist.

His body rocked into me. The slickness of our bodies was in perfect synchrony. I gripped the sheets as he reared back and pushed forward, every inch of him sheathed inside me.

My body shook and my legs quivered as my core pulsed, racing toward blissful release as he thrust faster.

"Mine," he growled as his thrusts grew stronger while his body slapped against mine.

I clenched the sheets as I rocked back into his body. My body burned for sweet release. A strangled shout escaped his lips before I came so hard I screamed his name at the top of my lungs. My inner muscles contracted, milking him. He roared as both of us crested.

I couldn't stop trembling. I wanted to laugh. I wanted to cry. I wanted to be held in his arms this way forever.

There was no going back... Not that I wanted to.

I knew with every fiber in my body that this man would love me hard and cherish me until his last breath.

I sighed, contented, as we held on to each other, lips touching and retreating as my tremors subsided.

# CHAPTER 38
## AURORA

After three days of being in heat and having sex in positions I'd never imagined, I was gloriously exhausted.

Sighing happily, I inhaled the sweet, woodsy smell of the forest as I traipsed across the grass.

"Hey, kitty." I greeted my mate, who was sleeping in the middle of the grass in his lion form. "Did your badass lioness wear your ass out?"

My sexy kitty didn't twitch.

"You know, there's this rumor that lions are the laziest of all the big cats." I grinned.

Still no movement from my lion, who was snoring without a care in the world.

"Well, okay then," I said while moving toward the hammock that hung between two massive trees.

His snore was louder than a roar.

"Who knew 'I'm a lion, hear me roar!' should probably be changed to 'I'm a lion, hear me snore!'" I remarked.

*Now you're just trying to hurt my feelings,* Mack's voice rasped in my head, causing me to stumble.

Turning to face him, I said, "What the hell!"

His eyes were open and staring at me. *Hello, my lioness,* he replied in my head.

I strode over to him. "How are you doing that?"

He yawned, displaying his four large canines. *Fated mates can mind-speak,* he revealed.

With my hands on my hips, I just stared at him. There were so many aspects of shifters that I didn't know, despite growing up in a pride.

"But how do you mind-speak?" I asked.

He rose to his feet. *That's like asking how do I shift,* he answered while scuffing the ground with his rear claws. *You just do.*

I pressed my palm against his nose. My lion nuzzled my hand while purring loudly. "You know you're not helping, right?" I asked.

*All I'm saying is that it will be easier for you to understand what I'm talking about when you shift into your lioness.*

I jumped up and down like a child in a toy store. "I'm ready." Shifting was the one thing I'd always wanted to be able to do. "What do I do?" I peeled off the T-shirt that I wore and now stood naked.

*Close your eyes. Take a deep breath. And call her forward in your mind,* Mack instructed me.

I did as he said. *Hello?* I called out in my mind.

I sagged with relief when I heard a female voice in my head reply, *I am here and ready.*

*Come forward,* I ordered my lioness.

I gasped as a vision of a lioness with a tawny coat, strong, compact body, and powerful forelegs flashed inside my head.

"Can you see her?" I asked Mack aloud.

*I can, and you are beautiful,* he replied. *Now hold that image of her in your mind to start your shift. And when you're ready to shift back to your human, call the image of your human form to mind. Got it?*

"Yes." Closing my eyes, I held on to the vision of my lioness. I flinched when I felt a sharp jab of pain in my legs, but I didn't lose concentration. Pain moved from my legs to my arms until my entire body was throbbing from the hot, piercing pain.

My limbs started trembling, and my head fell back as I screamed so loudly that my throat burned. My screams transformed into a roar. Deep inside my body, I felt the strange sensation of my bones rearranging. The movement was excruciatingly painful. Adding to the pain, my muscles started stretching and rippling.

Shifting was most definitely not fun.

I heard Mack's roar and my eyes opened, but now I was closer to the ground. When I moved my feet, they felt heavy, different, uncoordinated.

*Did I shift?* I asked Mack.

*Yes, and you are beautiful,* Mack said in my head. *Look down at your feet.*

My paws were similar to a pet cat's but much bigger.

*I did it,* I replied.

*You sure did,* Mack agreed before moaning softly and licking his lips. I copied his gestures, instinctively recognizing the greeting ceremony performed whenever lions met to reaffirm social ties and confirm pride membership.

We rubbed our heads together, then moved on to rubbing each other's sides with our tails draped over each other.

Mack's lion purred. We rubbed against each other so hard that I fell over.

I laughed with joy while getting back onto my feet.

*Let's run, mate,* I said, taking off in a run that ended with me tripping over my legs and falling flat on the grass in a heap.

Mack's lion strode over to me. *It takes a while to become used to four legs, my mate.*

Undeterred by my less-than-graceful run, I stood, shaking out my body.

*Come on, my lioness,* Mack said. *Move your sexy ass.* He took off, and I roared before taking off after him.

# CHAPTER 39
## AURORA



**EIGHT MONTHS LATER... ON A FULL MOON**

This was the moment Mack and I had been waiting for—our mating ceremony—and it was here. A celebration of our union to be shared with our family and friends.

"Did I tell you how beautiful you are?" Mack asked, running his palm along my spine.

I shuddered deliciously. "Yes, you did, my love," I replied while pressed against his chest with my arms wrapped around his waist. "And I'm the luckiest woman in the world to have you in my life."

"I think it's the other way around. You complete me, lioness."

My lips curled up into a smile as tears pricked my eyelids. I'd never imagined the life that I now had with Mack. We'd learned so much about each other after our mating, but the most important lesson was acceptance of ourselves and each other.

Neither of us was perfect, and that was what made our love and relationship work.

I'd spent so many years before coming to the Ridge denying the existence of the world that rejected me, that I hadn't realized this world, with Mack, the Bane pack, my new friends, and June, was what I needed.

My life in the Ridge was just beginning.

Who would have thought there would have been a life after the military? Yet here I was with my fated mate. Plus I had a newly renovated bakery that I called my own.

Reluctantly, I pulled away from him. "Our pack and family are waiting for us," I reminded him.

"Are you ready?" he asked, his eyes sweeping over my floor-length royal-blue ceremonial cloak that shrouded my body from neck to toe.

My lips curled up into a smile. "To officially make you mine? Hell yes." I eyed my handsome man, who was wearing a similar cloak to mine.

"I've always been yours, lioness." Mack pressed his forehead against mine. "Now let's make it official."

Breaking away from me, he entwined his fingers with mine before we strode across the moss-dotted earth that covered the small stretch of land within our territory. Green blanketed every corner of our forest.

The location of our mating ceremony looked like we'd been transported into a fairy tale. The large mossy circle was surrounded by the river, and large trees with pink blooms and heavy branches stretched over the small gathering—June, Bonnie, Piper, Imani, Nova, Nyx, Rose, Izzy, and the Bane pack —waiting for us to arrive.

I saw Aunt June openly wiping away the tears that stained her cheeks. When Mack and I made it to the spot where Freya was waiting and dressed in a skintight floor-length dress, Freya raised her arms skyward while looking up at the bright full moon.

"Luna, goddess of the moon," Freya began loudly. "We're here tonight to ask for your blessing in the joining of Mack and his female, Aurora."

Lowering her arms, she eyed Mack. "Mack Owen. Who is this female you ask to mate?"

He squeezed my hand lightly. "Aurora Darabont."

"Will anyone challenge Mack Owen's right to mate this female?" Freya asked.

There was silence.

"Aurora Darabont. Who is this male you ask to mate?" Freya asked.

"Mack Owen," I answered.

"Will anyone challenge Aurora Darabont's right to mate this male?"

No one spoke.

Freya nodded. "Mack Owen, will you take this female you have claimed to be your fated mate forever?"

"Yes. I do," he replied gruffly.

She asked the same question of me about Mack. "Yes. I do," I said, my throat clogged with emotions of happiness and love.

Freya raised her hands to the sky. Her fingers slowly glowed with a mystical bright white light that replicated the color of the moon.

Freya nodded. "By the light that shines from my fingers, Luna approves of this mating of this lion to his lioness. Take your mate, Mack Owen." She stepped forward, giving each of us a light kiss on the cheek before declaring, "Before your family and pack, we declare you officially mated."

Freya peered over at the gathering. "May our unmated males find their fated mates. And may the coupling between Mack and Aurora be strong, happy, and loving."

A cacophony of clapping, cheering, and whistling surrounded us.

June pulled me into her arms. "You deserve all the happiness in the world," she whispered in my ear. "And I love you more than life."

I hugged her back. "I love you too, Aunt June. Thank you for loving me as hard as you do." I kissed her cheek before stepping back.

Quinn, Emmett, Brody, Rhett, and Jasper each took turns hugging me, then clapped Mack on the back.

Bonnie, Nova, Piper, Freya, Imani, Nyx, Izzy, and Rose each hugged me.

I laughed when I read the slogan GLITTER IS ALWAYS AN OPTION on the white T-shirts that my friends were wearing. "Glitter? Really?"

"God help me if you start talking trash about glitter," Rose said with a grin.

I held up my hands. "No judgment."

Without warning, the girls screamed, "Congratulations!" while making it rain with pink and green glitter.

I laughed. "I think I got some in my mouth."

"It's tradition," Imani explained. "The T-shirts and the glitter. Welcome to our family."

"Now go have lots of dirty sex in the forest," Nova added.

"Yes, ma'am," I replied with a mock salute before joining Mack, who was beckoning me. When I reached him, he growled, pulling me to him, pressing his lips to mine.

Quickly, I broke our kiss. "Save it for our freaky sex in the forest, sexy kitty."

"Well, let's get going." He grabbed my hand, hustling me away from our friends and family.

We strode deeper into the forest to the spot where we'd had our second picnic outing.

"I can't believe I get to spend the rest of my life with you," Mack said while opening the two-piece metal closure attached to the front of my cloak, then pushing the material off my shoulders. The garment slid to the grass, leaving me naked before him. "I love you, Ro."

"And I love you, Mack." My fingers trembled while undoing the closure on his cloak, pushing it off his shoulders. His massive frame was naked, and his thick cock jutted out from his body.

"Time for me to claim my woman," he growled. "Get on your knees."

After I slowly got to my knees, Mack knelt behind me, using his leg to spread them farther apart. I moaned as he traced his fingers across my shoulders, then along my spine, before cupping the fullness of my ass cheeks.

"Aurora, do you take me as your mate?"

I groaned when I felt his cock nudge against my pussy. "Yes."

"Aurora Darabont, I take you as my mate, my other half, and the only female in my bed," he announced.

"Mack Owen." I panted in anticipation of being taken by him. "I take you as my mate, my other half, and the only male in my bed."

Mack inched his hard length into my body.

I braced myself against the ground by digging my nails into the grass beneath us. Mack's incisors bit into my shoulder. His cock slid in and out slowly, then faster, his teeth still sunk into my flesh.

"More!" I screamed as my pussy tightened around his cock. His thrusts became faster as he moved his body against mine in an erotic dance.

His cock grew thicker, filling me completely. I stilled, allowing him to dominate me and loving every minute of him claiming me. My pussy clenched and my stomach tightened as an orgasm tore through my body. Mack rocked his cock in and out before roaring as his hot seed shot into me over and over again. Releasing his teeth from my shoulder, he licked my bite mark before slowly rolling us over until I was on my back with him between my legs.

"Mine," he growled before sliding his cock into my pussy. Winding my legs around his waist, I raised my hips, meeting him as he slammed into me.

"And you are mine," I growled. "The love of my life."

"Damn right!" he replied. "Now ride me, lioness." He pulled

out of me before rolling onto the grass, lying flat on his back, allowing me to climb on top of him.

I straddled him with one leg on either side of his body. Desire pooled between my legs when I grabbed Mack's hard, throbbing cock that glistened with my essence. Lining up his manhood with my tight, slick pussy, I sank down, resting my weight on my knees and rocking my hips back and forth.

Mack wrapped his callused hands around my thighs. Grinding on him, I saw my breasts bounce up and down.

"Yes!" Mack growled.

I moved faster when my stomach tightened, on the edge of an orgasm. Leaning down, I licked his neck. I growled when a need to claim him curled in the pit of my belly. My gums throbbed and incisors lengthened before I struck the area between his neck and shoulder and bit down, breaking his skin.

Mack roared so loud that the ground beneath my knees shook.

"Oh God!" I screamed before climaxing hard. Collapsing against his chest, I licked the area where I'd bitten. "You, sexy kitty, are mine," I whispered.

"Yes, I am," he replied huskily before licking my bite mark. "That was hot, lioness." He pulled out of me before rolling us onto our sides, pressing my back against his heaving chest.

"Damn right, it was hot. I rocked your world," I bragged while wiggling my ass against his still-hard cock.

"That you did," Mack replied while peppering kisses all over my neck. "And now we're officially mated."

"And you're still hard," I noted.

"I'll always be hard as a rock when it comes to my beautiful woman." He rolled me on top of him. "I love you, baby."

"And I love you, kitty," I whispered, staring down at him. He rolled me over before getting to his feet and extending a hand to me. When I stood, he wrapped his arms around me.

With eyes twinkling in the moonlight, he asked, "So does that mean you'll marry me?"

My eyes widened. "Shifters don't believe in marriage," I pointed out.

"I do." He twined his fingers in my hair. "And you should know by now that I don't give a shit about shifter expectations. I'm greedy. I want it all. An official mating. Marriage. Forever with you. So what's your answer, lioness?"

"Hell yes, I'll marry you." Rising on my toes, I kissed him hard on the lips before tracing my tongue along the seam of his mouth.

In the time that we'd gotten to know each other better, we'd created something strong, beautiful, and precious.

With Mack by my side, I now truly understood what it meant to love and be loved unconditionally.

I pulled my lips away. "I love you, Mack." And I did, with all my heart, because every day, he showed me with actions and words just how much he loved me.

"And I love you, Ro."

The process of opening up to Mack hadn't been easy, but I wouldn't change a damn thing. I'd found the love that I deserved.

He kissed my fingers before saying, "Now we shift, mate. Let's celebrate and give thanks to Luna for not giving up on our love and bringing us back together again."

I nodded because I believed that everything happened—the good, the bad, the ugly—for a reason.

Life was messy, but nothing was perfect.

Calling on our inner beasts, we shifted into our lions, rubbing our heads together before running side by side under the moonlight.

* * *

Want to know what happens when Emmett meets his fated mate? Find out in **Shifters of Black Forest Ridge: Emmett**, the next book in the Shifters of Black Forest Ridge series.

Read Shifters of Black Forest Ridge: Emmett

# ABOUT THE AUTHOR

USA TODAY BESTSELLING AUTHOR Sedona Venez blends steamy scenes and paranormal elements. She lives the NYC life with her former military hubby—hooah—and her adorable fur baby. She loves writing steamy romance with characters who break boundaries to find true love, conquer fear and sacrifice everything for their happily ever after.

*Sedona loves to connect with readers!*
www.sedonavenezbooks.com